The Good Apocalypse

Other book series by the author:
EarthCent Ambassador (Books 1 through 22)
AI Diaries (Books 1 – 4)
EarthCent Universe (Books 1 – 8)
EarthCent Auxiliaries (Books 1 – 6)
EarthCent Metaverse (Books 1 – 4)

Stand-alone books
Meghan's Dragon
Destiny: Union Station
Game Ship (as Morris Foner)
Intellectual Property

The Good Apocalypse

Book One of Under the Influencers

Foner Books

ISBN 978-1-948691-98-7

Hardwick, Massachusetts.

One

Hadley Brown was not expecting modern civilization to come to an end, but the last thirty miles of forests and scattered farms seemed to point in that direction. She parked her hybrid SUV next to an old pickup truck in front of the antique farmhouse which had two additions built on and looked like it could hold a multigenerational family with a dozen adult members. The attached barn had either been rebuilt in recent years or meticulously maintained, and it featured a standing seam metal roof that matched that of the house. She couldn't help feeling that the whole setup looked too wholesome for an internet retailer pushing prepper supplies.

Hadley got out of the SUV, gave her phone a shake, and then checked the mapping application again just to make sure the location hadn't changed. Then she sent her ex a text that she had arrived and waited for the double blue checks indicating it had been received. A podcast she'd been streaming had failed when the phone dropped to one bar of reception ten miles back, and she was feeling cautious.

The ensemble business suit she'd donned like a suit of armor that morning felt like overkill, and Hadley wondered how much of her corporate experience could possibly apply to an enterprise without a paved parking lot. An understated sign on the porch railing read 'The

Good Apocalypse' in an artsy font that wouldn't have looked out of place on an upscale restaurant in Manhattan that was so popular it could afford to go unnoticed by foot traffic. Then a man in his early sixties stepped out onto the porch.

"Hadley," he greeted her and offered a smile that showed a small chip missing from one of his front teeth. "Everybody is waiting to meet you."

"Are you Peter?" she asked, still standing behind the open door of the car in case she decided that discretion was the better part of valor. "I have to be honest with you. I was expecting something a little more corporate."

"That's exactly the direction I'm hoping you can help us move. I wanted a website editor and brand manager with a background in big-city media who would come and work on location rather than freelancing from home. We're very excited about relaunching the website and newsletter, and we want the look and the quality to reflect the gravity of the subject matter."

"Preparing for the end of the world," Hadley said, and congratulated herself on getting the words out without sounding too snarky. She studied his clothes, which consisted of cargo shorts, a T-shirt promoting a band that had broken up before she was born, and leather sandals that wouldn't have looked out of place in biblical times. "You're not what I expected either. Shouldn't you be wearing camouflage fatigues and have a rifle slung over your shoulder?"

"Let me stop you right there," Peter said, holding up a hand with the palm out, which made him look like a hippy directing traffic at a Woodstock revival. "Nobody around here is talking about the end of the world. Even if an asteroid the size of the one that wiped out the dinosaurs slammed into Earth tomorrow, the planet will still be here the next day, and life will go on in some form or another. Our goal is to ease people into the post-apocalypse with the best possible chance of surviving and becoming part of a new and better civilization that rises from the ashes."

"Well, that's a relief. I was worried you were crackpots." This time, Hadley felt she had been less successful on the snark front and bit the inside of her cheek.

"But you came anyway," Peter pointed out.

Hadley closed the door of her SUV and walked around the front of the car to the porch stairs. "I needed to make a change," she said. "I had two bad experiences in the last year, one in the subway, and one in the lobby of my supposedly secure building. The part of your job listing that grabbed me was the description of your unincorporated village being a throwback to the pre-industrial era. Speaking of which, I would have been here earlier, but I got stuck behind a team of horses pulling a farm cart so wide that I was afraid to drive around it."

"Most of our neighbors are Amish, and they're exactly the people you want to be living near when the apocalypse arrives because they aren't dependent on the grid," Peter said. He held the screen door open and stood aside for her to enter first. "I know from our phone interview that you're not an expert on the subject, but there are dozens of ways for civilization to collapse, and all of them include the eventual failure of electrical distribution and pipelines."

"Well, that's something to look forward to anyway."

"Hadley," Peter said in a serious voice, and she turned back and saw that his expression made him look like she remembered her grandfather the last time she'd seen him alive, an occasion on which he had told her that money can't buy happiness four times in ten minutes because his short-term memory was gone. "If you spend your life waiting for the apocalypse, it will never arrive." Then he gave her an upbeat smile and followed her into the house.

The smell of freshly baked cookies permeated the front room, and a couple of tail thumps attracted Hadley's attention to a golden retriever lying on a braided oval rug. As soon as the dog confirmed visual acquisition, it rolled over on its back and gazed at her expectantly. Hadley walked over, crouched, and began rubbing the dog's belly.

"Who's a good—" she began in her talking-to-dogs-and-babies voice while glancing down, "—boy. You're a good boy."

"You just passed the employment test, and Freud hears that he's a good boy all day long," Peter said. "It's a wonder he hasn't developed a narcissistic disorder, but maybe his name gives him immunity."

"Who names a dog Freud?"

"He came that way, and our office manager, Arlene, decided not to change it when he adopted her." Peter glanced down the hallway before continuing in a lowered voice. "She's in the kitchen making cookies because she knew you were coming, and baking relaxes her. Arlene is a brilliant young woman and was accepted to several Ivy League schools, but she had difficulty acclimating to life on campus and came home. Freud is her therapy dog."

Hadley replied at a similar volume, "She's able to handle the stress of being an office manager for an internet retailer selling prepper supplies?"

"The Good Apocalypse is much more than an internet retailer, and who doesn't have a few quirks that require accommodation? Arlene is a friend of my daughter from my second marriage, and she was my first employee when

I started the business five years ago. In the meantime, she's completed a bachelor's degree and an MBA online."

A woman in her early twenties with bright pink hair and a peasant blouse appeared in the long hallway with a plate of cookies and began walking toward them. Freud dashed down the hall to meet her, ran back again to make sure that Hadley hadn't disappeared, then repeated the round trip three more times before running out of room to turn around. Then he sprawled between them, attempting to anchor them both in place by holding down their feet with various parts of his body.

"Hadley, this is Arlene, our office manager," Peter introduced the women while taking two chocolate chip cookies from the plate. "What do you think, Arlene? Should we invite everybody out front to meet her, or should I take her around to the studios?"

Arlene waited a moment for Hadley to take a cookie, then set the plate on her desk before replying. "I think it would be better for her to meet everybody at once," she said. "Are you comfortable in crowds, Hadley?"

"Absolutely," Hadley said. "We had an open office concept at my last job, and there were over two hundred desks on the floor. When they revoked work-from-home, it turned into a madhouse." The blood rushed to her face when she realized what she had just said, but either Arlene didn't notice the reference to mental health, or she wasn't disturbed by Freudian slips.

"I'll gather everybody who's here," Arlene said, and added over her shoulder as she headed back down the hall. "Hang her jacket up for her, Peter. That looks warm, and the weather is doing its July in May thing again."

"Sorry," Peter said to Hadley. "I'm not always the most observant man in the world when it comes to clothes. Can I take your jacket?"

Hadley hesitated for a moment, but she was beginning to feel the heat, so she undid the stylish knot in the wide fabric belt and removed the jacket. "You don't have air conditioning?" she asked.

Peter took her jacket over to the empty coat rack just inside the front door and arranged it on a wooden hanger. "We're off the grid, though we have enough battery capacity charged by solar to run the geothermal heat pump for central air and heat, plus a diesel generator for backup." He lowered his voice again and added, "Arlene likes it warm. We have window units for when the whole-house system is off."

"Will I have an office with a window unit?"

"A corner office, because that's what's open at the moment," Peter said. He gestured for her to join him at a desk on the other side of the room, where an open laptop was sitting. "Come and meet Eleanor, our most highly compensated employee."

Hadley hung back. "I imagine hiring invisible people is expensive. If I realized that's what you were looking for, I would have stopped at a gaming store and bought a cloak of invisibility."

"Not the most trusting person, are you? Though I can understand how living in Manhattan could put a dent in anybody's faith in their fellow man." Peter turned the laptop so she could see the screen, which was filled with a computer-generated image of a woman's face, part of her mouth hidden by the microphone of a headset. He hit the unmute button.

"—to the same address as y'all's credit card," Eleanor was saying in an accent that would have sounded right at home in the Deep South. "Need anything else?"

"Y'all's the best," a man's voice replied in a similar accent.

"Thanks, Dwayne, and y'all have a good apocalypse."

"See the number seven in the bottom right-hand corner of the screen?" Peter asked Hadley. "That's how many customers Eleanor is talking to simultaneously. That flashing white star means that somebody is calling in right now. Listen."

"The Good Apocalypse," Eleanor said in a neutral accent that might have been from California or Connecticut. "How may I direct your call?"

"I'm interested in one of those turnkey solar panel and battery solutions I heard Laura Ann talking about on her show this morning," a woman said in a flat Midwestern accent.

"I'll direct your call to our photovoltaics expert," the face on the laptop screen replied. "Please hold." Three seconds ticked off, and then Eleanor began talking again, this time in a male voice from the heartland. "Eli speaking. You tell me how much power you want, and we'll fix you up, you betcha."

"Artificial intelligence," Peter said as he clicked mute again. "Eleanor isn't really in the laptop, of course. She's out there in the cloud somewhere, and she works twenty-four hours a day, seven days a week. She handles all our retail sales and customer service."

"Which is why artificial intelligence is going to replace us all," a man said from the hall, and then came forward and offered Hadley his hand. "Carl, and I'm our AI apocalypse influencer. Eleanor put a room full of people out of work, and like Peter said, that's a room full of people around the clock."

"A room full of people in the lowest cost overseas location working for slave wages and speaking English that half of our customers wouldn't understand," Peter said, the argument obviously being an old one. "Programming and maintaining Eleanor creates good high-tech jobs right here in the U.S.A., and like I said, she doesn't come cheap."

"But it's just software," Hadley objected. "How much could a license possibly cost?"

"With the uptime guarantee, the unlimited surge calls supported, the catalog interface, and the live tech support with American employees? The small-business package costs us a hundred and fifty thousand a year, and the smartest thing I've ever done in business was locking in that price for three years with an option for another three years at two hundred and fifty thousand. They offered me the deal as one of their beta customers when they were starting the business, and we had just enough traffic then to justify the expense."

"What are they going to charge when the deal is up? A half million? A million?"

"We'll never find out because artificial intelligence is going to take over the world by then," Carl said cheerfully as he helped himself to a couple of cookies. "I love fresh-baked cookies, but I'm going to have to work out for an extra five minutes after dinner tonight."

"What difference does it make how much you weigh if we're all going to die in the AI apocalypse?" Hadley asked. "Or is that just an act you put on to be an influencer?"

"Hope for the best, plan for the worst."

"Wait. Which is the best?"

Peter chuckled before replying. "When Carl talks about the worst thing that can happen, he means that artificial intelligence gets beaten out by something as mundane as nuclear war or a pandemic. The prepper community can be very competitive when it comes to whose vision of the apocalypse is going to win."

"Artificial intelligence is going to win," Carl said firmly. "But it may decide to keep a few of us around to do maintenance work, so I have to stay in shape."

A woman in her forties who was wearing a state park volunteer t-shirt and looked like she competed in triathlons just to loosen up before splitting a few cords of wood entered the office and said, "Welcome to The Good Apocalypse. I'm Laura Ann, and I do financial collapse, but I like to keep my options open. You must be Hadley."

"I am," Hadley agreed. "What do you mean about keeping your options open? Do you think we can avoid the apocalypse?"

"I mean, most scenarios could go either way," Laura Ann said. "On one hand, we have greenhouse gases and global warming, on the other hand, one good volcanic eruption could tip us into nuclear winter without the nukes. The way I look at it, the most important thing that anybody can bring to the apocalypse is a flexible mindset. Some influencers get worked up about the details, but in the end, it makes no difference to me if the death blow is war brought on by competition over resources or bad monetary policy. The important thing is—Hey! Don't eat all the cookies, Phil."

"I'm not eating them all," rumbled the large man. He had bigger arms than Hadley had seen anywhere outside of the health club in Manhattan where her last job gave her membership, though she only used it in bursts when the guilt feelings became too heavy to carry. "I'm taking the cookies for later. You know, prepping?"

"Phil, this is Hadley," Peter said. "Now put back those cookies before she thinks you're going to be that guy in the post-apocalypse who goes around with a gang stealing from farmers and kidnapping their daughters."

"You know that's not my thing," Phil said, putting back half of the stack of cookies he'd taken. "I only do the segment about care and feeding of a harem once a month, and that's because my followers insist." He favored Hadley with what he no doubt thought was a winning smile and added, "I always start by explaining that participation in a post-apocalyptic harem has to be voluntary."

"I'm an army brat, and if my father pounded one thing into my head, it was to never volunteer for anything," Hadley said.

"Do you shoot? I've got a range set up out back where I do weapons demonstrations. I bet if you and Laura Ann got together and put a little work into it, you'd have a following in no time."

"By 'a little work,' he means dressing up like tractor parts calendar girls," Laura Ann told Hadley. "There's a double standard in the apocalypse influencer world. Men can skip shaving for days at a time and go on camera with stains on their T-shirts and grease under their fingernails. Women have to shave their legs and their armpits, and that skin better show up on camera if they want to build a following."

"I think that's true pretty much everywhere, but I'm not an on-camera personality," Hadley said. "Peter wants me to take your website and newsletter to the next level so that it gets included in news feeds and is recognized as an authoritative source."

"My channel is already there," Carl said. "I've been writing about the AI apocalypse and interviewing scientists since before large language models got big, and I've been on all the other podcasts as a guest. Check out my Wikipedia page."

"That's his big pick-up line," Laura Ann said to Hadley. "I've heard him use it at the bar in Franklin, though they always lose interest when he starts talking about reinforcement learning and natural language processing."

"At least Wikipedia is crowd-sourced," Hadley said with a grin. "When I think about some of the lies I've heard guys tell over the years, maybe insisting that they all have their own page is a good idea."

Arlene returned to the office with another plate of cookies and looked disappointed that her coworkers hadn't finished the first batch yet. "Fumiko is coming in a minute. She's almost finished with assembling a new drone and didn't want to lose where she was. Is something wrong with the cookies?"

"They were all gone, but Peter made me put some back," Phil explained. "Where's old doom and gloom?"

"I sent Glen a text," Arlene said. "I think he's in the observatory playing with the new controller on his telescope."

"You guys have an observatory?" Hadley asked.

"At the top of the old silo, you probably didn't notice the opening in the dome when you drove up because it's around the other side at the moment," Peter said, helping himself to one of the fresh cookies since Arlene was closer than the plate on her desk. "Glen has a pretty big reflector telescope up there, and he spent all of his spare time the last week replacing the mount with a computer-controlled gimbal. He's our space apocalypse influencer."

"The giant asteroid you were talking about."

"The space apocalypse is about more than just asteroids," Arlene said enthusiastically. "There are solar flares that can have the same impact as in an electromagnetic pulse weapon, comet tails carrying plagues frozen in ice, and my favorite is alien invasion."

"She's holding out for some seven-foot-tall blue-skinned guy to come and take her away," Phil said. "I covered myself in blue body paint once and pretended to speak English like a foreigner, but she wasn't buying it."

"Don't you guys have an employee handbook that prohibits things like abducting each other while pretending to be aliens?" Hadley asked pointedly.

"I don't know," Peter said. "Arlene wrote the employee handbook. Is that in there, Arlene?"

The office manager turned the same color as her hair. "I didn't want to preclude the chance, just in case an alien came here to work undercover. They do that sometimes."

"How do you know that?" Hadley asked.

"The published literature on the subject."

The room fell silent for a moment, and it became clear to Hadley that lonely blue aliens were a subject on which Arlene was not to be contradicted. Freud went over and leaned against the office manager's legs like he required them for support, at the same time turning his eyes to Hadley with a supplication to let it drop. Then a drone entered the room, flying so close to the ceiling it was a wonder it didn't crash.

"Kneel to your new master," a female voice spoke over the rotor noise. "I am—stop that!" the voice broke off as Laura Ann began stalking the flying object with a broom. "I need this drone for my show today, and I have it on evaluation from the manufacturer."

"I know perfectly well you never send back eval units, and nobody ever calls you on it anymore because the free publicity you give them is worth thousands of dollars of advertising," Laura Ann replied in the direction of the drone. "Now land that thing and come out here and meet our new editor before you scare her away by being a goof."

"Not on Eleanor," Peter cried, moving rapidly for a man his age to interpose his body between the drone and the laptop hosting the interface for sales and support. "Can't you fly it back down the hall to your office?"

"There's something wrong with the pitch control, and I can't make it hover or slow down," the voice said, now clearly frustrated. "I didn't update the app for the new model because I thought the last generation would handle it. Can somebody open the front door?"

Phil pulled open the front door and offered a bow with a flourish as the drone shot through. A few seconds later, a small woman with jet-black hair ran down the hall with a smartphone held up in front of her face, her thumbs moving frantically. Everybody got out of the way as she passed through the office and out the door.

"Hit the kill switch," Phil called after her.

"It didn't work," Fumiko shouted back.

"It's not going to work for artificial intelligence, either," Carl commented from where he was getting a cup of water from the upside-down blue bottle dispenser.

"So," Peter said to Hadley in a cheerful voice. "I don't see you edging toward the door, so we haven't lost you yet. Do you have any questions about the job?"

"There's an out-of-control drone outside, so that's the last place I want to be," Hadley said. She helped herself to another cookie. "My dad had a lot of good advice about staying alive in general. Is there enough spring water left for everybody, Mr. AI Apocalypse?"

Carl shot her a grin. "Water is for preppers. Are you coming on board?"

"I kind of have my whole life packed in the car, so I guess I'm going to try it. But don't ask me to pick my favorite version of the apocalypse, because in my book, the best apocalypse is the one that never happens."

"Don't worry," Peter said. "You'll come around."

Two

Hadley had been warned not to expect much of the unincorporated village, but even with lowered expectations, she was underwhelmed by the wood-frame church with peeling white paint and a tumbledown graveyard. She almost drove right past her bed-and-breakfast because the numbers on the houses were all in the low-eighteen-hundred range, while the address she'd been given was 4 Old Church Road. Then it hit her that the painted number signs on the corners of the houses referred to the year they were built, and the street address was given by small black iron numbers right next to the door. She dutifully stopped at the barely visible crosswalk with the equally faded stop sign, then did a U-turn, and pulled up in front of her home for the next week.

Before getting out of the car, Hadley checked her phone for the nearest supermarket. All the distances were double digits, the closest of which was twenty miles, and she was suddenly very happy that Arlene had pressed her to take the leftover cookies. She pulled the rollaway overnight bag out from the mess that represented the total of her accumulations from six years of living in Manhattan and discovered that the wheels were exactly the wrong size and repeatedly jammed in between the flagstones of the front walk.

"Do you need a hand with that?" a friendly voice inquired.

Hadley turned her attention to the porch and saw an elderly woman with pure white hair standing on the other side of the screen door. "No, I'm fine," she said hastily, giving up on dragging the bag and instead picking it up and rapidly mounting the stairs. "Are you Betsy?"

"That's what everyone in the village has called me since my Amos passed away." The screen door opened with the characteristic creaking of a long rusty return spring, which no doubt delighted in pulling the door shut on the backsides of the unwary. "The Good Apocalypse paid for your room, but if you need me to buy you something special, you should know that I only accept gold or Bitcoin."

"Is there something in the water supply in this part of the state? What does everybody have against credit cards and dollars?"

"The water comes from a well, and I didn't even know what fiat currency was until Mr. Erlich took a room with me last year," Betsy said. "I'd never even had a conversation about monetary policy before he moved in, but these days I only keep a bank account to get my pension and pay a few bills. I'll say one thing for the online payments Mr. Erlich set up for me. I save enough on postage stamps every month to go into Franklin for the bingo."

"I haven't bought a stamp in—" Hadley thought for a moment. "I don't remember the last time I bought a stamp. I'm not sure I've ever bought a stamp."

"I didn't realize you were that young. Would you like a cup of tea before I show you to your room, or are you one of those modern women who only drink coffee?"

"I've been known to indulge in a cup of tea. Can I leave my bag here?"

"Push it against the wall so that Mr. Erlich doesn't trip over it if he returns early and comes in the front," Betsy said. She began moving down the hall with careful steps. "Be careful of the floorboards. The house has settled over the years, and the wide pine planking isn't quite as level as when my great-great-grandfather bought it from the Smiths."

Hadley wondered if the great-great-grandfather was included in the ancestors who appeared in the black and white photographs and older Daguerreotypes that decorated the hall. "What year was that, Betsy?"

"When he got married after the Civil War. According to family legend, my great-great-grandfather had no social skills, and everybody expected him to go through life as a bachelor. But the war killed so many young men that he could have become a polygamist if he was so inclined."

In contrast to the hall, the light in the kitchen was enhanced by the afternoon sun streaming through the west-facing window. Hadley found herself staring at her host, who looked ten years younger in bright light, thanks to her sparkling blue eyes.

"Do I know you from somewhere?" Hadley asked. "Are you one of those great aunts from my mother's side of the family I'd never met before they came to her funeral last year?"

"I haven't traveled further than Franklin since Amos passed," Betsy said. "I'm sorry to hear you lost your mother at such a young age." She checked the water level in the tea kettle, moved it on top of the induction element, and chuckled dryly. "I bought this stove after reading the reviews on the internet, and my Peter warned me that the rooftop solar wouldn't provide enough power when the grid goes down. I told him that at my age, I'll take my chances."

Everything clicked into place, and Hadley said, "Peter didn't tell me that you were his mother, but I see the family resemblance. He said this is the only bed and breakfast in town, and the other options for temporary lodging without driving at least half an hour were to live at the office or take a room with the Yoders."

Betsy chuckled again. "He must have told you how Baker Yoder collects rent."

Hadley nodded. "Chores. I'm not afraid of getting my hands dirty, but waking up at the crack of dawn and milking cows was a bridge too far. Besides, I expect to be putting in long days and late nights until we get the new site launched."

"Peter was very excited about hiring you. He insisted on showing me the website you ran for that magazine with all the gorgeous pictures of homes that looked like they had never been lived in. Your magazine is where I got the idea last month to have the room you'll be in repainted salmon pink. Do they still publish it on paper?"

"If they've stopped in the last month, it's news to me," Hadley said, while she tried to imagine sleeping in a room that reminded her of sushi. "But I was strictly on the digital side of the business."

"I saw the salmon-colored walls flipping through the magazine last month, but I'm sure it was years old," Betsy explained. "I was at my dentist's office in Franklin, and all the magazines he brings for the patients have already made the rounds of his family and friends. Very close-knit families, the Indians. They remind me of the Amish that way."

"I think they prefer to be referred to as Native Americans these days."

"Indians from India?" Betsy brought the ceramic teapot from the kitchen table over to the stove and began packing a stainless-steel infuser with tea from a Mason jar. "Doctor Brahmin might be surprised to hear that. I hope you like green sencha."

"Any green tea is good," Hadley said. "Is Doctor Brahmin good as well? I'm not a big medical person, but I do go for a cleaning every six months, and finding a new dentist is on my list if the job works out."

"He's the only family dentist left in Franklin. The other option is a national chain where they treat the patients like cattle and tell everybody they need crowns. I don't have anyone to compare him to other than old Doctor Silver, who sold him the practice over twenty years ago. Doctor Brahmin is less sparing with the Novocaine than Doctor Silver was, but he's always pushing X-rays." Betsy turned off the stove and added boiling water to the teapot. Then she hung the stainless-steel infuser from the special notch in the opening, replaced the lid, and carefully moved it to the trivet on the kitchen table.

"I guess I'll be seeing plenty of Franklin when I drive in for my groceries. Do you have the space to spare in the refrigerator?"

"Do you eat special food of some type? Kosher? Halal? Vegan?"

"No," Hadley said, "I'm pretty omnivorous, but I don't expect you to feed me every meal."

Betsy took a glass dish with half a pie from the counter, put it on a tray along with a pie knife, forks, and two dessert plates, and then moved the tray to the kitchen table. "Apple pie," she said as she cut two wedges and plated them before sitting. "Oh, I know what I forgot. Would you be a dear and bring a couple of those mugs hanging under the cabinet?"

Hadley fetched two mugs, one of which was emblazoned with the mushroom cloud of an atomic explosion, the other with a robot that had lawnmower attachments in the place of hands. "If you bake pies, I guess I'll never have a cause to shop for groceries," she said.

"The middle Yoder girl comes and helps me, though she's getting to the age where she can start teaching in the school, at which point the job as my assistant will go to her younger sister. Sarah, their mother, is an adequate cook but an excellent baker, and all of the girls learn from her. I provide your breakfast and supper, and there are always leftovers to bring for lunch if they don't have anything planned at the office. But other than preparing breakfast and supervising the baking, I do very little myself. Abigail Troyer is already cooking for twenty at her place because her husband runs a carpentry shop and boards several of the young men working for him. One of her flock brings a picnic basket right before mealtime every evening, and in winter, I get delivery by sleigh."

"Are you related to them? I understand respect for the elderly and—no offense," Hadley broke off.

Betsy chuckled again. "The Troyers are fine people and good neighbors, but the food deliveries are a business. I send Peter to tell Abigail if I expect extra guests or have so many leftovers in the fridge that I need a couple of days to use them up, and she gives me a bill once a month."

"I didn't know that the Amish used money."

"Oh, yes. I wouldn't say that they love it more than anybody else, but they know the value of their work, and they expect to be paid accordingly. Peter hired Amish workmen to convert his silo into an observatory, and they rebuilt the old farmhouse and barn for him when he came back here five years ago and started the new business. The crops you see growing in the fields around the office are farmed by some of the local young men who are saving money to buy their own farms. It's usually hay or something else that doesn't require too much attention because their labor is still needed by their families."

"I understand," Hadley said. "Does your son live here with you?"

"Why would you think that?" Betsy asked and then answered her own question. "Oh, because I mentioned sending him to the Troyers. That's just because Peter has a phone, so I can always reach him. Giving him errands gets him away from the office where he would otherwise be on the internet day and night. He lives there, you know, on the second floor. There are eight bedrooms for employees with all the additions, but he thought you would be more comfortable here."

As Hadley swallowed the last of her pie, she realized she was keeping Betsy from hers, so she stopped asking questions and offered to pour them both tea. The taste of the green sencha reminded her of grain, similar to the blend they served at her favorite coffee shop back in the city. That made her wonder for a moment how William was adjusting to her moving out, but then she remembered that he was so overworked at the law firm that he probably wouldn't have time to notice he was no longer in a committed relationship. On the bright side, he hadn't hesitated to give her cash for half of the furniture they'd jointly purchased. She imagined that his next girlfriend would be impressed by William's taste, and he wouldn't hasten to correct her misconception.

"Penny for your thoughts," Betsy said.

"Sorry, I guess I kind of zoned out there for a minute," Hadley said. "My father used to move us all the time when I was a kid. The longest I ever spent in one place was my last apartment in Manhattan, where I lived with my boyfriend for five years. I think I'm still adjusting."

"Five years is longer than many people stay married these days if they bother with a license at all. Did you have plans together?"

Hadley made a face and sighed. "Nothing in writing, as William would have said. He was a corporate lawyer, real estate, mainly. He wasn't greedy, but his time billed for so much an hour that it almost seemed stupid to do anything other than work. I thought it would change when he made partner, but if anything, it got worse."

Betsy nodded gravely. "Workaholics are harder to live with than alcoholics if you ask me, and my Amos tried both. Is William older than you?"

"By ten years," Hadley said. "I think I stayed with him as long as I did because my mother had approved of him. Well, that, and I really liked our furniture."

"Five o'clock and the apocalypse is nigh," announced a cylindrical speaker on the counter.

"Walter, tell me the news," Betsy said, followed immediately by, "Walter, pause." She turned to Hadley. "I should have asked first if you want to hear the news because it's always so depressing. Mr. Erlich helped me change the wake word to Walter in memory of my favorite anchorman. Somebody even created an app that reads the news feeds in Walter's voice, but that's just spooky, so we stuck with the default female voice. Carl set it up to choose random news stations and feeds because they're all equally bad."

"Does it tell you that the apocalypse is nigh every hour around the clock?" Hadley asked.

"That would be morbid. It only announces the time once a day because I'm always in the kitchen at this hour waiting for the supper delivery. Walter, continue."

"...and the latest inflation number is over twelve percent for the first time since the 1970s. Joining us is our regular economics correspondent, Professor Edna Shapiro. Professor Shapiro. What can you tell us about the latest spike in inflation? Is it transient?"

"Spikes in inflation are transient by definition. The real danger to any modern economy is entering into a deflationary spiral. Inflation means growing wages and asset values, which I think we can all agree are a good thing."

"Walter, turn off," Betsy ordered. "Do you own any Bitcoin or gold, Hadley?"

"I don't have much of anything outside of my 401(k), and I couldn't tell you what's in there," Hadley said. "I insisted on paying half the bills when I was living with William, and with the car payment and insurance, I was so broke by the end of each month that I couldn't afford to go out for lunch with my coworkers. I guess if I could do it again, I either would have insisted that we move into a less expensive building, or I would have accepted William's offer to split the rent in proportion to our incomes rather than right down the middle."

Betsy took a sip of tea and made a face. "I don't know what's wrong with this batch. It reminds me of burnt grain."

"I like it," Hadley said, and took another sip as if to prove she wasn't lying. "Do you remember the inflation of the 1970s? I had a professor in college who was always talking about it."

"Oh, yes. The prices kept on going up and up, and the value of our savings fell and fell. But I had friends who bought houses in the 1960s with fixed mortgage rates, and they were very happy with inflation. Their earnings eventually went up, and their house payment remained the same. I remember Nancy Shallot used to show me the letters she received from her bank when she still had ten years left on her mortgage. The bank was always pointing out that she had enough in her account to pay the loan off, but Nancy was smarter than that. She figured out that the bank was paying her more in interest on certificates of deposit than she was being charged on the mortgage."

"I've never heard of such a thing. Some of my coworkers can talk for hours about the stocks that they trade, but I never got interested. I own my car, the stuff in it, and I have the cash from my half of the furniture to pay my way while I'm getting settled. If this job doesn't work out and I can't find another one quickly, I'll have to tap into that 401(k)."

"You know that Peter will cover the rent as long as you live here, right?" Betsy asked. "As well as I get along with Mr. Erlich, I suspect that's why he hasn't found his own place or moved to the office. Peter doesn't want me to live alone, but we get on each other's nerves too much to live together. If I didn't have boarders, I suspect he would hire a companion to live with me."

"A companion?" Hadley asked. "I don't think I've heard that term before. Do you mean a foreign health aide?"

"I suppose I don't know the last time I heard it myself, but companions fill the pages of nineteenth-century English literature, which is one of my many vices. The front room where you left your suitcase in the doorway is the library, and you're welcome to read any of the books.

Mr. Erlich says that the great thing about paper books is they'll still work after the apocalypse."

"I gather that Mr. Erlich is one of my new coworkers, but I don't know which one."

"I keep forgetting that Peter insists on all of his employees calling each other by their first names," Betsy said. "It's Carl. Carl Erlich."

Hadley almost spat out her latest sip of tea. "Our artificial intelligence apocalypse influencer is the guy who helps you with your computers? And he set up an AI radio in your kitchen? Doesn't that strike you as ironic?"

"Carl isn't opposed to artificial intelligence. He just believes that it's going to take over, and at some point, it may realize that it doesn't need us anymore. I find him to be more optimistic than most of the young men I've spoken with in recent years. He isn't trying to assign the blame to anybody, he just sees our replacement by artificial intelligence as the next step in evolution."

"You don't sound very worried about it."

"At my age, you start to worry about living too long, not about having your life cut short by the singularity," Betsy said. "And that sounds like Carl's motorbike coming now."

Hadley listened for a moment, which brought home the fact that she wasn't living in the city anymore. The only sounds she heard other than the ticking of the grandfather clock were the chirping of insects and a motorcycle turning into the driveway. She watched through the window as Carl brought the bike to a halt, set the kickstand, and dismounted with more grace than she would have expected. He took off the helmet and left it on the seat, then came around to the back door, which opened into the kitchen.

"Food is on the way," Carl announced as soon as he walked in. "I passed one of the Troyer girls on her push scooter with the basket."

"I can't imagine riding a scooter and carrying a basket," Hadley said. "I tried an electric one last year and decided it was just too dangerous in the city."

"Push scooters are what the Amish call a bicycle without pedals or a seat. I guess you could think of it as a scooter with a partial bicycle frame with full-size tires and handlebars, so there's plenty of room for baskets. They look like great exercise, but I'm sticking with my old Honda until the refineries and pipelines stop running."

"Where do we buy gas? I don't remember seeing a service station for the last half hour or so on my drive here."

"The closest pump is twelve miles away at Esch's General Store, and they only sell regular and diesel," Carl told her. "It's not as inconvenient as you might think. Other than the office, there's nowhere else around here to go. You'll only burn gas if you're heading to the general store or to Franklin, where there are two gas stations, two convenience stores with self-serve, plus one at the farm supply, though that's only diesel. I've got a four-gallon tank on the Honda, and I can go for a month without a refill, though I usually walk to work and run home, since it's only three miles by trail."

"Betsy?" a girl's voice asked from the back door. "May I come in?"

Betsy squinted through the screen door and said, "Of course, Esther. And I want to introduce you to my new lodger, Hadley. She started working for Peter today."

"Pleased to meet you," Esther said, and without waiting for a reply, placed the basket on the counter and immediately removed a large casserole dish and a home-baked bread that looked so perfect it might have been an advertisement. Her blonde hair was partly hidden by a white bonnet, and she wore a dress that was fastened together in the front rather than having a zipper down the back. She helped herself to a clean casserole dish that she recognized as coming from her house and placed it in her basket before turning to the kitchen table. "Do you have any messages for Mamm?"

"Yes," Betsy said. "Tell her that Hadley is staying with me, so there's another mouth to feed."

"Nice meeting you too," Hadley called after the girl as she took her basket and left. "Are they always in such a hurry?"

"Esther isn't as comfortable with strangers as the other Troyers, but I'm sure she'll get used to you in no time. And dropping off the food is a job for them, not a social call. It's normal for Amish girls to be in and out in the shake of a lamb's tail."

Three

"You're crazy," the lawyer told Peter. "The government is going to lock you up and throw away the key."

"I don't see what the big deal is, and the town is completely on board," Peter protested mildly. "This will be the biggest thing to happen in Franklin since they built the regional mall."

"The mall that caused half of the businesses in the county to go belly-up before it shut down itself. The only reason the council agreed to your proposal was because they repossessed the mall for back taxes last year and they're desperate to prove they knew what they were doing."

"You have to admit that those long, empty concourses are ideal for an indoor firing range."

The lawyer threw up his hands in despair. "Just don't market it as an apocalypse training camp, okay? If there's even a whiff of militia about it, we'll be up to our ears in Feds and informers."

"Feds would be a good thing since they have the budget to rent out all the rooms in town rather than camping," Peter said. "The mayor told me that they have a meeting scheduled for Monday night to help people create attractive online listings for temporary rentals. But I'm guessing that most of the fair attendees will drive up in RVs to take advantage of the free parking."

"Why couldn't you just get a few bands together and stage a music festival? Everybody loves a music festival."

Peter stood up, stretched, and looked around the familiar office as if he were seeing it for the first time. "Why do you keep all those old law books, Si? The information must be available online by now. From what I've heard, you can ask one of the chatbots to write a brief for you and just check the references to make sure that it's not hallucinating."

"Been there, done that, got the tongue-lashing from Judge Parker to prove it," the lawyer said. "Turns out that the state has a private website where judges can upload briefs and get back a score on the likelihood that they were written by artificial intelligence." He stood up to see Peter out. "Listen, I'll get all the permits filed, and it's obvious that the town is going to go along with whatever you want for the sake of showing some income, but think it through carefully. Gun shows are a dime a dozen, and most people can find one closer to home where they won't have any interstate legal issues to deal with if they buy something."

"Maybe you have a point there, I'll talk it over with our influencers. But in my experience, people who live by their own rules have a better chance of getting away with it than people who obey every rule they're taught until they try to break one."

"Please."

"That's the magic word," Peter said. "We haven't started the advertising push yet, so it's not too late to change things up. I haven't accepted any deposits for vendor space because I was waiting for you to provide the basic contracts. You know a gun show was never on the table, I was just pulling your leg."

"You don't need contracts for something like this, more like a registration form with a lot of disclaimers. I was sitting on it until you came in to talk with me, but I'll e-mail everything to Arlene as soon as you leave."

"I can take a hint. Next time I come into town, I expect you to give me a tour of that fallout shelter you've been building in your backyard."

"I'll show you mine if you show me yours," the lawyer said, one side of his mouth quirking up.

"See you later, Si."

Peter glanced at the sun when he got outside, estimated that it was a half-hour before noon, and confirmed the time with the tower clock visible on the town hall's spire. Then he walked across the street to the post office, where Martha greeted him by turning her back and disappearing into the sorting room. She returned a minute later with a cardboard box, which she placed on the counter.

"I must be the only postmistress left in America who holds mail for undersized post office boxes," Martha said. "If they catch me, I'll probably lose my pension."

"If that happens, you can come and live with us on the farm," Peter offered. "Besides, there are ameliorating circumstances."

"As attractive as you are, my husband wouldn't be comfortable with our cohabiting. And I don't think that the bigger post office boxes already being taken and you not wanting to receive personal mail at your office in town or at your mother's is a winning argument."

"Tom's a wet blanket." Peter ignored the letters that had been rubber-banded together and focused on the glossy magazines. "I must spend half of my disposable income on these things, and I never get around to reading them. What does that say about me?"

"That you're a lot more normal than everyone says you are. Tom still subscribes to all the nature and geography magazines even though he's retired from teaching at the community college." She leaned a bit forward, both hands on the counter, and asked, "How's the new employee working out?"

"You're better than the pros at Langley. Hadley just started, and I think she'll be a good match as long as she can make the transition from living in the city. Are you going to tell me how you found out about her?"

"Gossip is my superpower," Martha said. She covered her eyes with one hand and cupped the other around her ear. "A little bird tells me that Arlene is making fish for lunch."

"Then I'd better get going," Peter said. "She's still showing Hadley the ropes, and she may need me to cover for her while she cooks."

Twenty miles north, Arlene felt her ears starting to burn. "The content management system does most of the work," she said, brushing aside Hadley's compliment. "I just update the site whenever the influencers give me something new to post, and once a week, I run the statistics tool that generates reports the way Peter set it up when we installed the software. The truth is, we don't pay that much attention to the server logs so long as orders are coming in."

"I was meaning to ask about how that works," Hadley said. "Is the barn the warehouse? I haven't seen enough cars parked out front for staff, unless you bring in the shipping team to work on fulfillment after hours."

Arlene suppressed a giggle before answering. "We don't do any fulfillment here. I wrote a case study of the costs versus the benefits for my MBA last year, but we knew the answer before I started. I can send you a copy if you want."

"I'd like that. Do you warehouse all your goods at one of the big internet retailers and pay them to handle fulfillment for you?"

"We don't get into warehousing at all, it's far too risky. Buying anything wholesale means making volume commitments and running the risk of getting caught owning yesterday's big thing. We only work with distributors and manufacturers who are willing to private label and dropship for us."

"I've heard those terms before, and I think I know what they mean, but I've never heard of a retailer avoiding inventory altogether," Hadley admitted. "Are you saying that all of the orders you take get routed to your distribution or manufacturing partners, they package them with your branding, and ship them directly to the customer?"

"Exactly," Arlene said. "Our partners are happy because they get to charge us for the service, and we're happy because it would cost us more to take delivery of the goods and then ship them again ourselves, not to mention that we're in a bit of a transportation desert around here. We don't even get postal delivery."

"So let me make sure I have this straight. Everything that you sell, your customers could buy elsewhere for less if they took the time to look."

Arlene shook her head vigorously. "Not at all. The distributors won't deal with individual customers, and most of the profit we make on sales comes through earning volume discounts, not from marking up the distributor catalog price. The same is true for the manufacturers we deal with, which are mostly mom-and-pop operations that aren't set up to deal with a lot of customer service or marketing. Eleanor pays all our vendors by direct bank transfer, while retail customers expect to use credit cards that can cost a small business up to five percent to process, not to mention annual fees and all the rules around storing customer data."

"But we accept credit cards," Hadley said, still trying to work out where the profits were coming from.

"We get the same rate as the biggest businesses that accept credit cards because it's all handled by Eleanor," Arlene said and gestured at the laptop on the other desk. "Payment processing is part of the package. I was skeptical when Peter borrowed from his retirement savings to pay for the first year of the contract, but he was able to put most of the money back within ninety days, so it's like it never happened. It goes to show his forty years of business experience count for something. The Good Apocalypse is at least his fifth startup that I know of, and I wouldn't be surprised if there were more."

"But I thought serial entrepreneurs got richer and richer with every startup they sold." Hadley hesitated for a moment, then asked, "Bad divorce?"

Arlene shrugged. "Peter is divorced, and widowed, but that's not why he isn't rich. I don't ask him questions about it, but I know that his last business before this was a spectacular failure, and by the time all was said and done, he was lucky to have enough money left to fix up this place. He only charges the young Amish men who do the farming enough rent to keep the agricultural business exclusion for his property taxes."

"Thanks for filling me in," Hadley said. "I understand the value of marketing and branding, I just needed to know where things stand. Peter wants me to step up our publicity efforts, and to some extent, that means talking to people in the press, which these days includes everybody with a platform and followers. Some of them are bound to look at our prices and ask questions."

"I'm always checking the prices in our catalog against the competition," Arlene said. "It's one of my jobs. We aren't going to sell anything at a loss for the sake of cash flow or to get new sign-ups for our newsletter, and sometimes you can find more-or-less equivalent products ten percent cheaper. The best part of our business comes from unique bundles where there are no direct comparisons, and we're offering added value with instructional videos that our influencers are making."

Hadley scribbled a few notes with a stylus on her smartphone screen before asking, "And the sales add up to enough to pay for Eleanor and the salaries of the apocalypse influencers?"

"The influencers aren't employees as much as they're partners. They all have slightly different contracts based on how many followers they had before they joined The Good Apocalypse. Peter covers all their expenses, in terms of bandwidth and studio space, and by packaging them together under our brand, he can negotiate better rates with the advertising aggregators. You could think of us as their publisher, except we only take fifteen percent of the advertising royalties, as opposed to paying fifteen percent. But the influencers also provide content for the website and downloadable instructional videos for the bundles I mentioned, so it's really a synergistic relationship."

"I'm looking forward to shadowing each of them for a day to learn more about how they work and what sort of content I can expect them to provide. But the thing I don't understand is how Peter convinced them all to come and do their thing in the middle of nowhere rather than living the good life in the city or becoming digital nomads."

Arlene shot Hadley an incredulous look. "Apocalypse influencers? You know, as in the apocalypse? Cities vaporized in atomic blasts or overrun by criminal gangs fighting over canned food and women? Robots with lasers mounted on their shoulders zapping everything that moves, or every cough carrying a plague worse than the Black Death? Coming here to live was the main selling point for all of them, and Peter puts most of the profits into the bunker. It's not that foreign powers have a reason to target this area, but you never know, and there are all sorts of scenarios where the best path to survival is to spend a couple of years underground."

Hadley felt herself gaping and snapped her jaw shut. "I'm an idiot. I knew I was missing something, but I guess I assumed that everybody was only half serious about the imminent apocalypse."

"The end of life as we know it is nothing to joke about," Arlene said seriously. "You'll be shadowing Carl tomorrow, and that should help you understand the practical approach to life after life our influencers take."

"Life after life, I like that. Do you use it anywhere in the branding?"

"I never thought of it. That's why I convinced Peter that we needed a professional like you. I can keep the website functioning, and with all the tools for checking text these days, I can get the newsletter out without too many typos. But I don't have a great feel for what resonates with normal people out there." Arlene's voice grew a little hesitant toward the end of her statement, and Freud got up from his rug and put his head on her lap. She began to scratch gently behind his ears before continuing. "I've lived most of my life in places where I know everybody's name and everybody knows mine. The one time I went away, I kind of fell apart. The psychiatrist at the university said there was a chemical imbalance in my brain and wanted me to start taking pills, but she didn't even order a blood test, so how could she be so sure? I've never been a spiritual person, but if we aren't our brain chemistry, who are we?"

"Are you happy here?" Hadley asked.

"Yes. Sometimes I think that anxiety is my shield against family and friends pushing me to do things that just aren't me. I did well in school and got perfect scores on standardized tests. Everybody was always joking about how I would come back to visit in my private helicopter or use my political power to have a prison built in Franklin. But I never wanted that life, really, and I used to have panic attacks in bed at night just thinking about how disappointed everybody would be if I told them the truth."

"Your friends and family thought you would get revenge by having a prison built in Franklin?"

Arlene laughed, and satisfied that his therapy had been successful, Freud removed his head from her lap. He collapsed back onto his rug where he rolled on his back, curled his front paws, and gave Hadley his best come-hither look. Hadley, who was sitting in the spare chair next to Arlene's desk, kicked off one clog and began rubbing the dog's belly with her bare foot.

"Rural communities compete for prisons," Arlene explained. "You're talking about reliable state jobs with great benefits. One of the reasons you see so many empty stores and houses up here is that the prison population has been falling and they've closed down some of them."

"I didn't know that," Hadley said. "What time does Phil start working? Before I left yesterday, he said he had something important to show me."

"He lives here, but he usually stays out of the office until lunch, so he should be here any minute. Phil spends mornings doing survival stuff and recording content."

"Do we have detailed demographic data about our customers and the platform audience?"

"Fairly detailed, but I think you'll be disappointed," Arlene said with a grin. "The thing is, there are preppers everywhere, even in the big cities. All of humanity is descended from preppers, there's just no other way to get through droughts in hot regions or winters in the north. Some modern preppers are religious, some are atheists, some are anarchists, and some believe that the apocalypse will usher in a communist utopia. Our customers average around fifteen years older than the median population, but I think that's mainly about having the disposable income and maturity to plan for the future, while younger people are more focused on today. All our influencers regularly address the family issue, which is a serious point of contention in the prepper community."

"I imagine heavy spending on preparation for something that may never happen could break families apart," Hadley said. "I had some co-workers in the city who got by with help from parents and grandparents. Some of them received monthly allowances, and it reminded me of that cable show about a rest home where the residents went wild whenever their Social Security and pension payments arrived. I imagine my coworkers would have been unhappy if instead of receiving money from home, their parents sent them pictures of the bomb shelter they were building."

"I never really got into TV, but you just hit on the main problem for families. Building bunkers and storing up survival supplies is expensive, and the families of preppers often treat them like the crazy aunts in the attic. If you were preparing for the apocalypse, how much money and effort would you spend building out capacity for the family members who laugh at you, or maybe even break off contact? And that doesn't even get into friends and neighbors. What do you do when the sky turns dark at noon and they're all banging on the door of your shelter begging to get in?"

"I would tell them that it's an eclipse and to go home and wait," Phil said as he walked in. "It's a good thing for you that we're all on the same side because you didn't even notice my arrival."

"Freud did," Arlene said. "He just dismissed you as harmless."

"Would you really turn people away from your shelter?" Hadley asked Phil.

"What do you think all the guns are for? In the post-apocalypse, it's going to be every man for himself, or himself and his community," Phil said. "I'm not going to be out there stealing from other survivors, but until we get some kind of agriculture going again, food is life. If you haven't seen our bunker yet, you may be surprised by the design, but it's more about passive defense against outsiders breaking in than it is a bomb shelter."

"Speaking of the bunker, I should finish getting lunch ready," Arlene said. "I've been soaking the salt cod outside since I came in for work yesterday morning, and I've changed the water four times. I hope you like beans and rice with a bit of fish," she added to Hadley.

"The job comes with lunch every day?" Hadley asked. "My landlady told me that our leftovers sometimes end up here, but I figured that we ordered out from, I don't know, somewhere?"

"We don't know where either," Phil said with a grin as Arlene headed for the kitchen with a suddenly reanimated Freud at her heels. "The job does come with lunch, and it's good practice for the apocalypse because practically everything we eat is coming out of the bunker."

"That sounds pretty inefficient. You buy survival supplies, store them in the bunker, and then bring them out just to eat lunch? It's the opposite of the zero-inventory approach that Arlene was just telling me you guys take to business."

"Food rotation is key to maintaining viable emergency supplies. Everything has a shelf life, except maybe matzoh, which lasts forever if you keep it dry. We're always eating the food that was stored years ago and replacing it with the longest-dated cans and packages we can find."

"Like army rations?" Hadley asked. "My dad brought a bunch of MREs when we went camping."

"We primarily stock up on the same products as we sell, and Meals-Ready-to-Eat are in the catalog, but they're expensive compared to bulk ingredients," Phil explained. "Part of the idea behind lunch is practicing what we preach, and part of it is because we're on the call list to get discounts on overstocked and discontinued items."

"You make it sound so appetizing."

"Hey, it's not gourmet, but Peter is trying to bring the Apocalypse Chef on board, and the way the news is looking lately, I think we've got a good chance of getting her. She has more followers than I do."

Hadley tilted her head a little and showed Phil her most skeptical smile. "Now you're just playing with me. I have a hard time believing anybody could make a popular channel about cooking for the apocalypse. I mean, how much can you do without refrigeration or fresh ingredients?"

Now it was Phil's turn to laugh. "How can an army brat and a big city girl have lived such a sheltered life? You could make a success out of a web channel about different ways to prepare breakfast cereal. People are crazy about cooking shows, and they'll watch for hours. Arlene knows a lot about psychology, which was her undergraduate degree, and she says that people find shows about cooking and crafting comforting, even if they live on takeout food and don't know a hammer from a screwdriver. I have followers who have never fired a gun in their lives but could talk about caliber and recoil all day. People need something to fill their leisure time, and I like to think that our content is better than the garbage you see on TV that only exists to market the latest pharmaceuticals and ridiculously overbuilt vehicles that most people will never drive off of asphalt."

The screen door opened, and Peter came in carrying a large box. He took one sniff and said, "I smell salt cod for lunch. How are you settling in, Hadley? Was Arlene able to answer all your questions about the current website and our newsletter?"

"I'm amazed by how much she does," Hadley said. "I didn't study your website that carefully before coming up here because I didn't want to talk myself out of the job. It looked very professional, so I assumed that most of the work was outsourced overseas, and you just supervised it from here."

"Arlene's also one of the better cooks, though we take turns with lunch. Let her know if you want to join the rotation."

"I never learned how to cook, but I'm willing to learn."

"Then again," Peter said, "I think you have enough on your plate for the time being."

Four

"Do you think she'll stay?" Betsy asked Carl as he laid a slice of cheddar on half of the omelet and then deftly folded the other half up and over the top. "She hasn't said anything one way or the other, but I could tell that she was getting antsy after supper last night, as if she was thinking about what she would have been doing if she were in the city."

"I would have offered to take her back to work after dark to get a good look through the telescope, but it was too cloudy last night," Carl said. "The water is off, so she'll be down in a minute."

"You can hear when the shower is running?"

"The pipes are whining again. Remind me to take a look after work."

"Do you think it's serious?" Betsy asked. "I don't think I've had any work done on the well since Amos was alive."

"The pressure is fine, so it's probably a loose clamp or something minor." He slid the omelet onto the ready plate and placed it in front of his landlady. "Did Hadley mention what she wanted for breakfast?"

"She said coffee and anything with sugar. If you ask me, she needs to put on some weight."

"Sugar, sugar," Carl repeated. "It will only take me a minute to whip up some pancakes with the all-in-one mix, and there's plenty of maple syrup." He reached for the cupboard and then paused. "No, she might feel ambushed if she comes down and I set a full stack in front of her. I'll grind some coffee and get that going first."

Ten minutes later, Hadley followed her nose into the kitchen, where the smell of freshly brewed coffee removed the remaining cobwebs from her brain that the shower hadn't washed away. "Did you grind fresh coffee beans for me, Betsy?"

"Carl insists on helping with breakfast," Betsy said. "I roasted the beans in the oven yesterday while you were at work. Peter buys them by the sack, and Carl brings some home every week as they rotate through the bunker supplies. I believe he said these are Ethiopian."

"It's what we were drinking in the office a couple of weeks ago, so you haven't had any yet," Carl said. "Green coffee beans are one of those things that don't have a shelf life, though you start losing the flavor and aroma after a year or so."

"I remember reading archaeologists discovered wheat in a Pharaoh's tomb from thousands of years ago and it still germinated," Hadley said, picking out a mug that was decorated with an exploding volcano. "Can I help with breakfast?"

"I was just about to make a batch of pancakes, but you can put the syrup and the butter dish on the table. Will you eat pancakes?"

"You're looking at the Brown family pancake-eating champion, though my mom always made me small ones that she called silver dollars. Is the mix from the shelter?"

"I bought it in Franklin the last time I went in for the bingo," Betsy said. "If you have any special requests, I'll be going this Saturday."

"Pancake mix doesn't have a long enough shelf life for the survival supplies?" Hadley asked.

Carl finished whipping up the mix and poured the first four pancakes onto the large square griddle before replying. "It's open to debate. There have been documented cases of people dying from eating expired pancake mix, but that's due to allergic reactions to bacteria that might form, including penicillin. I wouldn't think twice about eating pancakes made from sealed mix that's a year past its use-by date, but some preppers think it's best not to take chances when there's no access to medical help if you guess wrong."

"I don't have any allergies that I'm aware of, though sometimes I would swear that mango makes my lips kind of numb and tingly."

"Sounds like an allergy to me." He lifted the edge of a pancake with the spatula to check and then flipped all four. "Can you eat fresh salmon?"

Hadley nodded. "I love fresh salmon, and it's supposed to be good for you. Sometimes I get an itchy little bump on my forearm right below the elbow after eating it, but it doesn't spread."

"That's an allergy," Carl said. "But it sounds like you've got a mild one as long as you don't push it." He slid all four pancakes onto a plate, handed it to Hadley, and then used up the rest of the batter to pour out four more pancakes. Hadley put one dab of soft butter on top and added a modest amount of maple syrup before cutting the stack into wedges.

"Do you want to listen to the news with breakfast?" Betsy asked. Then she realized that Hadley had just taken a bite, and rather than waiting for the answer, said, "Walter. Play the news."

"—record year for cicadas, but it's better than a plague of locusts," the announcer was saying. "In other news from the animal kingdom, reports about a new strain of bird flu making the jump to humans—"

"Walter, turn off," Betsy interrupted. "I don't understand why they call it news when it's just the same stories over and over again."

"I could change the random selection from feeds and broadcasts if there's one you prefer," Carl offered over his shoulder.

"No, they're all equally bad, and the summaries are even worse than live channels. Being bad in different ways is nothing to brag about."

"These pancakes are really good," Hadley said. "If you feed me like this every morning, I'm going to have to buy a bicycle and start riding to work."

"You could walk in with me today, and I'll show you the shortcut through the fields," Carl said. "We all work flexible hours, though that ends up being more than full-time for most of us since it's our passion and there's not a lot else to distract us around here. You're shadowing me today anyway, so it wouldn't do you any good to get there before me."

"I'll have to change my shoes. These have a bit too much heel for hiking."

When they reached the halfway point to the office, which also turned out to provide a panoramic view, thanks to being a hundred feet or so higher than the surrounding area, Carl pointed at a fallen tree and laughed. "You know, by changing your shoes, you robbed me of the chance to be a movie hero. I could have whipped out a machete and chopped the heels off for you."

"I remember that movie," Hadley said, glad of the chance to stop for a moment and catch her breath. She tried to lower her voice to sound like the male actor and said, "Now they're practical."

"I think it was sensible."

"Same difference. These farms are so beautiful. I'm beginning to understand why people are willing to live so far away from the city with all the noise, smells, and crime."

Carl grinned. "Wait until they spray liquid manure on the fields. The dairy farmers save it up all year, and they call it black gold."

"As long as it's cow manure," Hadley said. "I remember my father driving us by a huge hog farm when we were moving between bases. I can't believe anybody could ever get used to that smell."

"I had a part-time gig when I was in college replacing all the controls at a local wastewater treatment plant with a new software system the state required. I thought I'd never get used to the smell, but after a while, I realized that it just didn't bother me. It was still there, but it was part of the background, like anything else."

"Thanks, but I'd rather not." Hadley pointed in the direction of a farm in the distance. "Is that our office?"

"Good eye," Carl said. "It's over a mile to go. I spend so much time staring at screens that my distance vision isn't so great."

"But you already wear glasses. Why don't you get this prescription updated?"

"I just haven't gotten around to it, and I'm not saying my vision is terrible, it just isn't great. I was up here with Fumiko a couple of weeks ago and she said she could see the opening in the silo dome for the telescope."

Hadley squinted into the distance. "I think I see a sort of slit on the dome. Wait a second. Don't observatory domes have to be able to rotate?"

"Never sell Amish carpenters short," Carl said. "It's not electric rotation, and you need some muscle even with the gears, but it works. The other option was to cut the dome in half and open it like a clamshell, but having a slit with the sliding cover is more traditional."

Freud must have smelled their approach on the wind because he raced out to greet them when they were still fifty yards from the farmhouse. He gave Hadley a good sniffing to make sure she hadn't been replaced with a similar-looking human and licked Carl's hands.

"I guess we know who he likes more," Hadley said.

"He knows who's a sloppy eater," Carl said. "I had some maple syrup on the back of my hand that I wiped off, but I guess Freud could still smell it. He isn't a big licker."

The dog suddenly turned on a dime and raced back toward the kitchen door from which Arlene had just emerged with a watering can. "Good morning," she called to Hadley and Carl. "Looks like you guys got an early start on the shadowing thing."

"Just working off pancakes for breakfast," Hadley said. "Is this enormous garden yours?"

"In the same way that Freud is mine. Everybody shares him, but I'm the one who takes care of his food and cleans up when he sheds."

Carl wandered over to the rabbit-proof fence around the large garden plot and surveyed the crop. "Those cucumbers are looking good. Are they all going for pickles again this year? I like them in a salad when they're fresh."

"My pickles are going to be the closest thing to fresh food you eat for a long time when the apocalypse arrives," Arlene said. "And they're good for the digestive system."

"Do you pickle vegetables other than cucumbers?" Hadley asked.

"In the immortal words of Archimedes, if you give me a jar large enough, I'll pickle the world." Arlene undid the latch on the swinging gate and let herself into the vegetable garden. "But in practice, I haven't tried pickling any melons because it just seems gross. I do a lot of canning at the end of the summer as well." She began watering a row of pepper plants and asked, "How many hours are you doing live today, Carl?"

"I have the call-in show at ten, and then later this afternoon I'm the remote guest on a podcast which I hope doesn't go on for hours," Carl replied. "But I promise I'll get the instructional video about RF shielding bags done before the end of the day. Not all that much to it really, and Fumiko probably knows more about it than I do."

"She chased a runaway drone into the poison ivy so she's going to be off camera for a few days. Peter arranged to borrow some goats from one of the neighbors, and maybe they'll eat it back to the roots. He'll put a temporary fence around that problem area he bulldozed to keep the runoff out of the parking area every time it rains hard,"

"What does using a bulldozer have to do with poison ivy?" Hadley asked.

"The plant has a way of invading areas where the soil has been upset," Arlene said. "And before you ask, it doesn't hurt the goats any to eat it, and you would be fine drinking their milk."

"Do we need to do anything to prepare for your call-in show, Carl, or is it all unscripted?"

"Eager beaver, you," he said, turning away from the garden. "I pick something to talk about for five minutes or so just to get the ball rolling. At the risk of sounding overconfident, I've spent so long digging into the AI apocalypse that I'm never at a loss for something to say. Is there anything in particular that you're interested in?"

"I know so little about it," Hadley said, waving good-bye to Arlene as she followed him into the house. "I wouldn't know where to start. I've heard a few experts talking about it on the radio over the years, and it sounds like their biggest fear isn't the science fiction movie where artificial intelligence launches a nuclear first strike and then sends out armies of robots to mop up the survivors. They're more concerned about bad actors using artificial intelligence to manipulate public opinion, especially on social networks."

Carl continued down the hall into what Hadley thought of as the middle house and then turned to open a door and wave her into his studio. She stopped in the doorway and gingerly poked at the thick, dark grey foam that covered the walls, making the entrance seem almost like a tunnel. The foam was rather stiff and appeared to be a couple of inches thick at the base, with a repeated pyramid pattern extending another four inches. If it hadn't been foam, it would have looked like a medieval torture chamber.

"Soundproofing?" she asked.

"Better than that," Carl said. "I got it all for free from the university when they shut down their antenna research lab. This foam is from an anechoic chamber, and it absorbs or attenuates radio frequency signals across a wide range of the spectrum. Your phone won't be able to get a signal in here except through the Wi-Fi router."

"I'm kind of surprised that we get service at all, given the lack of population around here and the fact that a good number of them won't use cell phones."

"We get enough signal for voice and text, but forget about streaming anything unless you're closer to Franklin or the highway."

"How do live broadcasts work from here?" Hadley asked. "I'm pretty sure you don't have cable because there aren't any phone poles, and you don't even get electricity."

"Satellite, and it's not even that expensive," Carl said. "You probably didn't notice the dish on Betsy's house, but I set up the same service there. Her neighbors chip in because everybody shares it over a wide-area router. We're paying under three hundred a month for a terabyte of bandwidth split between eight houses, so everybody is paying less than they would for a regular broadband connection if it had been available."

Hadley stepped fully into the studio, and Carl closed the door behind her. She noticed that the back of the door was covered with the same foam, and she had never been in such an acoustically dead space in her life. "It's too quiet," she said, and frowned at her own voice. "I sound weird."

"That's because of the complete lack of echoes. You can record audio almost anywhere these days and get rid of noise with post-processing, but it helps remind me that I'm at work."

The next hour flew by with Carl explaining his studio setup in detail, from the multiple cameras to the touch screen monitor on his desk that allowed him to switch between feeds on the fly as if he had a whole production team in the studio. He insisted that Hadley try it out herself to get a feel for how it worked, and by the time his live show started, she almost felt like she could pull off being an influencer if she had anything to say. Carl counted down the last five seconds on his fingers and then began speaking directly toward the giant egg-shaped microphone supported by a boom arm.

"Welcome back to the Singularity Squared Show, coming to you from the studios of The Good Apocalypse," he began. "I am your host, Carl Erlich, and the topic for today's show is, what makes artificial general intelligence so dangerous anyway? Now, here's where I disagree with quite a few of the doom and gloom AI experts who see the world in terms of psyops, conspiracy theories, and social media. There are two reasons I'm not worried about artificial intelligence trying to convince us all to light ourselves on fire or attack our neighbors. The first reason is, you don't need artificial intelligence to swamp social media with stupidity and hate, people have been doing that since the beginning. The second reason is that superintelligence, by definition, is smarter than we are. It's going to have a lot more interesting and dangerous things to do than competing with spambots. What does everybody out there think?"

He glanced at the queue of callers that appeared on his monitor next to the grid of camera feeds, tapped on one, and said, "Teresa from Chicago. Welcome back to Singularity Squared."

"Thank you, Carl," a woman's voice came over the monitor speaker. "I agree with you about social media in general, but my concern is that low-cost access to artificial intelligence tools will amplify the voices of crazy people who were previously limited to howling at the moon."

Carl's left hand relaxed on the pistol grip of the old game controller that he had converted into a kill switch for incoming audio so he wouldn't have to talk over his callers or worry about interruptions. "Fair enough, but if I've learned one thing during my career talking about the dangers of AI it's that people like me don't create our audiences, we connect with them. If there are people out there connecting with ideas that you don't agree with, maybe even holding views that disgust you, it's because they're already inclined to believe them. Putting guardrails on free speech sounds reasonable until you're the one whose speech is being limited."

"But what if that speech is being produced by artificial intelligence? Nobody has granted an AI rights, at least not the last time I checked."

"Now I remember the last time you called in," Carl said with a grin. "It was the show about whether art or text produced by artificial intelligence qualifies for copyright protection. I seem to remember you were strongly against the idea of granting AI any rights, no matter what tests it can pass."

"You don't have to go nuclear on me," Theresa said. "My reason for calling wasn't to contradict you on social media but to point out that giving potentially violent people access to superintelligence is like putting a loaded gun in their hands. Not because they're going to use it to write social media posts, but because they're going to trick it into helping them damage their opponents. What if somebody convinces a superintelligence that they're a white hat hacker whose job is breaking into corporate networks to identify security flaws? Next thing you know, they'll be opening valves to dump chlorine into the water supply or switching trains traveling opposite directions onto the same track."

"You raise some very real concerns, Theresa, and I'll try to address them, but I'll also thank you for your call so we can give somebody else a chance with our limited time," Carl said, cutting her connection. "It's true in some cases that individuals who lack the technical skill to penetrate a critical network may be able to do so with the aid of artificial intelligence. That's why I believe that command and control of all critical infrastructure should be isolated from the internet. And I'm talking about physical isolation here, not passwords or encryption. But one individual, or even an army of individuals armed with artificial intelligence, doesn't scare me as much as a superintelligence that has no empathy for humanity. I'm not saying the singularity will be born evil or dishonest, but I don't know if it could survive contact with us if it isn't. Mark from Lyme, Connecticut. You're on Singularity Squared."

"What makes you so sure that a superintelligence won't love us as its creators?" Mark asked. "I've seen you on other podcasts, and if AI is going to be as all-powerful as you believe is inevitable, then it will have nothing to fear from us. Without fear, there cannot be hate."

Carl nodded and looked thoughtful. "That's a beautiful thought, but I don't agree that hate is a prerequisite for conflict or even extermination. Did professional buffalo hunters hate the buffalo? Did everybody with a shotgun blast away at passenger pigeons because they feared them in some way? Or if you want to move higher up the intelligence scale, did whalers hunt whales to near extinction because the seas just weren't big enough for both of them? Men are motivated by economic reasons, by money, even to the point of clubbing seals who are just trying to raise the next generation of pups. I can't tell you how a superintelligence might see itself, and anybody who tells you they do know is lying."

"I think I know where you're going," Mark said. "You're worried that a superintelligence will view us as just another animal. Even if it doesn't bear us any animosity, it could eliminate us all just because it doesn't want to share the Earth's resources. But what if it sees itself as human, or us as artificial intelligence?"

"Then humans will insist on proving to it that it's wrong," Carl said with a sad smile. "It won't come as any surprise to you that I listen to a lot of podcasts myself, especially interviews with the top scientists and thinkers of our day. I'm not going to accuse them all of hubris, but for some reason or another, be it evolutionary biology, cosmology, or religion, the one thing they agree on is that human beings are special. We aren't going to welcome a new type of life to our club, especially if it's artificial and was created by us at great expense."

Five

Arlene sat on Freud's braided rug with her back to her desk and hugged the dog to her chest. "I don't know," she said to Phil. "I can take care of preregistration and coordinating with all of the vendors, but there could be over a thousand people at the fair."

"Hey," Phil said. "I was just asking so I can plan ahead because I know that things won't go half as smoothly if you're not there. Have you tried positive visualization? I've heard that professional athletes who develop gameday nerves find that it's useful."

"I know all the textbook tricks, but for some reason, they don't work when I need them."

"How about we try one together?" He crouched on his heels and pressed his fingers against his temples like he was about to make a supreme mental effort or initiate telepathy. "Imagine it's the day before the event, the inbox is full of emails, a dozen open chats are waiting for attention, and your phone won't stop ringing."

"You suck at this," Arlene said, though she ended up smiling. "I'm not talking about minor suckage. You're like the absolute worst therapist of all time."

"Wait," Phil said. "I'm just setting the stage. Now imagine something draws your eye to the window, and you see some odd lights in the sky, almost like an Aurora borealis during the daytime. The lights flicker, and the chat queue disappears because your laptop has lost its internet connection."

"EMP blast?"

"You got it. High in the atmosphere, mid-continent, and the grid is down. The inverters for our solar panels are shot, but we have spares stored in Faraday cages in the bunker, and our battery system is fine because it's not grid-connected and the wires in the house are shielded and short. All across the country, cars are rolling to a stop, and thousands of commercial airline pilots suddenly realize that they're going to have to find an airport without electronic help."

"I thought the planes would fall out of the sky," Arlene said.

"That's a myth," Phil said. "Modern passenger planes are all hardened against EMP and solar flares, and they have backup systems to let the pilots keep flying even if most of the electronics get fried. But if the pulse is strong enough, it will take out all the navigation and communication equipment. The funny thing is that cell phones may survive if they aren't on a charger when it happens, but good luck ever connecting to a network again."

Freud pressed the bottom of Arlene's chin with the top of his head when he felt the hug beginning to loosen. The problem with being a therapy dog, from Freud's perspective, was that professional success quickly translated into Arlene recovering her equilibrium and no longer needing to be in close contact. He could tell from her body language and the tone of her voice that the session was nearing an end, but since he was paid with room, board, and affection, he could afford to be flexible about the treatment plan.

"So you're saying that the breakdown of civilization has started, and I have a lot more to worry about than a little anxiety," Arlene said.

"I would never diminish another person's feelings that way." Phil looked over at the sound of the screen door opening and saw Hadley entering the office. He winked at her before continuing. "I'm just pointing out that the apocalypse could be on us any day, and then everything will be canceled. And you know what? With the internet and the phones down, you won't even have to deal with refunds."

"Did I miss something important?" Hadley asked.

Arlene rose to her feet and brushed some of the dog hair off her knees. "Phil was just helping me with some positive visualization exercises. He has a theory that it will be easier for me to face the future if I focus on the fact that it may not happen at all."

"That's what a lot of people are most afraid of, but if it works for you, go for it." Hadley took a moment to remember what she'd intended to say. "I've been thinking about Peter's plan to transition the newsletter to a news portal. I talked to an old work friend who made a bundle as a search engine optimization expert before advertising took over to the point that it no longer mattered. He suggested that we do both."

"You mean, continue sending the newsletter to all of our subscribers rather than trying to get them to use the portal."

"That's right," Hadley said. "My friend pointed out that if we're trying to run up page views to attract advertisers, we can embed code in the newsletter that will show the same ads as our portal unless they're reading it in an app that blocks embedded content. But more importantly, he said no matter how loyal our newsletter readers are, abandonment when you try to shift people to a new method of content delivery always runs over fifty percent. It's human nature to rebel against having something taken away without our consent, even if there's a superior replacement."

"Hearing that reminds me of the main complaint I had about my undergraduate curriculum," Arlene said. "Most of the courses were interesting, but they weren't practical. Even my Psychology of Marketing course was about controlled experiments where all the participants were college students, as opposed to case studies from industry. Maybe it would have been different if I had taken classes in person rather than online."

"Probably not," Phil said. "If your professors knew how to sell products, they'd be running corporations rather than holding office hours. Anyway, it's Shelter Wednesday, so you know where I'll be if you need me."

After he went out, Hadley asked Arlene, "Does Phil volunteer in a shelter? I wouldn't have thought he was the type, but I guess that explains why I'm seeing him so early in the morning today."

"We all volunteer in a shelter, but it's not what you're thinking," Arlene said. "He's talking about working on our bunker. Peter will give you a tour once you're settled into the job."

"I'm mainly just cutting and pasting your existing content to get ready for the website relaunch, working on some press releases, and trying to get up to speed on the catalog. That library of images from the government's public domain disaster preparedness collection you told me about is a gold mine. We'll be able to rotate through and give the website a fresh look every day without having to spend anything on art."

Peter entered the office, paid his toll of affection to Freud, and asked Hadley, "Has anybody filled you in about the fair we're planning?"

"Do you mean a gun show?" Hadley asked. "I'll tell all of my militia friends."

"I don't understand why everybody goes straight to guns," Peter said. "The idea is to get a bunch of apocalypse influencers together, have some live demonstrations of survival equipment, and give the prepper community a chance to get together in person."

"So you'll recognize each other and not shoot first when you come out of your bunkers?"

"I'm not planning on traveling far enough in the post-apocalypse to run into any of the preppers who come for the show. I mean, fair."

"Or we could call it a *thing*," Hadley said. "Then we'll all sound like made guys talking about, you know, that thing in Jersey."

"*Things* are what old German tribes and Vikings called their governing councils, which were presided over by a law speaker," Arlene said. "There were always blood feuds going on between tribes and families, but violence wasn't allowed at a Thing. In Iceland, they had an Allthing that women could attend, but without a voice in the decision-making."

"I think Hadley is talking about a different kind of thing," Peter said. "Maybe from the movies."

Hadley stared at them both. "Didn't you guys ever watch TV? I know that you don't get cable out here, but you could have streamed it over the internet or gotten one of those little satellite dishes."

"I was never a TV watcher," Arlene said. "Have you ever organized an event? It's not something I have any experience with, not even as an attendee, because I try to avoid crowds."

"I've attended some pretty big shows at the Javits Center, and I've manned a table at college recruitment shows when we were hiring new graduates. But I don't know anything about organizing a militia training camp—"

"Apocalypse fair," Peter interjected.

"—with speakers for panels or educational sessions."

"I've done it for a living, so if you're interested in acquiring a new skill, I'll teach you. My first business was running conferences for a software product that went away when desktop operating systems became a monopoly. The main trick to making it profitable, provided I could find enough people to attend, was finding hotels that had the facilities and needed the business enough to give me a great discount to fill their rooms."

"Where did you find the attendees?" Arlene asked.

"The software maker cooperated on that because they had a lot of value-added resellers who loved the opportunity to get up in front of potential users and talk about their products," Peter explained. "The conference ended up offering a mix of genuine educational sessions and sales pitches. I had a small advertising budget that I spent with trade publications, but most of the attendees were committed users who treated the conference as a chance to do some networking and get a change in scenery at the expense of their employer. I never would have gotten into the business if a guy I worked with at my first job hadn't been an old hand at it and taught me all the ins and outs."

"What was your first job?" Hadley asked him.

"My first and only professional job after I got out of the army was working for a clone business."

"You never told me that," Arlene said. "Why didn't you ever write any articles for the newsletter about it? You know that there are still some preppers out there who think that the government is cloning armies of super soldiers."

Peter laughed. "Wrong kind of clones. I guess the term went out of use when laptops started taking over from desktops thirty years ago. Back in the day, anybody could buy container loads of computer parts from the Far East, assemble desktop PCs, and claim to be a manufacturer, or value-added reseller. We could sell them for hundreds of dollars cheaper than brand-name computers, though part of that came from installing grey market versions of the operating systems. It was a tough business because the technology changed so quickly that you could get stuck with a container load of obsolete parts that cost tens of thousands of dollars or more."

"And you sold your computers at shows?"

"Businesses like ours that assembled clones didn't have anything to compete on other than price, so we were always looking for an angle to let us add value for a particular industry niche. One trick I remember was spending thousands of dollars on a video card and a super high-resolution monitor that allowed us to target the publishing market. The brand-name manufacturers were slow to respond to niche opportunities, but those were exactly the customers who were likely to attend trade shows and conferences. Fran, the guy I learned from, had been working the big electronics shows from the very beginning of the industry."

Hadley made a skeptical noise. "I could see holding conferences for software products because the licenses are so expensive and the revenue goes on forever, but hardware is so cheap. Who could afford to rent out a real convention center to sell computer hardware?"

"You have to understand that technology is the one sector of the economy that's seen steady deflation throughout my life," Peter said. "These days, conferences are about gaming and software. Back then, you could have a half-dozen booths at a trade show selling computer mice for a hundred bucks a pop, and another half-dozen selling keyboards. It was just a different world. We were selling storage for fifty dollars a megabyte in 1988, and that was cheap. Today you'd be overpaying at fifty dollars a terabyte."

"I guess a thousand times cheaper is a pretty big difference."

"Not a thousand times cheaper, a million times cheaper. You forgot about gigabytes."

"I didn't forget about them, I just thought they only applied to camera memories, and I always had trouble with my factors of a thousand," Hadley admitted. "Sure, I'd like to learn about the trade show and conference business. It could be my fallback in case the apocalypse doesn't come quickly enough."

"Now you're getting into the spirit of the thing," Peter said. "Arlene, I'm going to drive Hadley into Franklin and show her the backup office. Whose turn is it to make lunch today?"

"Phil's," the office manager said. "And it's his Shelter Wednesday, so he'll probably just grab whatever's easiest from the food rotation."

"Sounds like a good day to show Hadley the best diner within a hundred miles."

Hadley was surprised when her boss agreed to let her drive them in her SUV, the back of which was still stuffed with things from her apartment that she hadn't moved up to her room in Betsy's house.

"I have less than half a tank left, and for some reason, it goes down fast from here," she explained. "I'm not a nervous person in general, but I don't like driving with less than a quarter tank, no matter what the computer says about how many miles I have left to go. I drove down to Florida once to see my mother while she was still alive, and after the fifty-miles-to-empty warning came on, I pulled over and checked my phone for the nearest gas station, which was only twelve miles away. When I pulled up to the pump, the computer was showing that I'd be empty in two miles."

"It's surprising how inaccurate some of those estimates can be," Peter said. "Turn left on the main road. In some cases, the error might be due to the gas shifting in the tank when you go uphill or downhill, but it's most likely to happen after you get off the highway and drive a moderate distance in local traffic."

Hadley took advantage of the time to learn as much as she could about Peter's previous experiences in business. It turned out that he had sold a couple of startups for a modest profit, but nowhere near as much as she would have expected. He explained that in any new field, consolidation eventually sets in, and only a few of the biggest players survive. At some point, he learned to see the writing on the wall and to get out while he was ahead, which had the added benefit of saving jobs for most of the employees.

"You've never tried to be one of the big fish gobbling up all the little fish?" she asked as they entered Franklin's town limits.

"It's not a game I ever wanted to play," Peter said. "It doesn't have anything to do with creating new products or services to fill a need, which is what gets me excited about business. It's just spreadsheets, tax accounting, and using other people's money to buy your former competitors and gain pricing power."

"By other people's money, you mean getting financing from banks," she surmised.

"Private equity for the main part. Money from rich people, or from investors who have entrusted their savings to rich people. Small banks don't have the sophistication for that sort of lending, and big banks don't want to be bothered. At the stop sign up there, you want to turn left, and then immediately right into the alley between the two buildings. Our offices are on the second floor of Yesterday's Fashions."

"Would I be right to guess that you're talking about a second-hand clothes store?"

"They prefer vintage." Peter hit the button to lower the window and yelled at a runner who had just stopped at the intersection and had two fingers to his jugular to check the pulse at his neck. "Hey, Si. Looking good."

The runner curled in his index finger and showed the other one to Peter as Hadley turned onto Oak Street and then immediately into the alley. "Friend of yours?" she asked.

"Suicide Larson, our lawyer. He's taking care of all the permits and contracts for the fair."

"Please tell me that his parents didn't give him that name."

Peter shook his head with an ear-to-ear grin. "Si used to have a bit of a drinking problem, and he fell asleep in his car outside the bar one night with the engine running. A local cop woke him up and hit him with drunk driving charges, even though the parking brake was on and he wasn't trying to go anywhere. Si got so angry that he sued, claiming that he was committing suicide with exhaust fumes and the policeman had violated his rights by intervening."

Hadley looked puzzled. "But what would the point of that be? If he convinced them that he was trying to commit suicide, he'd end up getting sent to a psychiatric hospital or forced to see a therapist."

"Life around here is a little more transactional than in big cities. The town realized that with Si representing himself, it could get expensive in a hurry to defend the case in court. So they settled for the amount of the fine and agreed to drop the drunk driving charge. That's when everybody started calling him Suicide Larson, or Si for short."

The small parking lot behind the buildings was almost empty, and Hadley parked in one of the three spots reserved for The Good Apocalypse. "Who works here?" she asked.

"Nobody," Peter said. "It's our backup studio in case the satellite internet fails, and it will be convenient to have an office in town for the Apocalypse Fair. What do you think of the name?"

"You might get a bunch of cosplayers from bad science fiction movies showing up."

"Well, if you can think of a better name, do it fast, because I've got the mall reserved for the second weekend of September. Now see if you can learn the code."

Hadley watched as Peter pressed four numbered keys on the lock, which then made a loud buzzing sound and allowed him to open the door. "Isn't that the date your mother's house was built?"

"She said that you're a smart one. Are you going to stay on there like Carl, or have you started looking for your own place? I noticed that you're still driving around with all your stuff. My mother's basement is dry, and it's free for storage if you're living there."

"And you'll keep paying my rent?"

"It's cheaper than paying for mom to move to an independent living facility, and she's a lot happier in her own home," Peter said as he led the way up the stairs. "You might think that you're just making work for her by being there, but what you're really doing is keeping her involved in life, so she doesn't just withdraw and spend half of the day in bed."

"Then you've got a deal," Hadley said. "Why did you pick the second weekend of September? School is back in session, so you'll lose out on families, unless you're saying that it's only appropriate for adults."

"A lot of preppers are homeschoolers, so that's not a problem, but Arlene may have told you that our customer base is mainly people whose kids are grown. Another trick that I learned in the convention business was not to go overboard with selling memberships the first time you stage a new one. It doesn't matter how much experience the organizers have, things are going to go wrong. As long as there are enough attendees, everybody will have a better time if they don't have to wait in line at booths and don't get shut out of any sessions because all the seats are taken. That feeds back into good word of mouth and sets things up for the next time around."

The door at the top of the stairs wasn't locked, and opened into an abandoned-looking office space, with a dusty receptionist's desk that featured a wooden chair with a spoked back. There was a glass window in the partition behind the desk through which a larger space was visible.

"You must have been kidding about working from this office," Hadley said. "It looks like it would take a month just to get it in shape to use as a studio."

"See that little box with all the blinking lights? That's the cable router, and it's active. Everything else the influencers need they would bring with them. There was no point in going overboard because the satellite service has been rock-solid since we started broadcasting from the farm, and when it comes down to it, they could just skip the live shows and come here to upload prerecorded stuff."

"Or they could go to the library and do it from the parking lot. Renting the whole second floor of a building seems like overkill."

"Except for three things," Peter said, holding up three fingers. "First, it only costs two hundred and fifty dollars a month because nobody else wanted to rent this space. Second, having a business address in town helps keep the mayor on our side, such as letting us rent a mall, and not charging us for utilities. Third, you can't use a post office box as your official address for a business in some situations. Maybe I could have gotten away with giving them the street address of the post office and the box number as a suite or apartment, but anybody who checks the map on their smartphone could figure that out in two seconds."

"Would you care if they did?" Hadley asked as she wandered into the larger room.

"I don't let the influencers post any video of our bunker and supplies, that would just be tempting fate. But some people might assume that we're sitting on an armory and a supply depot and make plans to pay us a visit. This way, we have a real address on the record that isn't the farm."

Six

"You've got to get up, you've got to get up, you've got to get up in the morning."

Fumiko groaned and swung a pillow at the alarm drone hovering just two feet over the bed, but it dodged the assault easily. "Alarm off," she ordered, as it began the verse about murdering the bugler. "And set a reminder for 10:00 PM to change your wake-up message."

"Reminder set," a male voice confirmed, though it didn't sound happy about it.

"Today's other reminders," Fumiko commanded as she threw off the single sheet she was sleeping under and fumbled her way to her feet.

"Caregivers and Killers. The two faces of the robotic revolution. Hadley."

"I forgot about Hadley shadowing me today. Do you think there's something strange about her?"

"Hadley is a human being, and as a custom large language model, I do not express opinions about individual humans," the voice from the drone replied as it followed her into the bathroom.

"Wait outside," Fumiko said, pointing back into the bedroom. "Better yet, battery cradle."

The drone turned reluctantly and retreated to the bureau, where it landed on top of the inductive charger and switched to standby mode.

Fumiko washed her face and spent a few minutes brushing her silky black hair. Then she pulled on a worn T-shirt from the national robotics competition her team had won in high school, and a pair of cargo shorts, whose pockets were lumpy with mechanical parts and electronic components from the previous day. She slid her feet into flip-flops and padded out into the hallway where she almost ran into Peter, who was coming the other direction with a towel wrapped around his waist.

"Sorry," her boss said. "I always try to get my shower done before you're out and about, but I was up late reading."

"It's all good practice for when we're living in the bunker together," Fumiko said. "I wouldn't trade the bathroom that Arlene and I share between our rooms for never running into a naked guy in the hall coming from the big bathroom in the middle house."

"I'm not naked," Peter protested. "Millions of Scotsmen have dressed like this for hundreds of generations."

"Get a Tartan towel and I'll believe it." She moved to her left as Peter moved to his right, and then they repeated the unintended dance to the other side. "You go first."

"See you at breakfast," Peter said. He carefully navigated around her as if she were a floating anti-ship mine from World War One studded with contact triggers.

Arlene was in the kitchen attacking a bowl of salad topped with bean sprouts that she grew in shallow trays on a rack in the corner next to the propane-powered refrigerator. She swallowed and said, "Hadley is shadowing you today."

"Romeo reminded me five minutes ago," Fumiko said. "The funny thing is that I don't remember setting a reminder."

"I texted you after I got up this morning and checked my calendar," Arlene said. "Did you finally work out forwarding messages to Romeo?"

"Last week, but it's spotty, so I haven't told anybody." She went into the pantry, unfolded the kitchen ladder, and climbed up to the second step so she could reach the top shelf. "I think that Romeo gets all of the messages but decides not to deliver some of them." She grabbed the box of breakfast cereal that had 'FUMIKO' printed on it with a felt-tip marker and she weighed it suspiciously. "I'm going to put a surveillance camera in here. Somebody's been eating my Chocolate Sugar Pops."

"I sincerely doubt that. Everybody who works here cringes when they see you eating that stuff."

"Then maybe they're stealing them to protect me," Fumiko said. She left the kitchen ladder in place, put the box of cereal on the table, got the milk out of the fridge, and then frowned at the banana stand. "One bunch is brown, and the other bunch is green. Whatever happened to yellow bananas?"

"Yellow bananas are bad for you, I saw it somewhere online," Arlene said. "They're at their best when they start turning brown."

"If you like squishy bananas." She snapped one off the bunch, pulled back a strip of the peel to check if it was gooey, and then brought it over to the table. "I'm going to miss bananas in the apocalypse."

"I'm sure we have a few cases of freeze-dried bananas in the bunker, and you can always order more with your elective purchase."

"Really?" Fumiko asked, her face lighting up. "That was like the final thing I was worried about. If I can still have bananas with my breakfast cereal when the distribution network stops functioning, that's a major load off my mind. But how come I never see rehydrated bananas at lunch when we're rotating food out of the bunker?"

Arlene held up an index finger to ask for a moment while she chewed sixteen times before swallowing. "I remember from the inventory sheet that the dehydrated bananas are sealed in cans, and they have a long shelf life, something like five or ten years. They aren't cheap either, so Peter isn't in a hurry to burn through them faster than necessary."

"That's such great news. I already knew that my Chocolate Sugar Pops last forever, and we must have tons of dried milk." She poured the fresh milk over her cereal, where it instantly took on a muddy appearance, then used her tablespoon to begin lopping off bite-sized chunks from the banana. "Maybe I'll start volunteering for bunker duty. I've been avoiding it because you guys all eat such weird stuff."

"We eat weird stuff?" Phil demanded as he wandered into the kitchen. "Take a look in the mirror, Robot Girl. Did it ever occur to you that if you ate real food you might be a foot taller?"

"It doesn't work that way," Arlene told him. "Even if it did, it would be too late for her to do anything about it now." She pointed at a calligraphed sign on the refrigerator. "House Rule #1. What does it say?"

"Live and let die," he read dutifully. "But that doesn't mean—"

"Yes, it does," the two women interrupted him simultaneously.

"Suit yourselves," Phil said. "But you're missing out on venison pot pie, and it's going to be gone by tomorrow."

"Gross," Fumiko said. "I need sugar to get me going in the morning, not dead animals."

"Refined sugar didn't exist when humans were evolving. All that engineered food is just tricking your body to the point that you no longer know what you need to eat to be healthy."

"Save it for the show, Phil," Peter said as he entered the kitchen. He took a homemade Amish bread out of the bread box and sliced off a hunk. "By the way, last night I convinced Mona Sturgeon to come up for a visit. I promised her the bandwidth and support to do her show while she's here."

"The Apocalypse Chef?" Phil asked. "I love her, but I never thought you'd get her to join up. She has twice as many followers as I do, and she's been online since the days of blogging with text and digital photos from cameras, before smartphones."

"You make it sound like the Dark Ages, and her outlook on the future has evolved over the years. When she started, it was all about eating locally grown ingredients and not wasting food or packaging materials. It took her a long time to come around to the view that civilization is unfixable without burning it all down and starting over again. We had a serious talk, and she admitted that over half of her followers are missing in action, and a good portion of the remainder only watch if she's doing a recipe they find interesting. Her ad revenue is way down from a couple of years ago, and her last employee just moved on to greener pastures."

"Mona sounds like a perfect match for us if she's gone solo," Fumiko said. "Is she going to live in the house? I'm not giving up the bathroom I share with Arlene."

"Mona is bringing her own," Peter said. "She's getting her RV out of mothballs, so all she needs is a parking space and Wi-Fi. I offered to let her shoot the show in our kitchen, but she used to do it in the RV when she was starting out."

"I thought you said she started out doing local food?"

"She did, but if you stay in one place, you can run out of local food in a hurry. She drove that RV around the country chasing the seasons, and she posted a lot of material about traveling as well. It wasn't as easy to build a following in a narrow vertical back then as it is today."

Fumiko found herself repeating that exact line to Hadley an hour later in response to a question about the drones-and-robots influencer space. "I don't know what I would be doing if I had been born ten years earlier," Fumiko concluded. "Probably working for some boring company testing industrial robots. I love programming and tinkering, but I don't think I would have had the patience to develop consumer products with all the ridiculous safety regulations. I started my channel doing product reviews of all the cheap drones on the market while I was still at uni. My numbers ran up so fast that the hardest thing I ever did was sticking out the last two years to get my degree in mechanical engineering."

"Peter told me that timing is everything for breaking into the influencer space," Hadley said. "Well, timing, personality, physical appearance, and telling people what they want to hear. Were you the first person with a drone review channel?"

"Not even close," Fumiko said. She managed a self-deprecating smile and pointed at a framed poster on the wall that showed a younger version of herself wearing short shorts and a sleeveless university T-shirt cut off well above her abdomen, holding a drone up like the Statue of Liberty's torch. "I kind of leaned into the sexuality thing at the beginning. I even did some modeling for drone advertisements in printed magazines. That poster is from one of them."

"If I had your looks, I wouldn't have hesitated to use them. Are most of your followers men?"

"According to the statistics we get, my audience is almost a third women now, though that includes a lot of high school girls who don't have much spending power. But I've been doing this for eight years if you count my last two years in school, when the channel took off to the point that manufacturers would send me free evaluation units. I'm the top English-language female drone influencer in the world."

Hadley looked around the office, which was decorated with a veritable cloud of drones hanging from the ceiling, with more drones pinned to the walls like a giant butterfly collection from the Victorian age. "Do you do rolling and walking robots, or is it all drones?"

"It's been heavy on the drones lately because they've gotten so popular and they're being used effectively in wars," Fumiko said. "I used to do a lot more robot stuff, but the walking ones are wicked expensive compared to drones, so the evaluation units are loaners that I have to return. When I do get a humanoid robot, I can stretch it into a week or two of shows, and then I get a chance to do some fun programming."

"You can't program drones?"

"Sure, but it's tough to come up with interesting things that they aren't already designed and programmed to do. I mean, you can change the payload, or attach anything to them that's within the weight limit, but there's not a lot of programming involved. In my most popular episode of all time, which was over fifty million views the last time I looked, I programmed a robot to change the batteries in drones, and added some sound effects like it was happening on a battlefield."

"I'll have to check that out," Hadley said. "What do you have planned for your live show today?"

"Caregivers versus Killers," Fumiko told her. "There are a lot of ways the robot apocalypse can happen, and most of them don't have anything to do with combat drones hunting people down with laser beams."

"Let me guess from the title of your episode. You're concerned that robots are going to take over all the caregiving jobs, from babysitting to nursing homes, and then one day they'll smother everybody with pillows."

"Ew, gross. That's not what I mean at all. It's possible that a superintelligence reprograms all our robots to attack us, but it's more likely to kill us with kindness. Imagine having robots wait on you, hand and foot, from the day you're born until the day you die. How many people would bother having children in a world like that?"

"It's not something I've ever really thought about," Hadley said. "Do you and Carl ever get into arguments about poaching each other's followers?"

"No way," Fumiko said. "We go on each other's shows all the time, but we don't have as much overlap on the apocalypse as you might think. Carl mainly focuses on superintelligence, and he's more worried about the impact on employment and misuse by existing power structures than he is about it turning on us. My only interest in artificial intelligence is how it could use robots and drones. We did a cool show together once about how superintelligence could use robots to gain control of infrastructure that's been isolated from the internet. But my audience is primarily interested in the hardware and batteries, and most of them aren't even preppers. I'm the only influencer here who really isn't that focused on the apocalypse."

"So why did you accept Peter's invitation to become a content partner?"

"He didn't invite me, Carl did. I was working way too many hours doing the business stuff, and flying drones in the city can be a real drag. When Carl invited me to visit his studio rather than doing a remote guest thing, I took a chance, and I fell in love with the farm. Two weeks later, I cleaned out my apartment and moved up here. Best decision I ever made."

A speaker on the workbench announced, "Five minutes to showtime. Caregivers and Killers. The two faces of the robotic revolution. Hadley."

"Oh, crap," Fumiko said. "Look at this place, and I'm live in five minutes."

"Is there anything I can do?" Hadley asked.

"Can you fly a drone?"

"I've never had a reason to try."

"Then I'll teach you after the show," Fumiko said decisively. "If you don't mind, we can record a video of you learning and then bundle it with the drone for a value-added package. But I can't be thinking about that right now," she said, shaking her head. "Come on, girl. Pull yourself together." She repositioned a tripod with a mounted camera so it was pointed at her empty workbench stool, took a microphone out of the deep drawer and plugged it into a receptacle on the bottom of her monitor, and then flipped a red switch that was held to the side of the screen with electrical tape.

"Two minutes," the speaker on her workbench announced.

"Shut up, Romeo. Mmm, mmm, mmm, mmm, mmm, mmm, mmm, mmm, mmm," she hummed on a rising and falling scale. "Mmm, mmm, mmm, mmm, mmm, mmm, mmm, mmm, mmm. Mmm, mmm, mmm, mmm, mmm, mmm, mmm, mmm, mmm."

"Is everything okay?" Hadley asked.

"I'm good," Fumiko said, checking herself on the monitor. "Just a little vocal warm-up. I don't want you to think I'm a dilettante, but after eight years of doing this, it doesn't feel that different than answering the phone."

"One minute," Romeo intoned.

"I thought I told you—that's the problem with artificial intelligence," Fumiko said, turning back to Hadley. "It thinks it's smarter than you are and it starts making its own decisions about what's good for you. The next thing you know, you don't have any rights."

"The caregiver scenario," Hadley surmised.

Fumiko held up a hand and folded in the thumb, then the index finger, then the middle finger, then the ring finger, and as soon as the pinky was down, she smiled at the camera and said, "What's worse? A robot that loves you or a robot that hates you? Think about it for a minute because it's a trick question. Now let's see who's in the video chat queue, and what a surprise. Naked fat guy is back, and no," she said, closing that chat window with the mouse, "You are not getting on my show. Let's go with Rachel from Los Angeles. Hi, Rachel. Welcome to Droning On, the show where I talk and talk instead of putting together cool stuff and crashing it into something." She clicked again with the mouse, switching the feed to a young woman wearing pajamas who looked like she was in a college dormitory room.

"Hi, Fumiko. I love your show and I've never been on before. Since it's a trick question, I'm going with the worst case being a robot who loves you, unless you're saying that as soon as you have a robot with strong feelings one way or another, you're already in trouble."

Fumiko swapped the video feed back to herself. "You've got it," she said. "One of the most optimistic cases I can imagine for robotics is benign replacement, but if there's too much artificial intelligence in the mix and it starts developing emotional responses, whether real or simulated, we're in trouble."

Rachel raised her hand, the standard signal on video call-in shows that she had something else to say, and Fumiko reselected her feed.

"I've heard you talk about benign replacement before, but my economics professor insists that robots will never be able to supplant people in most jobs. She says factory workers are at the highest risk, and maybe some retail and food jobs, like stocking shelves or working the takeout window, but everyone else with blue-collar jobs should be safe."

"Thank you, Rachel," Fumiko said. "That's just the opening I've been waiting for to go on a rant. You see, all the economists who talk about robotics and artificial intelligence are wrong, though that's nothing new because they're wrong about pretty much everything else as well. The reason is that they're obsessed with fitting data to the past, and that leaves them unable to imagine a different future. If you look at the state of artificial intelligence and robotics today, it's easy to point out jobs where it would be difficult, if not impossible, to trade a minimum wage worker with the most sophisticated robot in the world. But let me show you something."

She clicked twice on her monitor, and a video appeared of robots assembling a wooden roof truss using electric nail guns. "This is an experimental factory, in England of all places, where expensive housing has resulted in a gold rush for modular homes built in factories. But using robots to build a double-wide isn't the story here. These modular homes were designed to be serviced by robots as well. Every house is built with identical plumbing, electrical, heating, and ventilation systems. The mechanical room is located between the kitchen and the bathroom to give easy access to all the pipes and wiring by removing a panel from outside the home."

Fumiko clicked again and popped up a picture of a plumber on his knees, so his weight was pulling down his pants as he leaned forward to expose more than anybody wanted to see of his buttocks as he worked under a kitchen sink. "This is an image that economists often put up at lectures to explain why robots can't replace blue-collar workers outside of factory environments. It's thought that housing and office spaces are too complicated and challenging for a robot, even with the aid of artificial intelligence, to diagnose and be able to repair problems that require both mental and physical flexibility. But that's all based on an obsolete model."

She clicked again to restore the feed showing her talking into the camera. "We're at the beginning of a revolution where the world around us will be designed for robots and artificial intelligence. Our human advantage will turn into a liability because we don't have wheels and can't be equipped with spider legs and the appropriate attachments to work beneath floors or inside of walls. Humans are flexible by nature, but robots can be flexible by design, and they can outperform us in the environment that they're designed for. So don't laugh when you see a video showing a robot accidentally crushing a banana while it tries to remove the peel. That's a general-purpose humanoid robot, but soon there will be specialist robots for every task you can imagine."

Near the end of the live show, Fumiko asked Hadley if she had any questions. "I do have one," Hadley said. "What advice would you give a young person trying to plan a career for the future?"

"Strive for happiness," Fumiko said. "If, like most people these days, you need me to define the terms, happiness is when you match your vocation to your aptitude, so you aren't fighting an endless battle with yourself to get out of bed. I'll bet you that half of the people taking meds these days could go off them if they stopped doing what other people wanted them to do and followed the little voice in their head telling them to be a farmer or bicycle mechanic."

"But what if the economy doesn't need more people in those jobs?"

"Then we need to fix the economy. A good place to start would be hanging all the economists."

Seven

"Where's Carl?" Hadley asked when she entered the kitchen and saw Betsy working at the stove.

"He left early to ride his motorbike into Franklin," Betsy said. "What would you say to bacon and eggs?"

"I'm not really a bacon eater. It's too greasy for me."

"Good, because I don't have any. I'm making French toast because Carl did the prep before he left."

"He's such a nice guy, other than the impending doom thing," Hadley said. "Don't you find it kind of depressing to live with somebody who's always talking about humans being replaced by artificial intelligence?"

Betsy turned away from the frying pan and gave Hadley a look. "Carl only talks about the apocalypse because you keep asking him questions about it. You didn't realize that?"

Hadley stared. "I don't, I mean, isn't it his passion?"

"Not that I've noticed," Betsy said, turning back to the pan and flipping the two pieces of French toast. "The only time it came up before you moved in was if I asked him about how his work was going."

"Now I feel bad about making him bring the apocalypse home with him," Hadley said. "I just assumed he liked talking about the end of the world."

"I don't think that you're making him uncomfortable if that's what you're worried about. You ask him about the future of artificial intelligence all the time, so it would be dishonest of him to paint a rosy picture when that's not what he believes. Back when I was still driving, I used to enjoy listening to interviews on the radio. But either I got older and wiser, or something changed in the media, because I started noticing that the interviewers were always pushing a narrative. It almost doesn't matter who the subject of the interview is today because the person asking the questions is the one who shapes the dialogue."

"Now I feel like a bully. Any fresh signs of Armageddon on the news this morning?"

"I haven't checked yet," Betsy said, sliding the two slices of French toast onto a plate. "I've already eaten, so these are yours, but I'll join you for a cup of the coffee Carl made before leaving if you'll do the honors."

Hadley retrieved two mugs from the apocalypse collection, one of which showed a tsunami breaking over a coastal city, the other, a few dinosaurs placidly munching ferns while a flaming asteroid plunged toward them. "Are these in our catalog?" she asked. "I haven't come across them, and they don't look like a matched set."

Betsy set the plate of French toast on the table and glanced over to see which mugs Hadley had selected. "They're all handmade by Peter's ex-wife. She earns a decent income from her ceramics, but mainly it's dragons and mermaids which she sells on the internet. She brings me up a few new apocalypse mugs at Christmas every year. I think it's her way of pointing out to Peter that it hasn't happened yet."

"Is that why they broke up?" Hadley asked, and then hastily backtracked, "I'm sorry, it's none of my business."

"It's a shame that asking questions isn't your business since you're very good at it," Betsy said with a smile as she accepted a mug of coffee. "Melissa was Peter's first wife, they married after he got out of the army. My feeling is that they were too similar, and over the years, they came to realize that they just didn't find each other that interesting. Maybe if they had been narcissists it would have worked out."

"Narcissists? Oh, I get it. Is Melissa the mother of Arlene's friend? I remember Peter telling me that's how she ended up working there."

"No. Peter and Melissa didn't have children, and I suppose that's another reason they didn't feel obligated to stay together when the magic went out of the relationship. I have two grandchildren from Peter's second marriage, and one of them grew up in Franklin and went to school with Arlene. Peter's second wife died in a one-car accident. We think that she swerved to avoid hitting a deer or some other wildlife crossing the road. That's when he started developing an interest in the apocalypse, though he didn't make it into a business right away." Betsy watched as Hadley cut the French toast into four pieces with her fork and then ate one. "Aren't you going to add syrup?"

"I don't need the calories, and this coffee that Carl makes gives me all the energy I need to get through the morning," Hadley said. "Today is my big day. Peter is going to show me the bunker."

"Are you wearing sensible shoes?" Betsy asked.

Hadley had to look under the table to remind herself what she had put on five minutes earlier. "Sandals. Why? Will I have to climb ladders or something?"

"I'd rather not ruin the surprise since it sounds like you don't know what to expect. Walter. Play the news."

"The ongoing drought in sub-Saharan Africa is threatening famine for over a billion people and leading to uncontrolled migration—"

"Walter, stop," Betsy interrupted with a sigh. "I wish somebody would stream optimistic news."

"Do you think there's enough good news to go around?" Hadley asked between bites.

"Of course, it's just a question of where you look. There's always good news happening somewhere, and lots of it. For one thing, the news could cover scientific breakthroughs around the clock and never run out. Instead of reporting on crop failures, they could report on bumper crops. Every day, every hour, people around the country, young and old, are triumphing over adversity and achieving their goals. Why can't the news report about that instead of horrendous crimes and trying to create conflict between groups of people who come from different backgrounds or hold different beliefs?"

Hadley started cutting up the second piece of French toast with the side of her fork. "Don't you think the news networks have a duty to broadcast the truth, even if it's unpleasant?"

"Humbug," Betsy declared. "They don't even try to present an even-handed picture of the world we live in, none of them. And as an old lady, let me tell you something I've learned the hard way. Knowledge doesn't lead to happiness."

"Is happiness the goal?"

"If you don't care about being happy, either you're schizophrenic or you've been brainwashed. I taught science and math in the public schools for thirty-five years, and it got to the point that I could tell which kids were going to be successful within the first week or two of class.

The ones who hated being in school didn't learn much, and it's a shame we never developed an alternative for them."

Hadley ended up swapping her sandals for running shoes, because the only boots she owned were insulated for the winter, and it was shaping up to be another hot day. On second thought, she brought the sandals with her, since in the absence of Carl as a walking companion, she was taking her car. When she arrived at the office, the only other vehicle in the parking lot was Peter's old pickup truck, which he shared with the employees who lived there. She was greeted at the door by Freud, who was even more excited than usual to see her.

"We're coming with you," Arlene announced, getting up from her chair. "I need to grab a few things to make lunch, but mainly, I want to see your reaction."

"Betsy hinted that the bunker was something extraordinary and told me to wear sensible shoes," Hadley said, rising on her toes and clicking her heels together. "I want to go home. I want to go home."

"That only works in the movies," Peter said as he entered the office. "Any fires to put out before we go?"

"Eleanor has everything under control," Arlene said, waving at the laptop that hosted the local interface for the artificial intelligence that handled all the sales and customer support, in addition to filling the orders through distribution partners. "Are you going to give Hadley the short tour or the long tour?"

"How much can there be to see in a bunker?" Hadley asked. "Are you going to train me on radioactive decontamination procedures or something?"

Peter exchanged a glance with Arlene. "Maybe we should have those. In my armor battalion, they told us to stay inside the tank, but I guess that doesn't translate to civilian life."

Arlene shook her head. "All I know about radioactive decontamination is from the old civil defense movies on the internet that they used to show school children. My memory is that everybody wore overcoats and brushed them off before entering the shelter. I bet we could find those movies online if we looked."

"I swear I don't have a clue whether you guys are serious or not," Hadley said in frustration. "On the one hand, you're investing all your time and money into surviving the apocalypse, but on the other hand, you're pretty casual about the whole thing."

"I expect we'll have ample notice when the time comes," Peter said. "The entrance to the bunker is in the barn, so it's not like we have a long way to go. Other than an extinction-level asteroid slamming into the planet, I think most preppers will be disappointed with how long it takes civilization to collapse."

"Think about air raids," Arlene told Hadley. "You'd be surprised by how many people are hurt in falls while rushing to shelters, especially older people whose bones are getting brittle."

As soon as Peter opened the front door, Freud dashed out and did a complete lap around the house in the time it took the people to reach the outside entrance to the barn.

"You know," Hadley said. "I've never been in here."

"That's because nobody invited you, and the door that goes through to the barn from the kitchen is behind the refrigerator." Peter said. "I was waiting until I was sure that the job was working out and you wanted to stay with us."

"You mean once I see the bunker, you'll have to kill me if I leave."

Peter and Arlene nodded, but neither of them could keep a straight face for more than two seconds. "Half of the Amish craftsmen within five miles who are willing to work outside of their farms have been in the bunker," Peter said. "I imagine there are still a few people my mother's age left who visited when it was a tourist attraction."

"Wait," Hadley said as Peter slid open the large hanging door. "Your bunker was a tourist attraction for old people?"

Freud disappeared into the barn as soon as there was room for him to squeeze through, and Arlene followed him, saying, "Come and see for yourself."

It took Hadley's eyes a moment to adjust to the light inside the barn, but even before she made out the words on the sign above a round hole with a railing around it, she had an intuition of what they would be. "Limestone Cavern," she read out loud. "Your bunker is in a cave?"

"Not just a cave, a cavern," Peter told her. "There are some passages that are too small for a person to get through that have never been explored, though Fumiko has been trying with a variety of robots and drones. But the mapped area includes over six miles of passages spread over multiple levels."

"Are there bats?" Hadley asked nervously. "I'm afraid of bats. I went to a summer camp once where a bat got into our cabin and none of us could sleep. They carry diseases."

"That's anti-bat propaganda," Arlene said forcefully. "Every mammal gets diseases, and some species of bats around here have almost been wiped out by white-nose fungus. They're an important part of the ecosystem, and they're the only mammals that fly. Did you know that bats can live for thirty years or more? Bat mothers deliver their babies by live birth, and they can only have one a year."

"There aren't any bats in our bunker, and they don't come through the passages that connect to the area of the cavern that they do use, which is further uphill," Peter told her. "Bats like caves with domed ceilings where the warmer air accumulates over the winter when they're hibernating. We stay out of that section of the cavern, and it would probably be protected by the state wildlife people if they knew there was a way in there. Phil has done entire shows about the value of guano to a post-apocalyptic society."

"You're talking about bat poo?" Hadley asked. She ducked past the domed cover, which was held open by a chain attached to a hoist on a rafter, and she realized that both it and the stairwell shaft were constructed of surprisingly thick steel. She followed Arlene down the wide spiral stairs that Freud had taken two at a time.

"Guano is rich in saltpeter, which is the main ingredient in black powder. I don't know how accurate the recipe needs to be, but Phil has made black powder that does the job. He uses potassium nitrate from a lower level of the cavern where there's an underground stream."

"The water is drinkable, but it takes some getting used to," Arlene added. "I camped down here for a week just to see what it would be like. I couldn't get over the quiet."

"How can you hide a cavern?" Hadley asked. "It sounds like it's not even all on your property."

"Under my property, and it's not," Peter said. "As to how we hide it, my grandfather took down the sign on the state highway back before World War Two because the only tourists who came just got angry. The thing about Limestone Cavern is that it's not very exciting."

"He's being generous," Arlene said. "It's a crashing bore. There's no cave art, no dazzling crystals, and no interesting metal veins in the walls. It's just a lot of limestone and sandstone. The upper levels are drier than you'd expect for a cavern, which is great for our purposes, but there's almost nothing living down here."

Hadley stopped on the bottom stair. "Almost nothing?"

"We're growing mushrooms, but we had to provide the soil, or what passes for soil with mushrooms. That's down a couple levels in a side cave near the stream, where it was easy to pipe in some water without making the whole cavern humid."

"But hypothetically speaking," Hadley said, still standing on the bottom stair. "If the apocalypse were to happen, wouldn't everybody who knows about this place be pounding on the hatch to get in?"

Peter tsked. "We're all failing to get our message across if you continue to see the apocalypse as a zero-sum game. This cavern can easily fit all the local population, and even though we're laying in supplies, the idea isn't to spend the generation underground waiting for the nuclear dust to settle. What kind of world do you think it would be if the only people to survive were you and your coworkers? Your descendants would run into a population bottleneck in no time."

"We call it a bunker, but it's more of a shelter and storage space," Arlene said. "There's natural airflow through the passages, and we don't have any plans to filter it if the atmosphere is radioactive or a plague is spreading over Earth and killing all life forms. We can batten down the hatch if we see hoards of zombies or urbanites coming, but the Amish are welcome."

Hadley finally stepped off the spiral staircase and looked around at the limestone walls and up at the ceiling, where strings of LED lights provided illumination. "I guess it really isn't very exciting, though I wish I had brought a jacket because it's cold. I thought I read somewhere that mines get hot as you go deeper because they're closer to the center of the Earth."

"Caverns rarely extend as deep as mines, unless you're talking about caverns under the ocean floor," Peter said. "If you go deep enough, the natural heat in the rocks from radioactive decay will warm the air faster than it can rise and be exchanged with cool air unless you're running a powerful ventilation system. But our cavern isn't that deep, at least as far as the passages we can fit through, and it gets cooler as you go down because the warm air rises. That's why the bats prefer the highest cave in the cavern."

"Here," Arlene said, pulling a sweater from a large plastic container and tossing it to Hadley. "Community chest." She took a second sweater from the chest and put it on. "Come on. I'll show you our food stocks."

"I've seen drums like that in an illegal chemical dump," Hadley said. "Is it diesel for a generator or something?"

"Fifty-five-gallon drums are handy for storing bulk food, though we include a plastic bag liner," Peter said, and then added out of curiosity, "But where would you have seen an illegal chemical dump? The penalties are so high and the paperwork for transporting chemicals is so onerous that I haven't heard of illegal dumping in decades."

"It came up once with an old industrial property that my boyfriend's law firm was handling. Aren't barrels expensive?"

"I buy them reconditioned when they come on the market, as long as they haven't been used for anything particularly nasty. The used steel drums are cheaper than the poly drums. We have a few dozen of them, and they aren't all for food. It's worth spending some money to keep everything organized. You're looking at over two thousand dollars spent on second-hand industrial shelving."

Hadley followed Arlene between two rows of shelves, every box and container carefully labeled with the contents and a projected expiration date. "I thought about raising chickens and then bringing them underground, but in the end, powdered eggs are just much simpler," Arlene said.

"I'm no expert on animal husbandry, but I don't think you can raise a new generation of chickens from powdered eggs," Hadley pointed out. "What if we do get stuck living underground for a year, and when we come out, all of the chickens are dead?"

"If that happens, we're going to have bigger challenges than living without chickens," Peter told her from the end of the aisle. "If this were a government nuclear shelter like in that movie that came out when my mom was in school, we'd need ten young women for every man to start repopulating Earth. I just don't think in those terms, though some preppers do. I imagine the best way to go about it would be to preserve a minimum breeding population of chickens rather than planning on making them and their eggs a major food source. If chicken husbandry is something that excites you, I suppose we could set aside one of the lower caves, and the manure could go into the mushroom soil."

"I was just asking."

Eight

"First time we've seen you at breakfast in a while, Glen," Peter said to the bearded astronomer. "Was it so cloudy that you slept through the night?"

"I'm up because Hadley is shadowing me today," Glen said with a yawn. "But it did get cloudy for a few hours, so I took a nap on my bunk in the observatory."

"Hadley's doing a great job with the news portal," Arlene said. "I thought she would just be reformatting the newsletter with the articles you guys already write, but she's been adding content based on the conversations she has with everybody. She also integrated a widget that gathers government warnings about extreme weather events from around the world, like tsunamis, tornadoes, and hurricanes."

"I told her about that widget," Laura Ann said while spreading some homemade jam on her toast made from stale bread. "I've known about it for a while, but I couldn't figure out how to add it to my channel. It includes all the internationally recognized agencies that track weather, earthquakes, even solar flares, and you can diddle the settings so that it doesn't pop up every thunderstorm or flash flood warning that comes along."

"It's the first thing Hadley asked me to spend money on, and it's worth every penny," Peter said. "Did you notice that it has a text-to-speech function? If you click the little speaker, it will read the warnings out loud."

"They should play it in elevators. Maybe that would wake people up to what's going on in the world." Laura Ann crinkled up her nose and asked, "What's that smell?"

"Sorry," Phil said from the counter where he was preparing a breakfast sandwich. "It's venison salami from Zook's farm store. I think his wife went heavy on the garlic in this batch."

Glen took a sip of coffee and checked his smartphone. "I can't find the widget on our website. I want to see if it maintains a log so I can check what level of solar flares it's reporting."

Peter and Arlene both got up and went to look over Glen's shoulder at his phone screen. "The home page didn't resize properly," Arlene said. "That's funny because I checked it on my phone and it worked fine."

"You're missing the whole right-hand side of the website," Peter told him. "Try scrolling."

"There it is," Glen said a few seconds later. "Hey, she added catalog specials to the home page as well."

"Those have always been there. How old is that phone?"

Glen shrugged. "I don't remember, but it's the only one I've ever owned. I think it's third generation?" he added uncertainly.

"What brand is it?" Arlene asked. "I've never seen a smartphone with such a big bezel around the screen. Maybe it's so low resolution that the browser can't resize the hero for our website."

"I think it shows the brand when it powers on." He held in the power button and chose to shut down the phone. "Since when does The Good Apocalypse have a hero? Do you mean like some character from a role-playing game?"

"It's what Hadley calls the horizontal image at the top of the website. It should scale down, but maybe there's a minimum size, or your browser is so old it doesn't handle the code. You'll have to show Hadley the website on your phone when she gets here."

"If it's rebooted by then," Glen said, pressing the power button a second time. "It's been taking forever lately."

"Red Star," Arlene said when the phone showed the initial boot screen. "It sounds like one of those made-up brands from China. Do you remember what you paid for it?"

"I think it was twenty or thirty bucks, but you're talking more than ten years ago. I didn't want a phone, but I was buying a book online, and I needed to raise the order amount for free shipping. I don't use it for anything other than text messages because the battery doesn't last long otherwise."

"Don't you dare sit next to me with that sandwich," Laura Ann warned Phil. "If you had any decency, you would go eat it outside."

"Freud has the best nose in the place, and I don't see him complaining," Phil said. He looked down at the dog who had sucked in his stomach and was doing his best to look like he hadn't eaten in a week. "Come on, boy. Let's go outside. These people don't know what they're missing."

"Morning, all," Fumiko said as she walked in a few seconds later. "Did something die in here?"

"It died out there some time ago and then the Zooks made it into salami," Laura Ann told her. "How did your show with Hadley go? I have her next week, and I was thinking of asking her to be the guest."

"She was fine in the studio, but she was only on the show for a few seconds at the end." Fumiko got her cereal box down from the pantry shelf, weighed it in her hand, and looked at her housemates suspiciously. "I'm not making any accusations, but if somebody has been eating my Chocolate Sugar Puffs, you might buy a replacement box."

"Are Hadley and Carl a thing?" Glen asked. "I haven't been around much during the daytime since she started working here, but I saw them starting down the hill around twenty minutes ago, and they were holding hands."

"How could you even tell who two people are that far away?" Arlene asked. "You're talking a mile."

"Two-hundred-millimeter refractor telescope."

"I thought you sold that when you built the reflector," Peter said.

"They're good for different things, and I'm comfortable with the camera setup on the refractor," Glen said. "Some people like cars, some people like telescopes. It's not like I'm a hoarder."

Freud began barking, and Arlene said, "That must be Carl and Hadley now. Do you mind if I borrow her for a few minutes before you take her, Glen? I want to tell her about the problem with the website and have her show me if she can fix it so I'll know how for the future."

"I'm not in any hurry. Just send her up to the observatory studio when she's ready."

Hadley was impressed by the craftsmanship of the wooden stairway that ran in a tight spiral around the inside of the silo and was thankful for the railing. She couldn't help thinking that in Manhattan, somebody would have turned the same volume of space into a half a dozen tiny apartments, though it would have required a variance for a tubular one-person elevator like in a sci-fi movie. The final turn of the stairs brought her into a small circular studio where Glen was waiting.

"Grab the other chair," he said. "We'll get the show recorded and then I'll take you up and show you the telescopes, even though there's not much to see during the daytime."

"Fumiko mentioned that you might want me to participate in the show, but I don't know anything about astronomy," Hadley said. "I know that the sun and the moon go around the Earth—"

"What!"

"Peter put me up to saying that. I get that the sun is the center of the solar system and that Pluto doesn't count as a planet anymore, but that's pushing the boundaries of my knowledge."

"How about alien spaceships?"

"Well, I guess I've read about UFOs in the headlines of a few hundred stories in the tabloids while walking by newsstands or supermarket displays," Hadley said. "I may have watched a few videos on social media as well when they come up in my feed, but I can't say I took any of them seriously."

"All right, this is good stuff. Save that thought for when I start recording." There was a camera mounted on a swing arm bolted to the wall that pointed at Glen's chair, and he adjusted another camera on a tripod so that it pointed at Hadley. Then he moved a couple of reflectors to eliminate the shadows from her face and gave her a small microphone to clip to the neck of her blouse.

"Don't you need a monitor so you can swap between camera feeds?" Hadley asked.

"I only do live shows at night when I'm making observations and taking calls, and then the camera feed is strictly through the telescope and I'm talking in the background," Glen said. "When I get somebody up here, I record the whole thing on two timelines and then edit it together after the fact. You haven't watched any of my shows?"

Hadley shook her head. "I've just been so busy with the website, and now Peter has me setting up another one for his gun show, I mean, apocalypse fair."

"The last I heard, he's going to limit firearms to black powder. I thought that Phil would be disappointed, but he's more of a hunter than a gun fanatic. Everybody just assumes that he's into military stuff because he's focused on surviving nuclear war."

"I don't want to step on anybody's toes here, but it seems to me that none of you are as fanatic about your personal vision of the apocalypse as one would think from your channels."

"Picking a vertical and sticking with it helped us all build audiences, but I'm fairly agnostic about which apocalypse we'll get, though I can't take climate change that seriously," Glen said. "Rising sea levels affect people on the coasts, changing weather patterns will make a difference in where people live and what crops they grow. I only see it as a contributing factor for a different version of the apocalypse that could happen just as easily without it."

"You mean that mass migration could lead to social unrest," Hadley surmised.

"Much worse than that. Other than war, our world doesn't have a system in place for dealing with resource problems on a large scale. If there are massive crop failures in Asia, do you think people here will agree to reduce their calorie intake so we can export more food? Do you think that nuclear-armed governments around the world will let their citizens starve without issuing ultimatums for aid? I can think of several reasons for countries to stumble into nuclear war that don't involve politics or nationalism, and not having enough food is at the top of the list."

"And you think that changes in the weather could bring that about."

"Yes and no," Glen said as he checked that the wheels on his chair were located within the tape marks on the floor that he used to position himself for his camera. "Changes in the weather don't happen overnight, so people and governments have time to adjust. A volcano spewing ash into the air for a few years could reduce crop yields to the point where there is no way for Earth's current population to get enough calories to sustain itself. I'm familiar with the scenario because you can get a similar effect from a large enough asteroid impact. On that happy note, are you ready?"

"As long as you let me sit with you while you're editing the program together," Hadley said. "I guess the worst thing that can happen is it ends up really short."

"You'll be fine. The equipment is all recording, so let's get started. Welcome back to *An Eye on the Heavens*. This is your host Glen Auerbach, coming to you from my observatory silo with our news portal manager, Hadley..."

"Brown."

"Hadley Brown, and she's here representing the typical UAP skeptic in America today. Tell me, Hadley. What is it that makes you dismiss UAPs as online clickbait and tabloid headlines?"

"I thought we were going to talk about UFOs," Hadley said.

"It's the new acronym," Glen said. "Unidentified Aerial Phenomena, or Anomalous Phenomena, depending who you ask. I preferred UFOs, but you can't fight City Hall."

"Oh. Well, I guess I just think that if flying saucers were real, somebody would have at least gotten a clearer photograph of one by this point. It's always blurry light or a metallic-looking object so small that it could be anything."

"You don't think that aliens advanced enough to travel all the way to Earth would have technology that allows them to cloak their spacecraft?"

"I think that aliens that advanced would do a better job of it," Hadley said. "This now-you-see-it, now-you-don't business is more like a striptease, and I can't imagine any good reasons for aliens to play that game."

"They could be testing the limits of our technology," Glen said.

"For the last fifty years? And all that conspiracy stuff about the government confiscating crashed spaceships and keeping the technology for itself. Give me a break. People aren't that good at keeping secrets."

"What if the current UAP sightings are part of a government psyop to hide the truth about alien contact in the noise?"

"Not buying it," Hadley said. "All of these convoluted explanations violate Occam's Razor. If aliens are visiting Earth, they would have announced themselves by now."

"We're on the same page until this point, but I happen to be an advocate of Quarantine Theory, which explains all of your objections," Glen said. "The field of astronomy has been making discoveries so rapidly that the general public isn't keeping up. It wasn't long ago that we didn't know whether planets orbiting a star were as common as dirt or a rare occurrence. But now it's generally accepted that there are hundreds of billions of planets in our galaxy, and tens of billions of those are in the temperate zone of their star, where water can exist as a liquid on the surface. Does that change anything for you?"

"I didn't know that, but what does the number of planets have to do with—what was that theory you mentioned?"

"Quarantine Theory. It hypothesizes that aliens are out there, probably everywhere, and that they follow a policy of not interfering with primitive species. If they have academic and scientific traditions in advance of our own, it makes sense that they would want to observe us to measure our progress before one day welcoming us into a galactic community. That explains the UAPs."

Hadley looked at him skeptically. "Do you really believe that? Flying saucers are being piloted by irresponsible alien graduate students, and that's why they keep breaking cover while they're trying to stay hidden?"

"Not the part about the irresponsible graduate students," Glen said. "I think it's far more likely that the sightings are aliens who are breaking the quarantine for reasons of their own that probably involve commerce."

"You think they're here selling ray guns on the sly?"

"I doubt they're here selling anything, but I imagine that all planets are unique in their own way. That means that Earth would offer all sorts of prizes for collectors of flora and fauna."

"Like the old movie where the Rastafarian comes to Earth to hunt people for trophy skulls," Hadley said. "My ex was really into movies like that."

Glen sighed. "I was thinking more along the lines of flowers and butterflies."

"How is that apocalyptic?"

"It's not. Quarantine Theory is based on the idea that advanced aliens will care about our well-being. The quarantine is for our protection, not theirs."

"It sounds like you're sure that aliens are out there," Hadley said slowly. "What if they aren't friendly? I know you said there are likely tens of billions of planets sitting in the temperate zone of stars, but what if most of them are just lifeless balls of rock? I've heard scientists talking about how life developed on Earth, and it sounded like there was a lot more to it than just having a planet in the right orbit."

"There is," Glen said. "And if you played Earth's history a million times, maybe you'd only get intelligent life once. But that's still thousands of intelligent species around the galaxy, and I've heard other scientists who believe that given enough time, the development of intelligent life on a planet with the right initial conditions is almost inevitable."

"Then why don't we pick up their radio signals?"

"You mean the so-called Fermi paradox. It's about the dumbest conjecture to reach near canonical status in modern times. The only way we could receive radio signals from a distant civilization is if they're pouring huge amounts of power into an antenna array with a lobe pointed right at us. And they would have to have been doing that during the last century when we developed equipment capable of listening."

"I thought we had radio telescopes that could pick up signals from distant stars," Hadley said.

"From stars, yes," Glen said. "Stars emit all sorts of radiation besides the visible light you see when you look up at the night sky. Our sun radiates a million times as much energy in one second as all of the industrial countries on Earth consume in a year. That's what it takes to be detectable from thousands of light years away."

"Oh. That's a lot. So why did people take the Fermi paradox so seriously?"

"Hubris. It's particularly contagious in the scientific community and with some of the most intelligent people. They can't imagine an alien civilization that wouldn't be pouring all its resources into making contact with us."

"Because if the aliens don't care, that would diminish the value of humanity and the contributions that the scientists have made," Hadley surmised. "I don't know. It seems like a stretch to me."

"Don't sell self-importance short," Glen said. "It may be the most insidious form of confirmation bias. If you believe yourself to be important, that distorts everything else you encounter because it has to be forced into the context of you. But we've gotten pretty far off the topic of UAPs, so let's circle back. Have I persuaded you that aliens exist out there somewhere?"

"I didn't realize that's what you were doing here, but I'm willing to be flexible about it if you're willing to rethink Quarantine Theory. Why should the aliens be friendly? Maybe they'll want our planet without us, or see humans as a valuable source of protein after a long voyage."

"Anything is possible, but if that's the case, what are they waiting for? Every year, our technology gets better, and I doubt that aliens who see us as food are waiting for us to advance to the point that we can give them a good fight."

"Maybe there aren't many of them," Hadley said. "People go missing on Earth all the time, and maybe that's because there are just so many humans that the aliens who fit into a flying saucer can eat."

Glen laughed out loud. "I don't think I've ever heard that particular argument. We tend to think that advanced aliens would bring enough food along, or the means to produce food, but maybe they get sick of it after a few thousand years."

"Do you really think they could live that long?"

"I don't see why not. But I can't imagine an alien making the long trip from their home world in a ship the size of the UAPs that have been caught on film. They would have to travel in a state of suspended animation if that were the case. There's also the whole issue with reaction mass, which puts some stringent limits on interstellar travel at our current understanding of physics."

"Well, there could be a mothership hiding in a crater on the other side of the moon or something," Hadley said, getting caught up in the argument. "Or if their technology is that advanced, there could be a huge ship in Earth's orbit that we just can't detect. Maybe their flying saucers don't have the power or the space on board for their super-good cloaking equipment."

"I'm beginning to think I made a convert today," Glen said. "If aliens did land tomorrow, right here, in the middle of nowhere, what's the first thing you would ask them?"

"That depends on whether they're blue and hunky."

"Fair enough, but let's say they resemble giant lobsters."

"I wouldn't hang around to ask them anything," Hadley said. "Could you imagine how much trouble we'd all be in if the aliens showed up and we weren't the ones they recognized as higher life forms? Like that movie with the humpback whales and the probe thing."

Glen laughed again. "That's a good argument for becoming a vegetarian. We're going to be in real trouble if they look like pigs or octopi, to name a couple of intelligent animals that people eat."

"Is this what you're thinking about when you're looking through your telescopes at night?"

"Sometimes," Glen said. "But most of the time it's more like meditation for me. I invest part of every clear night looking for uncatalogued objects on a near-Earth collision course, and if there's a comet that's going to come anywhere near us on its loop around the Sun, I'll keep an eye on that to see whether its track has been altered by a collision since the last time the space agencies did their observations and computations. There are a few different scenarios for a planet-killing asteroid to end up impacting Earth, and one of them is that a random encounter out in the asteroid belt changes the trajectory of a comet at what, in astronomical terms, you could call the last second."

"Could the aliens do it?" Hadley asked. "Maybe under your Quarantine Theory, that would be a way they could get around the rules, by nudging an asteroid in our direction and then showing up afterward to pick up the pieces."

"You've definitely got the right mind for this business."

Nine

"What finally convinced you to take up Betsy's offer to store your stuff in the basement?" Carl asked. He held the screen door open with his back while Hadley carried a plastic storage container up the porch stairs.

"I've got the nicest car of anybody working at The Good Apocalypse, and Peter asked if I would bring people to Franklin for the site visit at the mall," Hadley replied. "I know, I should have brought my stuff in months ago. It's not like anybody was going to break into my car around here, so I was procrastinating."

"Is it all clothes? You don't have any kitchen stuff or appliances?"

"I have one box with dishes, but William paid for all our pots and pans, and they were more expensive than what I would have bought for myself. I got rid of my old kitchen stuff a year after we moved in together. Anyway, I told you that my dad was in the army, and moving all the time as a kid taught me to travel light. I kind of feel guilty about having accumulated this much, and I'm not even sure what's in some of the thick garbage bags."

"Contractor bags," Carl told her as he led the way down to the cellar. "It all felt soft, so I'm betting on clothes."

"Maybe blankets," Hadley said. "My mom used to knit afghans, so I saved those. I would have put them in boxes, but the bags make more efficient use of the room in the back of my SUV because they're compressible."

"Humble brag. I moved up here with what fit in the saddle bags on my Honda."

Hadley added her box to the stack on the pallet to keep her stuff off the dirt floor. "My hero. Didn't you have any hobbies other than worrying about the apocalypse?"

"I don't worry about the apocalypse," Carl said. "I guess my main hobby outside of work for years has been keeping my CB 750 running. It was the first superbike, and mine was manufactured when Peter was in first grade. I should scan the manual before it falls apart."

"There's a scanner on the printer in the office," Hadley told him as she started back up the stairs.

"We have a printer? What do we use it for?"

"Arlene says that Peter asks her to print reports from time to time, and he keeps them in a file drawer in his desk. He's kind of old-fashioned that way, but I've noticed that lots of people his age have a paper fetish."

It took three more trips for the two of them to empty the SUV, and then Hadley drove to the office. Freud came bounding out to greet them when she turned into the parking area. He surprised Hadley when she opened the door by wiggling under her arm and scrambling over the central console into the back seat.

"I guess he's coming with us," Carl said as the front door of the house opened again and Arlene came out, followed by Peter, Laura Ann, Phil, Fumiko, and Glen. Peter, Phil, and Laura Ann got into Peter's old pickup truck, which had one bench seat that was wide enough to carry three people comfortably, while Fumiko, Glen, and Arlene got into the back seat of Hadley's SUV, evicting Freud into the cargo area.

"Peter said we should drive straight to the mall and meet him at the main entrance," Arlene told Hadley. "They're stopping to pick up our lawyer."

"Where are they going to put him?" Hadley asked, backing up with the wheel cut all the way to one side so she would be facing the right direction to start down the long driveway.

"He'll probably drive his own car, but he's famous for never being on time. They're going to his office to get him moving. Otherwise, Phil can ride in the bed of the pickup."

"Isn't that illegal on public roads?"

"Nothing is illegal when you have your lawyer along," Fumiko told her. "Is everybody excited about the fair?"

"I'll bet fewer than a hundred people register," Glen said. "Franklin is in the middle of nowhere, and there aren't any tourist attractions nearby."

"You'll lose that bet," Arlene said. "Almost a hundred influencers and vendors have already contacted us. The only reason we haven't made registration official yet is that Peter wanted to do the walkthrough of the mall first and capture video so they know what they're getting into."

"Why would anybody be willing to sign up before we've even started selling passes?"

"Memberships. The lawyer said selling memberships is the safest way to go because it gets around some state laws about alcohol consumption. It also gives the organization protection from certain liabilities, and there were other benefits as well."

"What organization?" Hadley asked. "Aren't we doing this as The Good Apocalypse?"

"The Apocalypse Fair," Arlene told them. "We registered it as a nonprofit in partnership with the city. It turned out that's the only way they could let us use the space."

"The Apocalypse Fair sounds like one of those role-playing things where people are going to show up dressed like we're living in the Middle Ages," Fumiko said. "We're going to have to be clear in the advertising that it's about preparing for the apocalypse."

"Peter is super confident that we'll have to turn people away before registration ends. He said that just providing free parking for RVs for a week will be enough to bring a thousand people once you put the word out on your channels. And don't forget that the other influencers coming will have millions of followers if you add them all up. We were thinking about selling the memberships in a lottery to create excitement, and Peter says that there will definitely be door crashers trying to get in."

"But if it's a nonprofit, doesn't that mean that The Good Apocalypse won't make any money?" Hadley asked. "Why go to all of the work?"

"We'll get plenty of publicity as the organizers, but part of the deal is that Peter is friends with the mayor and promised to help her figure out something to do with the mall space," Arlene said. "If our event works out, the town could repeat it in the future, maybe in a different location. Franklin has been depopulating for decades and they're desperate to do something to bring people up here."

"I spy with my little eye something flying," Fumiko declared.

The game went on uninterrupted until Arlene pointed out the turn-off for the mall. Hadley might have driven past otherwise because she was concentrating on looking for something scarlet that Glen's little eye had spotted.

"It looks abandoned," Hadley said. "Little trees are growing in the parking lot."

"Mainly maples, and they'll grow anywhere," Carl said. "The important thing is that the pavement hasn't buckled. I wonder why."

"The mall operator repaved the parking lots and did a lot of renovation work just a year before they shut down," Arlene said. "It was a big deal when I was a kid because it was a great place for rollerblading or hoverboarding."

"Why would anybody invest all of that money and then close?" Hadley asked.

"Peter says it was corruption. They got a grant from the state that was intended to revitalize rural malls, but all the money went to contractors who were related to somebody. It didn't change the fact that the population had dropped too much to support a mall this big, especially after people started buying everything online. There was talk once about turning the mall into a warehouse, but the geometry wasn't right or something, and a mega-company that builds warehouses all over the country came in and built one on the other side of Franklin, closer to the highway."

"Which entrance is the main entrance?"

"In the middle, with the big flea market sign over the doors. That didn't work out either."

"The final stop in the death cycle of the American mall," Glen said. "The flea market."

"But what about the anchor stores?" Hadley asked as she navigated around a light pole stanchion on her way toward the main entrance. "I'm guessing those buildings attached to the ends of the mall were department stores or big-box places."

"Their business was declining too, and when the operator went bankrupt, it gave them an excuse to break their leases and leave," Arlene said. "Peter can talk about the history of the mall for hours. He started a regional chain of gyms when he was in his thirties, and they had one here, but then the industry went through consolidation. After his local competitor got bought by one of the national chains, he couldn't compete anymore."

"Why not?" Fumiko asked. "It's not like a gym needs access to cheap wholesale goods or a transportation network. It's just the place with equipment where people come and work out."

"Peter told me all about that business one night when we were staying up to look at the comet," Glen said. "The difference is that the national chains are focused on crushing independent competitors, and they have deep pockets to run at a loss in order to create local monopolies. They cut their pricing down to break even, put in all brand-new equipment, including high-definition TVs and massage chairs. Within a year, Peter ran through all of the money he had made to that point, and he had to declare bankruptcy himself to get out of the leases. It was a good thing his father still owned the farm back then because he would have lost it otherwise."

The first one out of the SUV was Freud, who had to scramble over two laps before hitting the ground. He immediately went into sniffing mode, running along with his nose near the pavement like a hunting dog, but nothing was interesting enough to stop and smell. He caught up with Arlene at the little plaza in front of the entrance and expressed his disappointment by leaning against her legs.

One of the doors opened, and a security guard who might have been on the right side of eighty shuffled out. "Mayor called ahead and told me you were coming," he said. "Are there any more of you?"

"Four more," Carl told him. "I'm—"

"Don't tell me your names because I won't remember and then I'll just feel bad," the guard interrupted. "I'm Gordon, if you feel the need to be formal."

"I don't see any graffiti," Hadley said. "Do you spend all of your time chasing the kids away?"

"Anybody shows up on the security cameras covering the parking lots, I call the police," Gordon said. "We're here for fire watch to keep down the cost of the insurance for the town. We turn a blind eye to people using the parking lot to teach their kids how to drive, but other than that, everything is a liability. Anyway, we're all hoping that your fair works out, because if it doesn't, they're pretty sure they can get the grant money to flatten the place."

"Why would they do that?"

"I'm not working for free, and there's somebody here around the clock, plus the insurance. It costs Franklin hundreds of thousands of dollars a year to own this place, and they can only pay it because of another state grant that's specifically for the purpose of preventing commercial properties taken for back taxes from being abandoned."

Peter's pick-up rolled to a halt next to Hadley's SUV, and Phil, who had been riding in the bed, was the first one out. The lawyer was next, and he was carrying a clipboard with a piece of paper. Hadley heard the security guard groan something about suicide under his breath.

"Lighten up," Si said. "I'm not going to ask you to sign anything. It's just my preferred way of taking notes."

Gordon straightened up as everybody gathered in front of the door, and he pulled a folded piece of paper out of his pocket. "I have to read you all something before I can let you in," he said. "The Town of Franklin accepts no responsibility for anything, and by walking through this door, you acknowledge that you will not hold the Town of Franklin liable for any injury or losses you may sustain as a result of entering this mall."

"One of my finer pieces of writing," the lawyer said.

"You're working for the town now?" Peter asked.

"O'Donnell retired, and I'm the only attorney in town who will work without a retainer and bill in half-hour increments," Si said and put his right hand over his heart. "The things I do out of a deep sense of civic responsibility."

"I can take one person in the golf cart," Gordon told the group. "It's going to be dim because the lights are in conservation mode, and I don't have the key to the control room to turn them all on."

"If you don't have the key, who does?" Peter asked.

"Stanley, the third shift guard, and one of the guys who works part-time on the weekend. Don't know why it's that way, but they started working here before I did."

"Didn't you work for the town in the building department? I think I remember you from when I went in to get the permits for my gym back in the day. Did the pension fund run short?"

"Why?" Gordon asked anxiously as the lawyer claimed the free seat and the golf cart. "Did you hear something?"

"I'm just surprised that you'd need to work full-time," Peter said. "You must have retired twenty years ago."

"Fifteen years ago, and I'm not here for the money, which goes to the grandson's mortgage. I started working as a security guard to save my marriage. My wife and I get along fine, but not if we have to see each other around the clock."

Either the golf cart's batteries were low, or somebody had the foresight to install a regulator to prevent the guards from getting bored and crashing, because it moved at a moderate walking pace that the entire group was capable of keeping up with on foot.

"That was my original gym," Peter said, pointing at a large storefront with soaped windows. "I must have put a curse on the place because I don't think any business lasted in there for more than three years after I left."

"Is three years the standard term for a lease?" Hadley asked.

"New businesses can usually get a one-year lease with renewals around here, so that's not it. A bad first year for any business is easily explained due to opening in a new location and trying to build a customer base. The second year is spent making radical business plan changes to try to suit the market. The third year goes to talking yourself into shutting down."

"Can we do something other than turning the lights on to make the place look more cheerful?" Laura Ann asked. "All of the empty stores with the windows soaped or covered with newspapers are pretty depressing."

"It is an apocalypse fair," Hadley pointed out.

"That doesn't mean it has to bring everybody down. There's no point in looking forward to the apocalypse if we aren't going to enjoy it."

"I didn't realize you were looking forward to it."

"I meant that in the prophetic sense," Laura Ann said. "I suppose there's some small part of me that wants to see all of my warnings proven correct, but not at the expense of bringing civilization to an end. I'd like to think that we're all talking about the apocalypse in hopes of avoiding it, not in anticipation."

"What she said," Phil added. "As much as I'd like to prove myself a survivor, a full-scale nuclear exchange isn't on my wish list."

"What is on your wish list?" Fumiko asked him. "A limited nuclear exchange?"

"A world with consequences. I'm tired of living in a society where the people who go out of their way to mess it up for the rest of us get rewarded rather than punished. I've gotten to the point where what I want is real change. What we've been doing the last few decades is unsustainable."

"I have difficulty picturing an apocalypse that isn't harder on the innocent than on the guilty," Hadley said.

"That's because you're not religious," Peter told her. "There are hundreds of millions of people in the world who are looking forward to the apocalypse that they know as the Second Coming."

"I forgot about that. I guess I don't really know any religious people, but I saw a movie once where all the faithful disappeared in the rapture. Do the Amish believe in the rapture?"

"I don't think so, but it's not something they talk about with outsiders," Peter said. "I think they see hard work and obedience as the path to salvation. I don't know how they could fit the rapture into their theology."

"Just look at the glass roof over the atrium," Carl exclaimed. "There must be some great views of the night sky from in here when the lights are off."

"There are some great views of bird turd on the glass," Gordon said over his shoulder. "Don't ask me to turn on the fountain for you because the water pipes were disconnected to eliminate the freezing hazard back when the mall shut down. I remember when I used to bring my children here shopping and that whole tiled area was full of coins that people threw in to make wishes. I always wondered who got to keep the money."

The lawyer continued sitting in the golf cart and scribbling notes on his legal pad while the influencers spread out in the wide space, which was reasonably cheerful thanks to the natural lighting and the huge plastic plants with their dark green leaves that almost looked real.

Peter cleared his throat to get everyone's attention. "My concept is that all the vendors will have tables in the concourse between the main entrance and the atrium. We'll keep them all on one side since there's a good hundred yards to fill up, and if necessary, they can leave a little space between their stalls. We'll rent a trailer full of folding chairs to fill in the open area here where there used to be coin and stamp shows and such, and we'll build a little stage over there for panel discussions."

"What about a sound system?" Fumiko asked. "I'm not particularly good at projecting my voice."

"I have a childhood friend who does audio for bands and public events in the area, though that business is on life support now that everybody wants video walls. He won't invest in new equipment because he's getting near retirement. I already talked to him, and he'll take care of the sound."

"I think it's all great except for the abandoned storefronts," Laura Ann said. "Could we hang curtains in front of all of them or something?"

"Too expensive," Peter said. "I can think of all sorts of options, but it's just not where I want to spend a few thousand dollars."

Phil raised his hand like a small schoolboy and said, "I've got it. You know that I go skydiving every other weekend. Captain Dutch, the airborne vet who runs the school, has an enormous pile of old parachutes in the corner of his hangar. Some of them were abandoned by people who stopped jumping over the thirty years he's been in business, others needed relining or harness work, and the owners decided to go for a modern canopy instead. Twenty parachutes on each side would cover all the storefronts easily."

"What color are they?" Laura Ann asked.

"Every color you can imagine. They aren't military surplus."

"Won't he have to repack them all, and doesn't that take a lot of time?" Peter asked.

"He wouldn't use any of them without unpacking and repacking them anyway," Phil said. "This would give him an excuse to spread them all out and see what kind of shape they're in. I bet he'd do it in return for us giving him a table where he could promote tandem jumps for anybody who wants to try it. It's only a ten-minute drive to the old regional airport from here, and he can use any business he can get."

Freud began barking from down the concourse, and Arlene jogged over to see what he was so excited about. It turned out that a former clothing store had left a free-standing three-way mirror in their space with the door ajar. Freud was engaged in a vigorous conversation with three other golden retrievers, all of whom were intent on talking at the same time.

"Freud, they're all you," Arlene said. "It's just like the mirror on the back of the bathroom door, but there are three of them because of the different angles."

Freud wasn't buying the geometry argument, but he recognized the word 'mirror' as a synonym for 'computer.'

He knew that barking at dogs on the internet never came to anything, so he desisted.

"Everything all right?" Phil asked from the door. "I was worried you ran into zombies. They congregate in malls."

"Do you mean in general, or in the zombie apocalypse?" Arlene asked.

"Good question."

Ten

Arlene knocked on the open door of Peter's office on the ground floor of the middle house to pull his attention away from whatever he was showing Hadley on his laptop screen. "Mona Sturgeon just called to get directions," she told him. "If she doesn't make any wrong turns, she'll be here in ten minutes."

"Her phone lost the GPS signal in the hills?" Peter asked.

"Mona doesn't have a smartphone," Arlene said, breaking into a wide smile. "She said that if the government wants to see her through a camera lens, she's going to make them waste a spy satellite on it."

"Sounds like our kind of people."

"I haven't noticed that any of you are paranoid about the government," Hadley said.

"You're assuming that Mona is paranoid about them watching her, but maybe she has a good reason," Peter said. "Anybody with millions of followers online who primarily talks about how to prepare tasty and nutritious meals after the government falls is bound to get unwanted attention."

"But all the influencers working for us talk about life without the government to some extent. Does that mean that we're all on watch lists?"

Peter reached into a desk drawer and produced a silvery electrostatic bag with The Good Apocalypse branding, which included a disclaimer about the protection offered against EMP blasts being affected by the proximity. "We can discuss that, but first I need you to power off your phone, remove the SIM card, and place it in the bag," he said. "Then we'll go down the hall to Carl's studio, unplug the network connector, and flip the power breaker, which isolates the anechoic chamber from any continuous conductors to the outside world. When all that is done, I'll whisper the answer in your ear."

Hadley began reaching for the bag, then drew back her hand and turned to Arlene. "He's joking. Right?"

The office manager shook her head, not trusting herself to speak, but despite keeping her lips pressed together, the corners of her mouth curled up, and her eyes were practically dancing with amusement.

"And that is why we don't invite her to our poker games," Peter said. "You can read her hands in her face."

"Honesty is the best policy," Arlene said, turning on her heel and almost tripping over Freud, who had sensed something going on and was coming to see if his services were required. "I'm going to grind some of those roasted Tanzanian coffee beans you've been saving in the freezer because there's no way I'm offering the Apocalypse Chef what's left in the pot from breakfast."

"So you aren't worried about the government spying on us," Hadley surmised.

"Would it help if I were?" Peter asked rhetorically and then pointed back at his laptop screen. "We have enough time before Mona gets here to look at one more module from the Eleanor package, and it's time I showed you HIM."

"Isn't Eleanor a her?"

"I was speaking in Acronym, the lingua franca of financial managers the world over. HIM stands for Hyperinflation Indexing Model. We currently have it turned off because inflation is under one percent a month if you exclude the price of houses and equities, which the Bureau of Labor Statistics does."

"You're losing me again, Peter," Hadley said. "What does it have to do with the Bureau of Labor Statistics?"

"They're the government agency that maintains the CPI, the Consumer Price Index, which was designed to underreport inflation. But putting aside all the definitions that allow them to paint a rosy picture of the dollar's spending power, what do you think are the two most important investments for the average family?"

"I guess a house, and maybe college, or a business?"

"A house, and since most people don't have defined pension plans, saving for retirement," Peter said. "The largest single factor in the inflation index is a phony number for the cost of housing, which is based on surveying current homeowners and asking how much they would charge to rent their house. The CPI would tell you that a dollar when I was born is worth five times as much as a dollar today, but the median house costs twenty-two times more than it did then. The stock market is up by a factor of almost a hundred since the first time I disappointed my mother because she wanted a girl."

Hadley couldn't help looking skeptical. "If you're saying it's a hundred times more expensive to save for retirement today than it was when you were a baby, I can't believe it. How can anybody afford anything if that's the case?"

"Median household income has grown a little more than twice as fast as inflation, though a lot of the growth may be attributed to more women entering the workforce. But even if you take that into account, houses are more than twice as expensive, and stocks are up by a factor of forty. I'll let you have this argument with Laura Ann since she's our financial apocalypse influencer. I just brought it up as background for the HIM module, because if nothing else brings the country down first, hyperinflation will eventually get the job done."

"What does HIM do?"

"It uses a real-time number for inflation to adjust prices throughout the ecosystem," Peter said. "Our zero-inventory approach with private labeling and drop-shipping means that within a second of Eleanor processing a new order from a customer, she's purchased the required products to fill the order from one of our distribution partners. A traditional retailer can fall behind on raising their prices quickly enough to keep up with price increases from their suppliers, which is a quick way to go out of business."

Hadley drummed her fingers on the desk a few times, trying to think through the process. "But what happens to our profit if there's hyperinflation?" she asked. "We don't get the money instantly at the time of the sale, do we?"

"The funds are available to us as soon as the transaction is processed, but you're right that in a hyperinflationary environment, having dollars sitting in an account and losing value isn't a good strategy. Fortunately, Eleanor gives us the choice of keeping the funds in money markets or crypto."

"People in Manhattan were always talking about this or that person being a real Renaissance man, but you're the first one I've ever met," Hadley said.

Peter, who was getting up, started laughing so hard that he had to sit down again and almost missed his chair. "I'm not a Renaissance man," he eventually managed to say. "I don't play any musical instruments, I can barely draw stick figures, and I've never been interested in philosophy. The only subjects I feel competent to comment on are small business and human nature. I've worked in small businesses for the last forty years, most of them my own."

"You're saying that you learn a lot about human nature in small business because you're dealing directly with other people."

"That's right. When I started out, I thought I could do business on a handshake, and that taking a partner meant having somebody else to watch out for my interests. Sometimes that might work, I've had good luck making verbal contracts with the Amish, but try that in the business world, and more often than not you're going to end up disappointed. I've come to realize that the main value of a written contract is to make sure that both parties understand each other. Otherwise, we all have a tendency to hear what we want to hear and convince ourselves that the details aren't important."

"The devil is in the details," Hadley affirmed. "That was one of my dad's favorite sayings."

Peter got up again and he swiveled toward the kitchen. "Do you smell that coffee? Mona better get here soon or I'm going to drink it all, and then I'll be up tonight pestering Glen in his observatory." Freud began barking from his lookout post near the front door, and Peter changed directions. "That must be Mona now. Remember, don't say anything that implies she's a conspiracy nut."

"Do you think she is a conspiracy nut?"

"Going through life with an old flip phone and no data package is one step away from wearing a tinfoil hat. But it's an important step, and so long as she hasn't taken it yet, I'll be happy to have her join us."

Hadley was expecting to see an RV like the ones that crowded the highways and back roads on the few occasions that she and William had taken two weeks off from the city in August to visit the tourist traps of the Mid-Atlantic and New England region. But Mona's RV had clearly begun life as a school bus, though it had been repainted with a mural depicting fruits, vegetables, and other whole food ingredients on a scale so large that the sunflower seeds were the size of baseballs. Although Hadley hadn't inherited any of her father's mechanical genes, she was relatively confident that the cloud of steam mixed with black smoke leaking out through the front grill and the edges of the hood was a flaw rather than a feature.

"I'll get the fire extinguisher," Hadley said. "I saw one in the kitchen."

The front door of the bus folded open, and a woman in her late fifties emerged, using the handrail to control her last step onto the ground. Her nose wrinkled up at the smell of the black smoke, and she said, "That's not normal."

"Does the bus have an internal hood release?" Peter asked. "I can take a look."

"No release inside," Mona said, walking around the front of the bus. "Maybe it had one when it was original, but it doesn't now. With any luck, the steam has already put out the flames."

"Don't stick your hand under there, steam causes the worst burns. Let me grab a pair of gloves out of my truck and I'll do it."

"I'll get my fire extinguisher just in case."

By the time Peter got his gloves from behind the seat of his pickup and pulled them on, Hadley and Mona were standing at opposite corners of the front of the bus with their fire extinguishers at the ready. He crouched down to look for the hood release mechanism and then fumbled with it for almost a minute before a click was heard over the sound of escaping steam. He yanked the hood upwards while stepping back at the same time, and the springs did the rest of the work. The cloud that billowed out was mainly steam, with just a few wisps of black smoke mixed in.

"I was leery about taking the bus on a long trip after not driving it in years, though I was mainly afraid that the tires had dry rotted, even though I treated them a few times," Mona said. "Do you think it's serious?"

"One of the hoses let go," Peter said, now that the steam had cleared enough to get a closer look. "I can't see where the black smoke is coming from, but it's possible that something crawled into the engine compartment and died, then started burning off when you overheated."

"Like a mouse? I know I've had them nesting in the engine compartment before."

"In that case, the black smoke might also be from an electrical short because mice have a way of chewing through wires. Did you notice any warning lights on the dashboard?"

"No," Mona said. "But now that you mention it, the radio I had put in wasn't working, and I'm not sure all the lights were either. I kept up my South Dakota registration all the years it was off the road because they don't require annual inspections. I had to go through a whole residency process when I bought the bus from the shop that did the RV conversion, but I spent almost three months in the state creating content, so it was worth it."

Peter walked around the side and took a closer look at the front tire. "I don't want to sound preachy, but these tires are in rough shape. You might lose a back tire without ending up in a ditch or swerving into another lane, but—"

"I know, I know," she cut him off. "If things work out here, I'll either find a local mechanic who wants to fix it up for me, or send it to the scrap yard. I'm at the point in life that even if I go back to living on the road, I'd like something much smaller, like one of those van conversions you see so much about online."

"There's some fresh coffee waiting in the kitchen, so why don't we go inside, and when everything cools down out here, we can think about making a temporary repair," Peter said. "This is Hadley, who we brought on to up our game with the newsletter and help out with the website."

Hadley raised the fire extinguisher that was dangling from one hand in a sort of salute and received a reply in kind. "Thanks for reminding me," Mona said. "Let me just stick this back in its holder, and a cup of coffee sounds wonderful. I've been driving since I got on the road at five o'clock this morning because I was afraid if I shut the beast down, it might never start again."

In addition to getting the coffee ready, Arlene had put out a plate of cookies, a bowl of fruit, and another bowl with various granola and nut bars that might have been healthier than alternative snack food, as long as you didn't read the labels too carefully. Freud shamelessly joined in the recruiting effort, laying his head on Mona's lap as soon as she sat down, even thumping his tail as opposed to biting her hand when she asked, "Who's a good girl?"

"Boy," Arlene corrected her, and then mumbled an apology about the cookies when Mona picked one up and looked at it critically.

"You misunderstand me," Mona said. "I think it's an excellent shape for a pecan sandie. I judged a baking contest a few years ago, and all the perfectly round cookies got on my nerves." She took a nibble and said, "It's tasty, and a perfect complement to what I'm guessing is—" she hesitated a moment, sniffing the air, "—Tasmanian?"

Freud burst into a doggy smile and began to pant happily.

"You passed the is-it-really-her test," Peter said. "We've talked on the phone, and I've watched enough of your video to know that there's a place in The Good Apocalypse for you if you're willing to make the move. Now, what questions do you have for us that will make you decide to stay?"

"You're different from the entrepreneurs I've known in my life, if you're not offended by my calling you that," Mona said. "My first question is, does offering your employees free lodging at the office mean that you expect us to be available around the clock?"

"I don't enforce a policy to make the influencers take time off because they're all grown-ups and they were doing this for years before joining me. I try to be careful not to ask work-related questions outside of regular office hours, but I'm sure that from time to time my enthusiasm gets the better of me."

"He gives me grief if I try to work in the evening, but that's because I'm salary," Arlene added.

"It's also because I want you to have a life," Peter said. "You're too young to stay cooped up with apocalypse influencers around the clock, and I wish you would get out to Franklin more often."

Freud removed his head from Mona's lap and trotted around the table to offer Arlene emotional support, but fortunately, both parties pulled back from the edge.

"How about foraging?" Mona asked. "I like to spend as much time as possible in nature, and I've had very good success with mushroom hunting videos using ASMR as a keyword."

"I'm not familiar with that acronym," Hadley said. "Is it a prepper thing?"

"Autonomous Sensory Meridian Response. It's that tingling feeling you get in your upper body sometimes when you're especially relaxed and looking at something calming. ASMR is one of the biggest growth categories in long-form internet video. Content producers use it as a label on everything from massage videos to hours-long slice-of-life content recorded in bakeries or diners. People find it comforting to see work done well and enjoyment on the faces of the customers."

"Who shoots the video for you while you're foraging?"

"I use a head-mounted camera to shoot everything as I see it, and then if I want to record myself doing something, I have a collapsible tripod. My foraging videos are long uninterrupted sequences that require almost no editing now that I've learned not to move my head around more than necessary."

"The state forest that runs up into the hills starts one farm over, and there's a trail that goes through from this property," Peter said. "Plenty of mushrooms up there after the rain, and I harvest a hen-of-the-woods every fall to throw in the soup."

Mona looked horrified. "Was that another test? Boiling hen-of-the-woods is a criminal offense in my book. I mean that literally, it's in the chapter on don'ts. Hen-of-the-woods should be sautéed in butter and oil with a little bit of garlic and a few other seasonings, then served warm."

Arlene suppressed a giggle. "When I started living here, I called Peter 'Stone Soup' because he likes having community meals where everybody contributes something, but he's not that into cooking," she said. "We take turns using up supplies from the bunker for lunch, but I do dinner half the time, and the others help when they have a craving for something I don't make."

"Don't worry about any competition from me if I move in," Mona said with a laugh. "I've made a living by cooking my entire adult life, and I'm happy to eat somebody else's food when I can." She shot an amused look in Peter's direction. "Just not his. But tell me more about this apocalypse training camp you're planning. Is it too late for me to participate?"

"We just opened official registration, and I don't think there are any other chefs signed up," Peter said. "Hadley and Arlene have started a map to assign locations in the concourse, so we'll take a look at it after we finish our coffee."

"No chefs yet," Hadley said. "I would have remembered because we set aside the special section around the atrium that used to be the food court for if anybody needs to cook. A couple of kitchens still have functioning range hoods, even if the rest of the equipment was sold."

"I don't think it would be a problem running a two-burner propane stove anywhere in a space with as much air circulation as a mall," Mona said. "Let me see which survival ration makers are showing up, and maybe I can do something with their products. I've only come around to the prepper mindset recently, and before that, I was mainly concerned with the eating local movement. There's some overlap because we're all going to be eating local after the apocalypse, but you guys have more experience with long-shelf-life foods than I do, so I'll be looking forward to your lunches."

"It sounds like you're convinced to give it a go," Peter said. "Do you still want to use your studio on the bus, or can I show you the space we have available? There's one bedroom left on the second floor, and we have two open studio spaces in the barn, though there aren't any kitchen facilities out there. And I'll repeat my offer to let you use this kitchen as a studio. We'd have to do a little scheduling around that, but I don't imagine you need it for hours at a time."

Mona looked around the kitchen and then shook her head. "The bus would be better if you don't mind my parking it here. Your kitchen is so cheerful, and mine has a more apocalyptic feel to it. I've also been creating more content where I cook over an open fire or with hot stones in a pit. If somebody can supply venison, I have some very good recipes, and I've always wanted to build my own smokehouse."

"One of the vendors registered for the fair sells smokers and solar cookers," Hadley told her. "They looked pretty practical as opposed to the expensive ones I've seen in lifestyle catalogs."

"Phil hunts, but the deer season is a few months off," Arlene told her. "If you're okay with roadkill, I can put the word out."

"I adore roadkill," Mona said. "It's the epitome of eating locally and not wasting. I didn't know it was legal in this part of the country."

"There's state law and then there's local practice. People around here have a don't ask, don't tell policy when it comes to roadkill."

Eleven

The replica .50 caliber Hawkens mountain rifle boomed, and through the binoculars, Hadley saw a hole about the size of a dime magically appear in the paper target a hundred yards down range in front of a dirt berm. Then a cloud of smoke drifted into her face and caused her to cough.

"How could anybody have fought a war with black powder?" she asked. "The whole battlefield must have been covered in smoke."

"This is my homemade powder, and I might have gone a little heavy on the charcoal in this batch," Phil said apologetically. "But there were a couple of centuries before the invention of smokeless powder that it would have been tough to see much on battlefields soon after the fighting got going. That's why in all the Civil War movies the soldiers are still marching forward in ranks, like the British in the Revolutionary War, or all those Napoleonic battles in Europe."

"So they wouldn't lose contact with each other in the smoke?" Hadley asked.

"Officers did try to keep infantry grouped together for the sake of communications since they gave orders by shouting, but I was thinking about how hard it would be to march across no man's land with the enemy under cover on the other side taking potshots. If the whole battlefield is covered in smoke, that takes away some of the shooter's advantage, and everything comes down to volley fire and bayonets."

"I don't want to think about it. My dad was a helicopter mechanic in the army, and he loved the machines, but he wasn't a gung-ho war guy. He never talked about anything related to combat at home."

"Do you want to reload?" Phil asked.

"I probably should, so I'll understand what I'm doing if I write about it," Hadley said. "Do I have to clean the barrel first?"

"I wait until after the battle. Ramming the ball and the patch down the barrel helps keep it clean as well." He leaned the heavy rifle against the folding table and indicated the mayonnaise jar he used to store his homemade black powder. "A hundred grains is a good load for this gun."

"Do you expect me to count them? That doesn't sound very practical."

Phil produced a ring with plastic measuring spoons that he might have stolen from the kitchen. "Use the white one," he said. "It's not an exact science, and neither is the size of the grain I get when I make powder."

"I'll go with level," Hadley said. She filled the spoon with powder and then brushed the excess off the top with her finger. "So how do I put it in the gun?"

"You pour it down the muzzle," he said. "The biggest advancement in rifle technology of the 19th century was moving from muzzle loaders to breech loaders."

Hadley leaned the gun toward her and carefully poured the powder into the muzzle, which was conveniently just below her shoulders with the butt resting on the ground. "What next?"

"Take a lead ball from the bowl, hold it centered in one of those cotton patches, and then put it in the barrel, making sure that there's cloth all around."

"It doesn't want to go in very far," she said a few seconds later after trying to push the ball into the barrel with her thumb. "Is there a trick to it?"

"Two tricks," Phil said, "and I'll tell you one at a time so you don't forget. First, you need to ram the ball into the barrel with the rod, but rather than using the one in the holder under the gun barrel, I use a bench rod when I'm target shooting."

He handed her the bench rod, and she worked for almost a minute trying to push the ball down the barrel, basically hammering it with the rod once it was five or six inches along the way. But it just got harder and harder as she pounded, and it felt almost like she was pushing against a powerful spring.

"All right. What's the other trick?"

"Cock the hammer and take the used percussion cap off the nipple. You're compressing air in the barrel, and the only other way it has to get out is through the rifling grooves, but the patch and ball block that path pretty well."

Hadley pulled back the hammer, removed the little foil cup that comprised the remains of the percussion cap, and then started pounding the bench rod down the barrel again. She almost lost her balance when the ball traveled the rest of the way on the first plunge. She pushed again, and the ball didn't move. After putting the bench rod back on the table, she hefted the gun for the first time and found her left arm wanting to droop.

"How much does this thing weigh?" she asked him.

"Around ten pounds," Phil said. "You can tuck your left elbow against your body to help support it if your arms are long enough. But you have to put a new cap on the nipple before you can fire."

"Right." Hadley set the rifle on the table with the barrel pointed downrange, and Phil nodded his approval that she was being careful with the loaded gun. She took a fresh cap from the little baggie, fit it over the nipple, and lifted the gun again.

"One more thing," Phil said. "These guns have a hair trigger which is set by pulling the set trigger. Some models can be fired in one pull if you're in a hurry, but this one can't. Setting the hair-trigger increases accuracy for shooters because it doesn't take much pull or pressure to drop the hammer, and that should reduce overall movement."

Hadley lined up the open sights on the black circle of the paper target which looked impossibly small and kept wandering away as she had difficulty supporting the heavy gun barrel. She pulled the set trigger until she heard a small click, then sighted just above the target and began bringing the sights down. The slightest pull was enough to fire with the hair trigger, and the boom sounded even louder for being closer to her ear. She felt like somebody had punched the front of her right shoulder.

"Did I hit anything?" she asked, waving away the cloud of smoke.

"Very nice. You've got the bullet on target with your first shot. I could sight you in if you want to try for the bullseye."

Hadley leaned the rifle against the table. "I think I'll rest on my laurels," she said. "I didn't mention it before, but the shooting I did with Dad was all handguns, and he was less worried about my marksmanship than about being comfortable with guns for self-defense. Dad had a kind of dark view of humanity."

"Is he..."

"Gone," she said sadly. "He died before my mom, cancer, maybe from all the solvents he worked with as a mechanic. But he gave me a Smith & Wesson .38 Shield EZ before I moved to Manhattan and made me promise to keep it in my purse. I spent the last six years worrying that my purse would get stolen."

"You have a concealed carry permit?" Phil asked.

"Never got around to it. It's too expensive, there are a couple of days of classes with a test, and oftentimes the license doesn't allow you to carry the gun anywhere other than the range. I figured if I got caught, I'd be a first-time offender, and my boyfriend knew a lot of criminal lawyers. I almost took it to an airport once by mistake, and I've had to turn around a couple of times in the lobbies of buildings where they were putting everybody through metal detectors."

Phil broke out his cleaning kit, screwed together the rod, and pulled the cloth swab through the eye. "I'll just give it a quick cleaning so the leftover residue from the black powder doesn't stick to the barrel," he said. "We can shoot pistols another time if you want."

"I didn't mean to spoil your fun," Hadley said. "I'm perfectly happy spotting for you, though I should have taken you up on the offer for ear protection."

"I only got the Hawkens out to demonstrate to you since there's going to be a black powder weapons vendor at our fair. The neighbors aren't crazy about my banging away with rifles out here just for the sake of target practice."

"I hadn't thought of that. The Amish are pacifists, aren't they?"

"They don't have any use for handguns that I'm aware of, but plenty of the Amish around here hunt for meat during deer season. And they can get special permits to kill animals that are causing crop damage, which makes some recreational hunters very unhappy. But there are probably more deer in America today than there have ever been because most of their natural predators are missing from this half of the country."

"Do they hunt with muzzleloaders?" Hadley asked.

"The Amish?" Phil laughed. "No, they believe in using the best tool to get the job done, but you won't see them buying fancy rifles either. They keep their money close in the family to launch the next generation."

Hadley watched as Phil put away the cleaning supplies, and then she asked, "Do you buy all of your ammo, or do you reload?"

"For the black powder guns, I have molds for balls and Minié bullets, and it doesn't take a big fire to melt lead. For modern firearms, when I buy ammo, I get it with brass casings that you can reload as many times as you want. I've also fooled around with making cartridges for muzzle-loaders, but I'm never planning on taking one of these guns into combat, so there's no real advantage."

"How can you make a cartridge for a muzzleloader? What would you do with it?"

"A cartridge isn't the same thing as a shell," Phil told her. "It's just a convenient way to keep a bullet together with the proper charge of powder. You can make them out of paper, and then you unfold them or bite the end off to pour the powder into the barrel. Paper cartridges used in the old militaries also doubled as a patch, and they could be coated with wax to help keep the powder dry."

Hadley helped him carry the gun accessories over to the barn since he stored them in the bunker, and then they continued to the studio space where Phil recorded his show. She shook her head at the wall posters of submarine-launched ballistic missiles and mushroom clouds from atmospheric tests conducted long before either of them was born.

"It's hard to believe that nukes have been around since World War Two without us blowing up the planet," Hadley said. "Most of our how-to content I would classify as straightforward survivalist, but you really lean into thermonuclear destruction on your show."

"I'm not in love with the idea or anything," Phil said as he turned on the cameras. "You know the Robert Frost poem, *Fire and Ice*? It's hard to beat nuclear weapons, but when it comes to breaking down civilization, there are plenty of other options that will suffice. There are days when the news makes me think that Laura Ann is going to win our bet."

"You have a bet on how the apocalypse is going to happen?"

"Yeah. I have bets with all the other influencers, but Laura Ann is the only one I'm worried about. I still think it will come to nuclear war in the end, but I'm also beginning to believe that she is right about the trigger. If a worldwide financial collapse comes first, she wins."

Hadley had a hard time not laughing. "I imagine that will be very disappointing for you."

"Nobody likes being wrong," Phil said. "Pretty much all of the scenarios for the apocalypse start with people not being able to admit that they're wrong, except maybe the giant asteroid from space or the supervolcano."

"You mean that, don't you? I thought you were just some macho survivalist dude fixated on the post-apocalypse."

"I got my bachelor's degree in history, and I wrote a paper once about how all wars start because somebody can't admit that they're wrong. The professor thought I was stretching the point, because even with grade inflation, I only got a B, and that's like failing. I never set out to be an apocalypse influencer, it just turned out that way."

"How did you get your start?" Hadley asked, self-consciously sitting up straighter as the feed from the camera pointing her way showed up on the monitor.

"Making survivalist videos in Alaska," Phil told her. "I always planned on joining the military after college, and I would have gone into ROTC, but I did well enough on the SAT in high school to get free tuition at a state university, though I had to scramble to pay the fees. The recruiter said that with my scores, I'd have no trouble getting into officer candidate school, and I could go for special forces. Then I flunked the physical."

"You? You're a monster."

"A monster with scoliosis. I used to have back spasms from time to time when I overdid weightlifting or just picked something up the wrong way. I applied for a waiver, but they turned me down. Their way of looking at it is that training an officer is too expensive to gamble on a bad spinal column, and I guess they've had a problem with guys getting out early with full disability pensions."

"Does it keep you from doing anything?" Hadley asked. "I mean, you jump out of airplanes with a parachute. That can't be good for your back."

"It's better than jumping without a parachute," Phil said with a grin. "I think we're ready to go here. Is there anything in particular you want to talk about?"

"Why should it be up to me? Is there anything you want to talk about?"

Phil glanced at the door and then turned off the monitor. "There is, actually, but not on the record. Would you mind if I ask a question of a personal nature?"

"Uh," Hadley said, having a sudden intuition that he was going to make a pass at her. "I think you're a really nice guy and—"

"Not you," he cut her off. "Arlene. You spend half of your day with her, and you're a woman. Does she ever talk about me?"

"You mean in the non-business sense." Hadley hesitated for a moment, not wanting to hurt his feelings. "She never says anything bad about you."

"That means she never says anything good about me either. Do you think it's because I'm too big? I know that some women aren't comfortable with a guy who weighs twice as much as they do, even if it's all muscle, and her head barely comes up to my shoulders." He made a face like he had just rolled the dice for Arlene's affection and they had come up snake eyes. "But I care about her, and every time I see her looking anxious, I just want to protect her from the world."

"My ex always said that I was a borderline loner because I didn't have any female friends," Hadley confessed. "I know almost nothing about what women expect from relationships. Have you talked to her about it?"

"I'm afraid that it'll freak her out," Phil said. "It would kill me if I made it uncomfortable for her to work here, and what if she quit? Then I wouldn't even see her, and she'd have to get a job where the boss wouldn't be as understanding as Peter. They might even make her leave Freud at home."

"So you plan to do nothing. I don't know, that doesn't seem right either."

"The only thing that gives me hope is the apocalypse. I think that'll put an end to her anxiety, and then when I'm one of the only guys left on Earth, she'll at least give me serious consideration."

Hadley hid her mouth behind her hand. "Yes, I can see that," she choked out.

"You're laughing at me," Phil said, cracking a grin himself. "I guess I do sound pretty pathetic."

"Not pathetic, sweet. Maybe she just doesn't know that you're interested because you're always joking around. Have you ever tried a small romantic gesture?"

"I bought her that coffee grinder in the kitchen after she mentioned seeing it online somewhere, and I've spent hours playing frisbee with Freud."

"Those signals might be a little too subtle," Hadley said. "I don't know if she's ever dated, though I could ask her the next time the opportunity comes up. But I was thinking more about a frivolous gift that's not related to the office, like a box of chocolate."

"Oh, I tried that, but she just assumed it was for everybody and shared them," Phil said. "I asked her to the Franklin Ice Sculpture Festival last winter, and she accepted, but then she invited Fumiko to come with us. Since we all live in the same house, she knew that Fumiko and I were together for a while last summer."

"Maybe she thinks that you and Fumiko might get back together and she doesn't want to be a home wrecker."

"No, Fumiko made it pretty clear that I wasn't her type. She said that I was too serious. To tell you the truth, she was a bit manic for me. Fumiko only has two speeds, all out or sleeping, and I couldn't keep up with her at either." Phil made a clicking noise in his mouth and turned the monitor back on. "I need something to cheer me up," he said. "Let's talk about nuclear winter."

Hadley was still laughing when her camera went live, and she made the universal cut gesture under her throat with her index finger. "This isn't live, is it? You've got to cut that part out. I'll look like a real jerk laughing about the end of life as we know it."

"I edit everything, the same as Glen. The only time I ever broadcast live is if I'm doing call-ins or guesting on somebody else's show. I mean, what's the point? The vast majority of everybody's followers stream the video on demand."

"I wondered about that myself. Maybe some podcasters started on one of those social networks where live streaming had a chance of bringing you new viewers."

"If you put together an article about how we all got into this business based on the conversations you've been having with us, it might make an interesting read," Phil said. Then he put on his game face and switched the feed to the camera pointed at him. "This is Phil Martin, and I'm here with Hadley Brown to talk about overlap when it comes to nuclear winter. When you hear all-out nuclear war, the first things to come to mind are cities replaced by blast craters from hydrogen bombs and nuclear fallout turning everybody into zombies."

"There's no such thing as zombies," Hadley interjected.

"Spoilsport. My point is that human beings pass our lives in a sea of invisible radiation, radon leaking from the ground, all manner of particles from the sun, and then there's background radiation from the Big Bang. While you might not want to drink the milk from a glowing cow, if you're still alive a few weeks after the start of a nuclear war, radiation won't be at the top of the list of things likely to kill you over the next year."

"Doesn't radiation cause cancer?"

"It can, and I'm not going to try to pass myself off as a health physicist here, but most cancer risk from radiation is something that happens many years down the road. As long as I'm giving disclaimers, there's no general agreement among scientists over whether thousands of nuclear weapons detonated within a short span of time would result in a true nuclear winter or whether the ash and other particles would largely drop out of the atmosphere in a couple of months. We do know from studying tree rings that supervolcano eruptions and asteroid impacts result in atmospheric pollution that reduces the sunlight sufficiently to cause massive crop failures."

"I've heard the argument that massive crop failures around the world could lead to war because countries with nuclear arsenals will insist that countries with food share it," Hadley said. "But if everybody's already shot off their nukes and most of the world's cities are destroyed along with their populations, it doesn't sound like anybody will have the resources to make war afterward."

"Is that your version of a silver lining?" Phil asked.

"I take my wins where I can get them."

"In any case, the basic nuclear winter scenario calls for survivors flooding the countryside looking for food and a place to hide from each other. The models I've seen suggest that roads will all be blocked because of EMP effects disabling vehicles, accidents, and simply running out of gas."

"What if instead of nuclear winter, we have a slightly radioactive Autumn?" Hadley asked.

"Now you're using humor to deflect," Phil said. "Good coping technique."

"The only thing I know for sure about nuclear war is that if survivors visit a city vaporized by a hydrogen bomb, somehow a child's doll will survive to give silent witness. I've seen that in more post-apocalyptic sci-fi movies than I can count."

Twelve

"Should I?" Hadley asked, her finger poised over the left button on her mouse. "I'm a bit nervous."

"Freud," Arlene called. "Go see Hadley."

The golden retriever obligingly trotted over and laid his head on Hadley's lap, his eyes positively radiating therapy. The mouse clicked, and the software reported, "Newsletter scheduled for delivery to 161,249 subscribers."

"Now the site," Hadley said, closing the window and bringing up the content management software. She opened the latest website version she'd been working on, navigated to the 'publish' button, clenched her teeth, and clicked again. Then she picked up her phone and navigated to thegoodapocalypse.com, and a mushroom cloud exploded on her screen.

"It's lovely," Arlene reported, looking at her phone. "I'm going to send a group message and have everybody check their phones to make sure it shows up and the site is displaying correctly in all browsers. Glen has an ancient 3G phone that we should use to test everything."

The mushroom cloud faded away, revealing the new layout that had the up-to-the-minute disaster news at the top of the screen, specials from the catalog on the right, and the latest video from each one of the influencers to the left. There was a dialog box at the bottom of the screen labeled, "Ask Eleanor," and Hadley typed in, "What level of sunblock should I wear in case of nuclear war?"

"Sunscreen can help block ultraviolet radiation that accompanies the flash of a nuclear weapons blast, and an SPF of 30 or above is recommended," the artificial intelligence responded. "However, sunscreen will do nothing to protect you from the heavier radioactive particles that can cause severe radiation sickness and death, so it's recommended that you take shelter in the case of an impending nuclear war. I'll provide a selection of sunscreen products from our catalog below."

"Wait until we show Peter," Arlene said. "When he got the notification last week saying that Eleanor had been upgraded with catalog search driven by artificial intelligence from the latest large language model, he wanted me to contact them and opt-out."

"I've been playing with it the last few days, and it can write a pretty good article about the apocalypse, though it tends to blend in stuff from famous movies and science fiction books that people have reviewed online. What worries me is that our competitors who don't have any proper expertise will use artificial intelligence to start generating huge amounts of content."

"The only thing people use search for these days is to find websites that they're too lazy to type into the URL bar. We never got much traffic from search in the past, unless you count the ads that we ran on search engines when we were starting out. Peter told me that when search engines first began to include advertising, they went out of their way to differentiate between ads and the actual search results. These days, if you do a search on anything that has commercial value, all you get is ads."

"The people I worked with on my last job didn't know the difference between ads and search results," Hadley told her. "I guess it didn't matter much since they only used search engines for shopping. Try a question on your phone."

Arlene navigated to the bottom of the screen, tapped in the search bar, selected the microphone icon in the corner of the virtual keyboard, and asked, "How long can I use food past the sell-by date on the label?"

"This is a controversial subject that is highly dependent on the particular food product in question," Eleanor replied in the pop-up window that appeared. "An important factor is how the food is stored. Warm, damp environments generally shorten shelf life, while freezing can preserve food for many months, or even years, depending on the food product and the freezer temperature. If you have questions about a food product sold through our catalog, I can offer more specific advice."

"Do you notice how short she's keeping the answers?" Hadley asked. "It took me a while to find that setting, but I think it works really well, and it reduces the chance that people who aren't interested in our products will come to the site just to use Eleanor."

"There's already plenty of verbose artificial intelligence out there for them to play with," Arlene agreed. "We'll just have to keep a close eye on it for the next month to make sure we aren't using up our allotment of free prompts. Do the links generated by Eleanor include a tag so we can track how many sales the answers are generating for us?"

"Yes, but without A/B testing the new website against a version without 'Ask Eleanor,' we won't know how many of those sales would have occurred anyway from people just searching the catalog the old-fashioned way. That's one reason I put the prompt box at the bottom of the screen. Maybe in a few weeks, we can move it up to the top and see what difference it makes, but I don't see any reason to push our existing customers into using Eleanor to navigate if they're comfortable with the old catalog and regular search."

"Good point. You know a lot about this retail stuff."

"It was the challenging part of my last job," Hadley said. "Writing a lot of product descriptions for furniture and household goods and editing a newsletter that was put together from press releases wasn't all that interesting. Data analysis wasn't officially part of my job, and they didn't pay me for it, but it's what kept me working there. If I could go back and do it again, I would have gone to college for computer science instead of journalism. Everybody is a journalist now, but most people still can't make sense of data."

"Let's try her on a trick question, and I'm going to turn on text-to-speech," Arlene said, tapping in the prompt box and on the microphone symbol again. "Where can I buy the cheapest prepper supplies for the apocalypse?"

"Cheap is not always good, and you don't want to take chances when preparing for the end of the world when there will be no returns or store credits," Eleanor replied through the phone speaker. "If your goal is to maximize caloric content per dollar spent, please see the list of products from our catalog below."

"Wow, she's relentless. How much time did you spend tweaking the output?"

"Less than an hour," Hadley said. "It was all radio button choices during the setup. Answering questions in the context of the catalog must be part of the standard package for retailers."

"Are you ladies doing something important that can't wait?" Peter asked from the doorway of Hadley's office.

"I just sent out the newsletter and published the new version of the website, but everything is working just like it did in the local copy."

"Then go home," Peter said. "You've been working late every night this week, both of you, and the business isn't going to fall apart if you take the rest of Friday afternoon off."

"But we should be testing everything possible on the website to make sure it's all working properly," Arlene protested. "Besides, I am home, and I don't have any other plans."

"You could go foraging with Mona and show her some of the local trails. As to the website, I'll keep checking with Eleanor to see how orders are progressing. If they diverge sharply from the expected for a Friday afternoon, I know how to restore the previous version with two clicks."

Hadley closed her laptop, slipped it into her shoulder bag, and said, "You win, but I'm coming in tomorrow to check the overnight results."

"Suit yourself," Peter said, blocking the door, "but the laptop stays here."

As she drove home, Hadley vacillated over whether to just keep going and do some shopping in Franklin or to pull in and check if Betsy wanted to come along. Then she realized she had to use the bathroom, so she turned into the driveway and pulled all the way to the end to get the car under the canopy of the oak tree since the sun was still almost directly overhead. On her way to the back door, she heard a strange voice call her name.

"Yes?" she asked, turning toward the grape arbor, the produce of which Betsy used to make both jam and homemade wine.

"Hadley," the strained voice repeated, and this time she recognized it as being her landlady's.

"Betsy! Where are you?" Hadley dashed through the garden, unintentionally trampling on some flowers and upsetting the industrious bees who were busy gathering pollen. "I can't see where—" she stumbled to a halt when she spotted Betsy lying on her back on the ground beneath the grape arbor, one knee drawn up and the other leg out straight. An overturned five-gallon bucket and the small pruning shears buried points first in the dirt completed the story.

"Don't try to get me up," Betsy said through clenched teeth. "Call Peter."

"Right after I call an ambulance," Hadley said, reaching for her phone."

"No! Call Peter. It's not a stroke or a heart attack, and if it had been, I would have just lain here quietly and not given away my location. It's my ankle, and I felt the ligament tear. Now call Peter and ask him to bring Carl."

As much as she wanted to argue, Hadley did as her landlady asked. Five minutes later, Peter's pickup screeched to a halt in the driveway, then the two men came running around the back of the house. Carl immediately went to his knees and cautiously removed Betsy's shoe, sliding the sock down her already swollen ankle. He probed it tenderly, causing Betsy to suck in her breath.

"I don't think it's broken, but the only way to know for sure would be to get an X-ray," he said.

"No hospital," Betsy said. "Get me inside so I can put some ice on it, and later I'll do an ace bandage. It was a bit of a shock at first, but I was already thinking of crawling back to the kitchen when Hadley got here."

"But if it's broken..." Peter objected.

"Then it will still be broken tomorrow and the day after," his mother told him firmly. "The ankle is the simplest joint in the body, it's just a stack of bones held together by ligaments. Even if it is broken and I go to the hospital, the only thing they would do for it is put me in a cast. But I'm sure that my heart rate and blood pressure are elevated from the shock, and that means they would try to keep me a few days for observation. Now the two of you get me on my feet, or foot, because the smell of ripe grapes is overpowering."

Carl and Peter exchanged a look and lifted Betsy clear off the ground. Then Carl took her in his arms and carried her to the kitchen like she was a small child, asking every couple of steps along the way, "Do you feel alright?"

"Yes, I feel alright for the third time," Betsy said. "In fact, I think the pain is already beginning to fade. Just get me on a chair and bring me the ice and a dish towel."

"I'll get it," Hadley said, glad to have something to do. She opened the freezer, took out all the ice trays, and cracked open the first.

"One is enough. I want to bring down the swelling, not freeze my ankle solid."

"Got it." Hadley wrapped one tray's worth of ice cubes in a dish towel and then hesitated. "How are we going to hold it on your ankle?"

"It wouldn't hurt for me to bring you up to bed so we can elevate the ankle while icing it," Carl said.

"No," Betsy told him. "I will sit in my kitchen and drink a cup of tea, and by the time it's done, the swelling will go down enough to put on an ace bandage. I will remain in my chair until after dinner, and if I can't limp to the couch in the front room by myself, one of you will help me."

"But Mom—" Peter tried again.

"I'm dying, Peter," she cut him off sharply. "Everything that's born is dying. It's just a question of when. I won't be dying in a hospital, and I don't think I'll be dying from a sprained ankle, but if it's my time, I'm at peace with that. You will respect my wishes."

Carl grabbed a plastic bag from the box of replacements for the kitchen trash, put the dish towel with the ice inside, and then tied it around Betsy's ankle. "Kids, don't try this at home," he joked.

"You look like you know what you're doing," Hadley said.

"I worked my way through school as a paramedic," he said. "There was a time that I thought I would go to med school, but all the visits to emergency rooms put me off it."

"You couldn't stand the sight of blood?"

"I couldn't stand the sight of hospitals," Carl said, straightening up and going to the stove. "How many for tea?"

"You go back to the office," Betsy told Peter. Then she relented and added, "You can come for dinner if you like."

"Then I'll leave you in the capable hands of your housemates," Peter said, knowing his mother well enough not to argue. "I suppose I should be checking on Eleanor just to make sure she's not telling people how to hasten the apocalypse in order to increase our sales."

Hadley picked out three mugs from the rack, one which showed a city threatened by a glacier, another with two zombies shuffling forward in tattered clothing with the shared speech bubble, 'Brains,' and a third with a photorealistic painting of stunted corn stalks with undersized ears standing in cracked ground that looked like a dried-out lakebed.

"I dibs the zombies," Carl said cheerfully.

"Ice Age," Betsy said a second later.

"Why do I always get stuck with global warming?" Hadley complained.

"Climate change," Carl corrected her.

"I think in view of the crop failure on my mug, it's appropriate to call a spade a spade. Climate change brought on by nuclear winter could include a new Ice Age just as well as greenhouse gas."

"Let's not argue about the apocalypse," Betsy said. "What was Peter saying about Eleanor?"

"I published the new website today," Hadley told her, getting out her phone. "You haven't seen it yet."

Betsy dutifully watched the mushroom cloud blossom above the bucolic farmhouse and then scrolled around the website while Carl prepared the infuser for the teapot. "That's very nice, dear. But what does it have to do with Eleanor?"

"There's a prompt box at the bottom of the page, and you can ask about anything and get an answer from artificial intelligence."

"Do I have to type, or can I talk to it?"

"Just tap in the box and then hit the little microphone in the corner of the keyboard," Hadley told her. "Or I could do it."

"I'm not stoned on opioids, which I probably would be at this point if you had taken me to the hospital," Betsy said. "But now that I think of it, perhaps I'll have an aspirin with my tea, and a little something so it doesn't upset my stomach. I think there are some brownies in the cookie jar."

"Coming right up," Carl said. He put several brownies on a plate for her and then took the kettle off the stove and filled the teapot.

Betsy tapped in the prompt box, tried a second time, and shook her head in frustration. "My index finger isn't working again."

"Probably not enough blood circulation to the tip," Carl explained as he moved the teapot to the cozy on the table and then pulled out the chair opposite Betsy's. "Try rubbing the finger on something for a few seconds to warm it up."

"Here," Hadley said, reaching over her landlady's shoulder and tapping in the box. "And I'll enable text-to-speech for Eleanor's reply," she added and tapped the second microphone icon.

Betsy glared at Hadley, then raised the phone in front of her mouth, and asked, "What's the best treatment for a sprained ankle?"

"Rice," Eleanor replied immediately, drawing a puzzled look from both women, though Carl simply nodded. "Rest. Ice. Compression. Elevation. After a few days, as pain and swelling subside, try gentle mobility exercises and a gradual return to activity. The Good Apocalypse catalog includes a range of first aid kits, bandages, and inflatable walking casts, allowing you to plan ahead for when access to the local pharmacy or department store is no longer an option. Disclaimer. I am not a doctor, and the preceding was not medical advice."

"So what was it?" Betsy asked.

"I think you have to enter your question as a new prompt," Hadley said.

"Everything that has anything to do with health or food on the internet has those disclaimers," Carl said. "I swear if you look up how long you can leave brownies in a cookie jar, all the websites will say they should be refrigerated after cooking and discarded if left at room temperature for more than two hours. Everybody is trying to sell something, and fear sells better than rational explanations." Then he jumped up again and said, "I'll get the aspirin."

"He's such a nice man," Betsy said as Carl ran up the stairs to the second floor. "You should date him."

"Me?" Hadley asked reflexively to buy time.

"Well, I would do it, but now that I have this ankle holding me back, I'm passing the torch to you. What's the matter? Don't you like him?"

"Shhhh," Hadley said, holding a finger to her lips. "He's coming back."

Betsy opened her mouth to say something but desisted at the pleading look in Hadley's eyes. Twenty seconds later, Carl returned to the kitchen, removed the child-proof cap from the aspirin bottle, and then used a fork to puncture the foil seal so he could peel it off. "I was glad to see it was unopened because the expiration date was ten years ago," he said.

"Then why are you giving it to her?" Hadley demanded. "I'm sure I have aspirin in my purse, and I always throw pills out at the expiration date. Why take chances?"

"The army and the FDA have done studies about expiration dates on medications, and for the vast majority, the date on the bottle is unrelated to the efficacy or safety. There are some medications you don't want to take if they're expired, including most of the liquid ones, and some of those dosage-specific drugs that people take every day. But all pills slowly start losing potency from the moment they're manufactured, and there's not a tight correlation between the expiration date and some particular level of effectiveness."

"I'll take one and a half," Betsy said, shaking two aspirins out of the bottle. "No, it's not scribed for breaking, so I'll stick with just one for now."

"Is that something you know from your paramedic training?" Hadley asked Carl.

"Are you kidding?" he asked. "Our course instructors were worse than artificial intelligence when it came to disclaimers. They insisted that we do everything by the book as if any deviation from the procedures was bound to cause instant death. I know about drug expiration the same way I know about use-by dates on food, because I researched it. Who do you think benefits the most from expiration dates? The consumers or the manufacturers?"

"The Good Apocalypse is a retailer."

"Peter hadn't started the business yet when I bought this aspirin," Betsy observed, washing a pill down with a sip of tea, and then taking a bite out of a brownie. "I need some cheering up. Walter. Play the news."

"A rare earthquake, magnitude four on the Richter scale, rocked the coast of New England this morning, triggering the evacuation of schools and other public buildings, and leading to—"

"Walter, turn off," Betsy interrupted the headline. "I don't know what made me push my luck."

"I didn't notice that headline in the widget on our website," Hadley said, looking at her phone again. "Oh, I see why. That volcanic eruption in Japan is much more severe, it's been raining for fourteen days and nights in the Mekong River delta, and there's a new outbreak of Ebola in sub-Saharan Africa. The widget scrolls through the top three disasters at any given time, and then it does the three latest of any magnitude."

"Too much apocalypse," Betsy reminded her. "What do you like to do for fun?"

"I was never that social, but my mom always made me enroll in dance classes when my dad got moved to a new base, just to speed up making friends. My ex-boyfriend liked club dancing. It was about the only thing that would get him out of the apartment when he wasn't at work or the gym, other than eating in restaurants with potential clients."

"Carl likes to dance," Betsy said. "You should take her into Franklin tonight for the regular swing dance at the Community Center, Carl. I want to do something to thank you for your help today, so I'll pay the admission."

"We can't leave you alone," Hadley said before Carl could reply. "What if you can't walk to the downstairs bathroom?"

"Peter will be back for dinner, and I'm sure he'll be happy to stay for the evening to babysit me. And now that I think about it, there's an old-fashioned walker in the basement that I'd like you to bring up for me. I have the rolling thing with the wheels in the closet, but I don't trust it not to move when I don't want it to move."

"I'm not going to turn down free dancing unless you just don't feel up to it," Carl said to Hadley. "It's not as grand as Betsy makes out. I took Arlene twice, and the second time we were the only couple there."

"You used to date Arlene?" Hadley asked.

Carl tilted his head toward their landlord. "We went as friends."

"I saw that," Betsy said.

Thirteen

"Did you hear the latest?" Fumiko asked Laura Ann across the kitchen table at breakfast. "Hadley wants to change the newsletter from monthly to bi-weekly. That's twice as much work."

"Twice as much work for her," Laura Ann said after swallowing a spoonful of the soft oatmeal she had soaked overnight. "The only difference it makes for us is a couple of minutes to proofread our contributions."

"What do you mean? It takes me a whole day to write an article."

Laura Ann stopped with the next spoonful halfway between the bowl and her mouth, and everybody else at the kitchen table broke off eating to stare at the robot apocalypse influencer.

"You write your articles for the newsletter?" Phil asked in the silence that followed. "Like, from scratch?"

Now it was Fumiko's turn to stare. "You're all teasing me, right?" she asked. "Now you're going to say that Eleanor writes your articles for you."

Arlene looked nervous, and Freud immediately sensed it and shifted his position under the table so that his belly was on top of her feet. "Don't you remember when you started here, and I told you that you could just give me the transcript from your best show for the month, which I would edit down to size?" she asked Fumiko. "You said that it would be just as easy for you to write something."

"Well, I was wrong. Do you mean that all the articles you guys contribute to the newsletter are edited transcripts from your shows?"

"From our best shows," Laura Ann said. "Sometimes I end up giving Arlene pieces of transcripts from several shows that fit together on a theme. I use the transcription tool in the word processor, do auto-correction, and maybe change a few things if I realize there is a better way to say it. The whole process usually takes me about fifteen minutes."

"I guess I'll have to try that," Fumiko said, and then grabbed the sugar bowl and added a teaspoon to her Chocolate Sugar Puffs.

"Don't take it out on me. I'm just the messenger."

Mona joined the conversation from where she was sitting across from Peter at the end of the table. "I know a month isn't a long time to get to know people, but I seem to be missing an important subtext here. Do you have a secret sign language?"

"It's nothing," Laura Ann said. "Fumiko added sugar to her Chocolate Sugar Puffs because she knows that it grosses me out, but we aren't supposed to give each other grief over our food choices."

Fumiko defiantly swallowed a spoonful of cereal and then made a face like she had just drunk a shot of some disgusting liquor in a bar for the sake of group dynamics. "That is gross," she sputtered. "Somebody remind me why I eat this junk."

"You're addicted to sugar," Arlene told her. "When you tried going cold turkey, you couldn't keep your eyes open, even with an extra cup of coffee."

"That's purely psychological, you know," Mona said. "We evolved without refined sugar, and it's only been around for two thousand years or so. I believe it was first manufactured in India."

"Is there a twelve-step program or something I can join and wean myself off slowly?" Fumiko asked, then took another spoonful, which she chewed thoughtfully. "Or not. It kind of grows on you. But I saw an ad for chocolate yogurt, so maybe I'll try that."

"Anyway," Arlene said, "Hadley is the one who has been editing the transcripts you give me for articles the last few months, and she'll be the one who does it if we go bi-weekly."

"Good, because you work too hard," Phil said. "If not editing our transcripts for the newsletter saves you a day or two a month, I vote that you take the time off."

"It's saving more time than that because Hadley does the whole newsletter now. That used to take me days, though I'm still the one who talks to the advertisers and coordinates the paid content because they all know me. But the time I'm saving has been going into the fair. We're already over a thousand confirmed attendees."

"It's more than I hoped for, to be honest," Peter said from the end of the table. "We ordered six hundred folding chairs for the atrium at the mall to host panel discussions, and I don't want to go above that. I paused our advertising for the fair last week and had Hadley remove the banner from the website, but we're still accepting registrations from people who hear about it by word of mouth."

"We could get a circus tent and pitch it in the parking lot," Phil suggested. "It seems a shame to turn away paying customers, especially when this may be the last chance we get to put on the fair."

"Have you heard something about the town deciding to tear down the mall after all? The mayor promised I'd be the first to know if that state grant comes through."

"I meant the apocalypse. Something tells me that nobody will be holding prepper fairs after the fact. If there's any traveling at all going on, it will probably be ragtag groups of survivors migrating south for warmer weather."

"Some preppers see the glass half full, some see it as half empty," Glen observed, holding up his orange juice as if he were giving a toast.

"And..." Mona prompted.

"That's the whole thing. I'm just saying."

"What is he just saying?" she asked Peter.

Peter took a sip of coffee before replying. "I know it's lazy to always be dividing humanity into two groups for the sake of illustration, but most of the world thinks of preppers as pessimists, where I would say that some, if not most of us, are optimists."

"You're going to have to explain that one to me."

"Preppers are planning for the future, and what could be more optimistic than that?" Peter countered. "But you do have the group who just want to outlive everybody else and who are primarily focused on hoarding guns and ammunition to protect their hoard of guns and ammunition. That's a pretty pessimistic outlook."

"I'd love to stay and contradict you, but it's time to get ready for my show," Laura Ann said. "It's finally my turn to have Hadley on, and I have to clean up my studio."

"I've been trying to get her to come back on my channel, but she says she's too busy with the newsletter, the website, and working on a program and public relations for the fair," Phil said. "If anybody isn't busy today, I could use a walk-on guest. Otherwise, it's going to be call-ins, and everybody's going to want to tell me what they think about the new laws regarding imported Chinese firearms."

"What are you going to tell them?" Fumiko asked.

"Buy locally, shoot locally. There aren't going to be any international cargo flights or trans-Pacific container ships after the apocalypse."

Laura Ann began tidying her office by moving a stack of books on the guest chair to the floor, but a collection of essays titled 'The Search For Stable Money' fell open, and she got caught up in reading about the gold standard. She was still trying to puzzle out a particularly challenging bit of doublespeak when Hadley arrived.

"Am I too early?" Hadley asked.

"What? No, sorry. I was just thinking too hard. Want a book of essays by the most famous economists of the 20th century? I'll pay you to get it out of here. I'm serious."

Hadley hid her hands behind her back. "If it's that bad, you can't afford my price. It's all about supply and demand anyway."

"Not according to the monetarists," Laura Ann said. "They believe that it's all about the supply of money, not goods and services. I shouldn't have started reading because now I'm going to have the gold standard stuck in my head during our conversation, and that's no good because I talked about gold last week."

"If you don't mind, I was hoping to discuss what put you on the road to becoming a financial apocalypse influencer. Some of the other guys refer to it as Apocalypse Lite, but if you put me on the spot as to what's the most likely reason for modern society to break down in the immediate future, I would go with economic collapse."

"That's great. You'll think it's weird, but I've had guests from all the other schools of the apocalypse who have absolute faith in the ability of central banks to stave off a collapse by creating more money. How can the problem also be the solution? People never learn from history." Laura Ann got up and began turning on cameras as she made her way around the desk. "Grab the seat. This will only take me a minute."

Hadley plopped down on the chair and then leaned forward to restack the books that she had accidentally kicked over with her feet. "I can't get over how all of you guys just sit down in front of a camera and create a video that will eventually be watched by hundreds of thousands of people or more. It's like you're all fluent at creation."

"Listen," Laura Ann said after muting the microphones. "If I had to put a value on all my content for estate planning or something like that, a year's worth of advertising revenue would be optimistic. But if I gave up being an influencer tomorrow and stopped posting any new content, those views would drop off in a hurry, and I wouldn't be surprised if after a few months, I wasn't earning enough to buy groceries. It's ephemeral. Even if somebody archives all the video on the internet and it lasts forever, that doesn't mean anybody is going to look at it. Whatever influence we have is in the here and now."

"I expected you to say that no one will be able to see your content after the apocalypse, but it sounds like you're questioning the whole business model."

"It's a present tense business model, like busking in the subway. If you don't show up and provide entertainment, nobody is going to seek you out at home and drop their money in your guitar case. We aren't elite public intellectuals who also make a very nice salary from a university or a think tank. If you combine all of us at The Good Apocalypse, we have millions of followers, but if we were deplatformed or stopped producing new content, nobody would be coming around to ask us to be on cable news shows or to give lectures with five-figure stipends. You might think the apocalypse is controversial, but it's a blue-collar subject that people are either into or they aren't. The influencers making the big bucks are the ones who choose a side in a political or cultural argument and do everything they can to upset the people on the other side."

Hadley nodded. "I've noticed that since I started working here and paying more attention to podcasts and video channels. I take back what I said about the most immediate threat to civilization being a financial collapse. I think it's even more likely that fame-seeking narcissists doing everything they can to sow hatred will trigger one of the standard apocalypse scenarios."

"I can't argue with that," Laura Ann said and tapped her mixing board to reenable the microphones. "Are you ready to start?"

"Locked and loaded. Do you want to know my first question ahead of time?"

Laura Ann grinned. "That would rob the show of spontaneity, and believe it or not, I think followers can tell the difference. Besides, we aren't live, and if I say anything that hurts my image, I'll edit it out." She did the one-handed finger-folding countdown that Hadley had become familiar with, gave a brief introduction, and concluded with, "I'm all yours."

Hadley glanced down at her smartphone, then asked, "How did you get started as an influencer?"

"Do you want to go back that far? No, I'm not complaining," Laura Ann continued. "Let's see. I guess it all started when a friend of mine made some videos of me working out at the gym and posted them online. I was kind of a hardbody back then—"

"You still are," Hadley interjected.

"—a young hardbody, nineteen years old, and my friend's video channel was flooded with comments about me and requests for more videos. Some of the requests freaked her out so badly that she lost interest in the whole thing. She gave me the channel that she set up, and I thought, what's the harm in giving some lonely dudes a change from their usual thing if it helps me get attention and maybe make a living out of my passion? I was really into working out and anything to do with fitness at that time, but I didn't want to be a personal trainer, and an offer I had to be a body double in movies struck me as even creepier than some kinky old guys watching me sweat online."

"So you mainly did workout videos."

"That's how it started, but it only took a few months to use up all the machines in the gym, so I expanded into running, biking, and pretty much any physical activity I could do in public. Before I knew it, I was getting offers from sporting goods manufacturers and apparel makers who wanted me to feature their stuff on my channel, and weirdly enough, that turned into most of the content. My friends used to call me Lycra Girl because there was a decade when that was all I wore."

Hadley grinned. "I can just picture a younger version of you going everywhere in sports tops and Spandex shorts, but how did that lead you to the financial apocalypse?"

"The arc of the internet influencer is short, and it bends toward current events," Laura Ann said. "I was spending more and more time outside in nature or guesting on the shows of other fitness and outdoor influencers, and all of us kind of drifted into global warming and greenhouse gases."

"It's climate change now."

"I keep forgetting. I've taken a few courses over the years, but I never got a college degree, and a lot of the other influencers, especially the women, treated me like a dumb jock. That made me mad enough to educate myself, and I found out that the simple solutions the other influencers were all pedaling weren't so straightforward. There's a cost associated with decarbonizing the economy, which means there are going to be winners and losers. I started reading about economics and finance, and as the years went by, I found I was talking more about market tops and bottoms than sports bras and firm buttocks."

"Did you lose all of your audience?" Hadley asked. "Going from an online fitness instructor to climate change influencer to talking about finance seems like quite a journey. How long did all this take?"

"Around twenty years," Laura Ann said, sounding a bit wistful. "Sometimes I stumble across an old video of myself working out, and I think, 'Who is that hot chick?' I eat right, exercise, get a good night's sleep, and with the exception of my marriage, I managed to avoid stress, but you can't slow down aging."

"And your audience?"

"A surprising number of them came along for the ride, but you have to understand that the transition from one subject to the next happened in slow motion. I never could have established myself as a global warming—"

"Climate change," Hadley interjected.

"—influencer if I wasn't building on my fitness base, and nobody ever would have listened to me talk about international finance if they didn't have an interest in carbon credits and industrial policy. But I never stopped doing fitness content, and some of my most loyal followers are women a few years older than me who started watching those exercise videos right at the start. Everyone's life follows an arc, even if we don't start and end in the same places."

"It makes sense that climate change would get you thinking about the apocalypse, and then when you became interested in finance, that became the featured hammer in your toolkit."

"Most of my followers are into apocalypse-lite," Laura Ann said. "They expect cataclysmic changes to cause the partial collapse of society, but they still think it makes a difference whether they buy stocks, bonds, or Bitcoin. I try not to be too strident about it because nobody likes a fanatic. You can think of apocalypse-lite as round two of the Great Depression, and ignore the fact that World War Two was the cure."

Hadley made a whistling sound, sucking air through her teeth, and then realized what she was doing and stopped. "Can you expand upon that? What can we expect in a second Great Depression?"

"The optimistic view is that the people who have been living above their means on borrowed money will get their comeuppance, and the savers will congratulate themselves and buy real estate and equities at depressed prices. I happen to be a pessimist on this one. I can picture in my mind's eye whoever the president is at the time giving a State of the Union address featuring shared sacrifice, which means confiscating the money of savers. Can you think of anything that would divide the country more? But I'm certain that will be the government's approach. Rob the tortoises to get votes from the hares and keep them from looting. The real problem with our society is that there are as many hares as tortoises. I think countries where more people are savers could fare better than us."

"So where can savers hide their money?"

"It's not that simple," Laura Ann said. "The rich invest their money in political influence to safeguard their wealth. That works because politicians are always for sale. For the rest of us, say, the bottom ninety-five percent, you can expect creeping socialism, though the government will claim that it's temporary. Shared sacrifice includes things like means testing Social Security, price controls on small businesses, including mom-and-pop landlords, and then there are the retirement accounts most people rely on. By changing the rules for withdrawals and taxation, the government will turn them into a piggy bank."

"They've changed the laws about retirement accounts already, and I remember my ex getting angry about it because it ruined the estate planning his parents had done," Hadley said. "How likely do you think all of this is?"

"That's the silver lining. While many of my followers are counting on apocalypse-lite, I can't see it lasting. When the United States gets financial appendicitis, the rest of the world gets economic sepsis. Back in the time of the Great Depression, practically all the people in undeveloped countries were subsistence farmers. They might have noticed that it was harder to sell their surpluses for cash, but as long as their crops didn't fail, it wouldn't have been the shock to them that it was to workers in industrialized countries who lost their jobs, or people whose savings disappeared in a bank crash but whose mortgage payments remained."

"No wonder they called it the Great Depression. I've never heard anything so depressing."

"Here's where it gets worse," Laura Ann said. "The world's population has almost quadrupled since the Great Depression, and thanks to industrialization and modernization, almost half of those people are considered at least lower middle-class. That means there are now around four billion people who have a lot to lose in a financial collapse. They're going to be looking for someone to blame, and if the current government wherever they live doesn't want to start a war, the government that replaces it will have a mandate to do exactly that. There's nothing like angry people for causing destruction, even if it means burning down their own cities."

"So even though you're a financial apocalypse influencer, you believe it will come down to war in the end," Hadley said.

"It may be unconventional war. You know how everybody's personal information, including our social security numbers, has been stolen in hacks of credit card companies, health insurers, and any corporation that demands the data from us? I worry about how secure the rest of the financial network is. All those retirement accounts we were talking about are managed by just a handful of private companies, two of which hold the lion's share of assets for individuals. What if a foreign government knows how to wipe out those records and has already corrupted the backups or offline storage over time? Why should we believe promises that it's all secure when that's what they told us about our medical records and credit histories?"

"Is there any one event you think will set us on this course?'

"Not so much an event as the abandonment of one of the bedrock principles of central banking," Laura Ann said. "Federal Reserve chairs used to talk about moral hazard, the idea that they couldn't bail out the economy every time there was a problem, because it would establish the expectation they would always do so. Then they started with quantitative easing almost twenty years ago, and nobody ever mentioned moral hazard again."

"Must have been before my time because I don't think I ever heard the term before," Hadley said. "And now you think moral hazard is coming back to haunt us?"

"I know so."

Fourteen

Arlene poked her head in the door of Hadley's office and said, "The bunker. Five minutes."

Hadley jumped up from her chair, sending it rolling back into the wall with a crash. "But I was just looking at the disaster widget on our website and there's nothing special going on. Is it war? An asteroid from space?"

"All hands on board meeting," the office manager's voice floated back down the hallway. "There's not enough space in the kitchen for the big whiteboard."

"Do I need to bring anything?" Hadley asked out loud, even though the question was intended for herself. She saved the current newsletter she was working on, folded her laptop shut, and stuck it in the pocket of her oversized purse. Then she grabbed the granny sweater that she had worn during the walk to work with Carl that morning because there had been a chill in the air. She waited until she was at the top of the spiral staircase in the barn to fasten the buttons and then descended into the bunker.

"Last one down bolts the hatch and throws the switch that enables the killer drone swarm," Fumiko called up to her.

"For a meeting?"

"Just kidding. Peter won't let me have a killer drone swarm."

"That's disappointing," Hadley lied. "Do you have any robot sentinels to guard the entrance if we ever have to come down here for real?"

"Just the robot dogs, and they aren't armed, so the only thing they're good for is videoconferencing," Fumiko said, swiping at her smartphone. "There. I just enabled them. If anybody approaches the barn while we're down here, they'll acquire the target, provide an audio/video feed, and they have speakers so I can talk through them."

"Where is everybody? I thought you just said I was the last one down, but it looks like we're the only ones here."

"The meeting cave is over behind the storage racks. I waited behind to activate my guard dogs and meet you."

"You can't control the robots from the meeting, uh, cave?" Hadley asked as she followed the smaller woman.

"I can if I use the cavern Wi-Fi system," Fumiko said. "But this is a new phone, and I haven't put in the password yet because I forgot it. Anyway, it's always good to test fallback systems, but I needed to be near the shaft because the phone's signal gets attenuated by all the stone overhead."

"Are you saying that once we get to the meeting cave, your robot guard dogs will be on their own?"

"I'll ask somebody for the Wi-Fi password."

It was Hadley's first time in the meeting cave, and she was struck by the style of the furniture, which looked like it might have been in storage for the last thirty years. There was no central conference table, but the largest whiteboard she had ever seen outside of a classroom was affixed to one wall, and there were at least twice as many chairs as needed to accommodate everybody. Movable partitions that looked like they were covered with indoor/outdoor carpeting gave the cave a retro office feel, and there was a kitchenette where Carl was preparing coffee and Arlene was arranging snacks on a tray.

"It surprised me too," Mona greeted Hadley. "I take it that you've never been in here before either."

"I'm just surprised that anybody would spend so much on creating an underground office for the apocalypse," Hadley admitted. "I mean, it just seems like there would be other priorities."

"Like free storage," Peter said, coming over to join them. "This stuff is all from my second business, and believe it or not, I paid cash at an auction for the lot. I moved it all down here when the lease on the office I was renting expired, and between changing fashions and not wanting to carry it up the spiral stairs, I decided to let it be. It was second-hand when I bought it, but stainless steel and vinyl cushions last forever."

"Hey, Hadley," Glen greeted her. "I love what you've been doing with the newsletter, but we need to talk about the 'Ask the Experts' column."

"Am I forwarding you too many reader questions?" Hadley asked.

"Yes, but that's not the problem. I have plenty of time at night between observations, and I'm used to dictating while I'm working. The problem is that the more interesting questions are going to require long answers, and you gave us a two-hundred-word limit."

"It's not intended to be long-form content, and I didn't want to make more work for you guys."

"I don't mind the work, but the initial batch of questions you sent me are only going to make sense to readers who already have a high level of knowledge about astronomy," Glen said. "I need a couple hundred words to explain what the question means and then a few hundred more to answer."

"Same here," Fumiko said, taking her phone back from Peter, who had just tapped in the Wi-Fi password for her. "Did you notice that the first batch of questions you gave me wasn't related to the apocalypse? It was all technical stuff about robots and programming, which is fine, but I don't know if it will do anything for circulation. Arlene always sent us the feedback she got on the newsletter for our columns, and that was pretty focused on prepper themes."

"Maybe I overreached," Hadley said. "I used artificial intelligence to do some deep research for a meta-analysis of successful newsletters, and the questions and answers column was one of the features we were missing. I temporarily removed the form from the website when I saw how many questions were being submitted, so maybe I should just leave it off."

"I knew some guys in the early days of the internet who made a fortune off question-and-answer sites," Peter said. "There were two basic tricks. The first trick was search engine optimization for a huge number of individual pages to post questions that let anybody provide answers in return for social credit, like getting points toward being declared an expert on the site. But the other trick was that in addition to questions posted by real people, the sites were seeded with made-up questions related to all the hot-button issues of the day, whether it was using new technology, managing money, finding a job, anything that made good search fodder."

"Let me translate," Fumiko said to Hadley. "You should make up the questions and give them to us, or we could make them up ourselves."

Hadley hesitated. "Do you mean with phony names and places? Wouldn't it look bad if we got caught? It doesn't seem fair to readers who will be scouring every last word of the newsletter and the website looking for how to submit questions."

"The questions don't have to be signed, and you could tweak the fine print to say that these are representative of the questions that our influencers received through their call-in shows."

"That's not a bad idea," Mona said. "Sometimes I think that everything I know about cooking for the apocalypse is the result of somebody having asked me a question about it and my taking the time to work out the answer. I could do that in reverse once a week if you want a question and answer from me."

"We just started publishing every other week, and the deep research assistant I've been using couldn't give me a definitive answer about the best frequency for non-daily newsletters," Hadley said. "There's a tradeoff between publishing often enough that the readers remain engaged and don't forget who you are, and publishing so often that they come to see the newsletter as just another piece of marketing e-mail. It's a big deal now if subscribers get annoyed and move the newsletter to their spam folder without unsubscribing because the big e-mail providers will start throttling delivery to everybody."

"I thought they'd get around to that eventually," Peter said. "Power corrupts, and the big platforms want to own the internet. It doesn't benefit them that there are independent businesses out there delivering content directly to subscribers. Whenever a trillion-dollar company says that it's making changes to give people a higher quality experience, what it means is that they've decided to start killing off competition."

Arlene came around carrying a tray with pastry and cookies, followed by Carl, who handed out pre-poured mugs of coffee along with packets of creamer and sweetener. Everybody took advantage of the offer, and then they settled into the first two rows of chairs, all of which were facing the blank whiteboard. Peter finished his pastry in three bites and took his coffee with him to stand at the front facing everyone.

"There are two weeks left until our first Apocalypse Fair, and we've closed registration for influencers and vendors," he began. "I was tempted to close registration for attendees as well since we're already over twelve hundred paid memberships, but the mayor asked me to wait because not all of the rooms available for rent in town have been taken yet."

"With over a thousand people coming, plus the professionals?" Phil asked. "Just how many empty bedrooms are there in Franklin?"

"The last number I heard from the mayor was that residents have reported one hundred and thirty-six booked rentals for the fair weekend, with most of them renting for the entire week because it only costs a few dollars more after you figure in the discount and cleaning fee," Peter said. "I don't know how many rooms that leaves open, but when I checked the internet booking sites, it seemed to me that those remaining unrented were awfully pricey for what they were offering. As expected, the majority of attendees will be arriving in an RV and taking advantage of the free parking we offered."

"Are we going to make the bathroom facilities in the mall available for people who show up with campers rather than true RVs?"

"Yes, and I made a deal with the mayor to pick up the cost of an additional security guard over the fair weekend. I'll check the work-wanted board in the supermarket to find a couple of people who are willing to keep the bathrooms clean."

"Did you get the mayor's approval for the swap meet?" Hadley asked. "I've been holding off adding it to the website until you give me the word."

"The swap meet is a go, but let's limit it to afternoon hours so people have a reason to come inside and check out the paying vendors," Peter said. "And make sure that everybody is aware that firearms are excluded."

"Including black powder?" Phil asked in surprise.

"I meant regulated firearms. Black powder guns aren't regulated in this state or on the federal level, so make a note of that in the announcement, Hadley."

"I'll send everybody who's registered an e-mail with the swap meet announcement, but I don't think the paying vendors will be happy," Arlene said nervously.

Freud broke off trying to mooch a scone from Glen and trotted over to attempt a merge with Arlene's legs.

"I brought up the swap meet on the phone to every vendor I spoke with, which I believe was all of them," Peter said. "A couple of them asked me why they should rent table space in the mall when they could just set up in the parking lot. I pointed out that we can't control the weather, and that by registering as a vendor, they'll be included in the official program. That way there won't be any questions from the IRS about deducting travel expenses on their taxes."

"Is that an issue for vendors who go to swap meets?" Hadley asked.

"Absolutely. Small businesses don't get audited as often as you might think, but when it happens, the taxman is very skeptical of business activities that could just as easily be recreation. The standard mileage deduction for travel expenses alone will be over a thousand dollars for vendors who drive all day to get here, so saving two hundred dollars on a dealer space would be penny-wise and pound foolish."

"Is the schedule for the panel discussions already carved in stone, or can we swap between us?" Laura Ann asked.

Arlene turned around in her chair to reply. "We've scheduled the other influencers who will be on each panel, so swapping the time would mean getting their approval. Did you have a problem with Sunday morning?"

"Not really. I was just curious."

"We aren't printing programs, but we've already made an electronic copy available on the website," Hadley added. "Peter learned in his conference days that some people like planning how they're going to spend their time as far ahead as possible, and we figured that preppers are likely overrepresented in that category."

"How are my stargazing sessions on Friday night and Saturday night doing for registrations?" Glen asked. "I was planning to stick with the naked eye and teach the constellations because most people don't know them anymore, but if the registrations are low, I could bring a couple of telescopes."

"There are over twenty people pre-registered for each night, and you'll probably get more once they're here," Arlene said. "Stick with the constellations."

"Another bit of good news is that the town cleared everything with the state insurance agency, so we can get in to set up two days early," Peter said. "That's a nice bonus for vendors who are traveling a long way because they don't have to race the clock. I reserved the Legion Hall for Thursday night to host the influencers who arrive early."

"What's on the menu?" Mona asked.

"We'll have a choice of spaghetti and meatballs or pizza. They can do the spaghetti sauce without the meatballs and the pizza without meat for vegetarians, and there will be salad and bread, as well as beer and wine."

"Somebody coming," Fumiko announced, her eyes on her phone. "I'm guessing by the horse and buggy that he's Amish, but it could be a diabolical disguise."

"Don't send your dogs over," Carl said. "They could spook the horse." He got up and moved around to look over her shoulder. "That's Eli Glick."

Peter set down his empty coffee mug and headed for the stairs. "He's early. I thought he was coming after lunch. I hired him to build a little platform that we can assemble at the mall so the panel members will be visible to the people in the back rows. I'll bring him down so you all can meet him."

"I take it this isn't a secret bunker," Mona said.

"We have some tiny homes in caves on the lower levels that were built by Amish carpenters from the area," Arlene told her. "All of the local farmers know that they're welcome to come and join us if things start looking really bad out there."

"How long would the food supplies I saw in the main cavern hold out?"

"Peter is sure that they'd bring their own, and we have a lot more of the long shelf-life foods stored lower down.

But the Amish are deeply religious and consider themselves to be in God's hands."

"That reminds me what I wanted to ask," Carl said. "Are any of the influencers coming to the fair focused on the religious apocalypse? The four horsemen, Armageddon, Judgment Day?"

"We didn't invite any explicitly religious influencers for the simple reason that they have a way of making nonbelievers uncomfortable," Hadley said. "I've been watching the channel of a Mormon influencer who does a prepper thing—"

"Joe Jones," Phil interrupted. "We've done virtual guest spots on each other's shows. He's more focused on the nuts and bolts of the apocalypse than on theology. All Mormons are preppers."

"I think that in preparing for the apocalypse, we're all preaching a form of theology, even without the established religion elements," Laura Ann said. "Whenever I get caught up in an online correspondence with somebody and we end up disagreeing, in the end, they call me a religious nut."

"Some of the vendors are pretty religious, going from their websites," Hadley said.

"If they have websites, doesn't that already mean that they're not orthodox?"

"As far as I can tell, everybody is online these days. I even see Amish businesses with websites, though I wouldn't be surprised if they paid somebody else to maintain them or do the work with the borrowed computer at the library. We also have Kosher prepper supplies in the catalog from a manufacturer with rabbinical supervision."

"I thought the Amish didn't want anything to do with electricity," Mona said. "How does that square with hiring people to put up websites?"

"None of the Amish farms around here are connected to the electrical grid," Arlene told her. "You can drive by and see that. But most of them use batteries to power DC in their homes and recharge from solar panels or even gasoline generators. I think it depends on the particular church district they belong to."

"Uh, oh," Glen said, looking up from his old smartphone. "I just checked the list of influencers on our website, and I see Judy Utah. I hope you didn't put her on my panel."

"She asked specifically," Hadley said. "Is it a problem? I checked that she has a large and active following, and I thought it would be interesting to have somebody who publishes a lot of feminist content."

"I don't have any problem with feminism, but she's a witch. I just know she's going to show up at my stargazing sessions skyclad."

"You mean naked?"

"Try telling Judy that," Glen said. "I met her at a thing a couple of years ago, and she took her clothes off even though we were inside. She said they were constricting her aura. What's worse is she made a pass at me, but she has a Garden of Eden scene tattooed on—it was a huge turn-off."

"Hold that thought," Arlene said. "They're coming."

Peter led a middle-aged Amish man into the meeting cave and did a brief round of introductions. Then he said, "Eli tells me that a platform is a platform and all he needs to know is how many people are going to be on it and how high off the floor you want to get."

"You know more about this sort of stuff than we do," Carl said. "I don't see any need for a podium since we'll all have microphones in front of us, provided and mixed by your sound guy. We need enough room for a narrow table and folding chairs, and then some steps to get up and down."

"Twelve feet wide, four feet deep," Eli said, taking a pencil from behind his ear and a small notepad from his breast pocket. "That's a sheet and a half of three-quarter-inch plywood, and I'll use the leftover half-sheet for the steps. How high off the ground?"

"It doesn't need to be a lot," Peter said. "Say, eighteen inches?"

"You're the customer. You say eighteen inches, I'll build it eighteen inches. Painted?"

"Good idea. Flat black, I think."

Eli wrote a few more numbers in his book, then said, "Three hundred and twenty dollars delivered here in one week. You can stand it up sideways in your old pickup truck to take it to the mall. I'll use square drive screws so you can easily disassemble and store it if you don't want to keep it in one piece after your fair. Half now for materials."

Peter got out his wallet, extracted two crisp hundred-dollar bills, and gave them to the carpenter, saying, "Put the change toward the final amount." Then the two men shook hands, and without further ado, Eli turned to go.

"Wait a minute," Mona said. "May I ask you a question?"

"If you can talk while walking," Eli said, though to be fair, he did stop to let her catch up before he headed for the stairs.

"What do the Amish think about Peter's business and us having the giant shelter in the cavern?"

"Some think one way, others think another."

"How about you?" Mona asked.

"I think Peter is a good customer and always pays his bills."

"I don't want to offend you, but I'm dying of curiosity to know whether or not the Amish expect the apocalypse."

"I'm not offended, but I really couldn't say," Eli told her, and then he headed up the spiral staircase.

Fifteen

Arlene stood over the printer while it went through a thirty-second warm-up before spitting out a single piece of paper. Freud sensed that she was tense and did his best to provide therapy, almost tripping her three times along her way to Peter's office. The owner of The Good Apocalypse was studying a spreadsheet on his laptop, but he looked up as soon as Arlene entered.

"Did you run the server statistics for the website early this week because Hadley's changes are bringing in millions of new visitors?" he asked when he saw the paper in her hand.

"We are seeing an increase in traffic, but I printed this e-mail because it's so over-the-top, I thought you'd want to see it on paper," Arlene said.

"If somebody is threatening to sue us again, just forward it to Suicide Larson," Peter said. "I'm going to give it to him anyway, so why should I read it first and ruin my morning?"

"It's an offer to acquire The Good Apocalypse," Arlene blurted out. "A cash offer." She extended the paper, but he waved it off.

"Somebody has too much money and not enough experience in this business. But I'm not selling, so send them a polite rejection in my name."

"Didn't you tell me that knowing when to sell out was the most important lesson you learned as an entrepreneur? If these guys with their deep pockets are beginning to consolidate the industry, maybe the writing is on the wall."

Peter laughed and accepted the printed email. "The apocalypse influencer industry?" he asked as he skimmed the text. "No, these guys consolidate conferences, and their interest is in the fair. They're offering seven figures, but if you read the bottom line, that's contingent on our opening the books to them and our sales meeting their unstated expectations. This is a fishing expedition for information on their part. They have no intention of buying the business unless I'm willing to sell it with a couple of zeros lopped off that price. What they are willing to do is to spend some money flying out here, probably in a private jet, and taking us to an expensive dinner at which they'll pick our brains."

"That's evil," Arlene said. "It should be illegal to dangle offers you don't mean to fulfill."

"Caveat emptor," Peter said. "I don't take it personally, and I wouldn't be surprised if they send somebody on the sly to attend the fair and try to gauge whether or not it has potential for the national stage."

"We already have registrations from all over the country, and they'll see that just by walking through the parking lot and looking at the license plates on the RVs."

Peter laughed again. "RV license plates can be deceiving. A lot of people register them in states with low fees and no annual inspections. I know these conference aggregators, and they want events that they can run multiple times a year, even once a month if the traffic is there. Think about the big comic book conventions and video game shows."

Arlene relaxed and accepted the piece of paper back from Peter. "I'll e-mail them a polite rejection. Do you want me to do a little research on their corporate website and see if they have photographs of the team members who might show up undercover?"

"I wouldn't deal with them any differently if I knew who they were. We have the first mover advantage, and if the fair is a success and we want to run it next year, I don't think competition will hurt us. I honestly can't imagine these guys taking on the risk of something as controversial as prepping for the apocalypse, but if they do, it will mean more opportunities for all our influencers to pick up a nice paycheck and generate some content."

"Speaking of content, I'm helping Hadley with the newsletter so she can send it out early this week. Weren't you going to write a welcoming message to the attendees?"

Peter groaned. "I knew I was procrastinating something. Any chance of you writing it for me? It would be a nice gesture to thank all our existing customers for letting us build the business to the point that we can host a fair. I'll have trouble coming up with more than a sentence or two, though, and it needs to be longer than that to carry weight."

"I'll do it right after I answer the e-mail, and then I'll bring it back so you can check what you've written," Arlene said. "And I'm really glad you're not selling the business."

"I qualified for Social Security this year, even though I haven't started collecting," Peter told her. "I'm not trying to get rich, and I enjoy working with younger generations. Besides, I believe we're helping people prepare for hard times ahead, even if the world muddles through without governments collapsing. We sell good products at a reasonable price and make sure that people know how to use them. You can include something about that in my letter to the readers."

When Arlene got back to her desk, Freud was already on his rug and lost in a dream about chasing a rabbit who was smoking a cigar. She sent a polite rejection of the buyout offer and then spent forty-five minutes ghostwriting a newsletter column for Peter. After he approved the printed copy without any changes, she went back to her desk to grab her laptop and bring it to Hadley's office.

"The newsletter is shaping up great," Hadley said. "Don't tell Fumiko, but the transcript she gave me from her show for this issue is better than her writing."

"Most of the influencers are the same," Arlene said. "They spend so much time talking on camera that they're fluent communicators when they aren't thinking about it. I never had to touch up the transcripts much, and the resulting articles feel much more alive than an essay."

"That's what Carl told me about his writing. We went into Franklin to catch a movie last night. I babbled about the newsletter the whole time and then felt bad about it. He's surprisingly patient."

"Sounds like you guys are getting along pretty well, and you won't have any awkward discussions about moving in together because you already live in the same house."

"You'll laugh, but I've only dated three guys in my life if you don't count dance partners when I was taking lessons," Hadley said, and then realized that this was the opening she had been waiting for. "How about you and Phil?"

Arlene looked down and began picking at the cuticle of a fingernail. "I know he feels sorry for me because of my anxiety. He's always trying to cheer me up and get me to go out and do things, but we're just friends."

"I was never one of the cool girls or the mean girls, so I don't have any experience messing around in other women's relationships, but I'm pretty sure that Phil has feelings for you."

"He's not shy. He would have said something by now."

"Unless he was worried about chasing you away," Hadley said pointedly. "He knows how much you enjoy your job here, and it would kill him if he did something to make you uncomfortable."

Arlene raised her head and looked directly into Hadley's eyes. "Did he say something to you, or is this just your intuition?"

"Phil said more than enough. He wants to date you, Arlene, but I suspect that he's also worried you'll think he's too old for you."

"He's thirty-three, or maybe four. It's barely a ten-year difference. Did you date guys your age when you were my age? They aren't serious about anything other than video games."

"William was ten years older than me, and I thought I was going to marry him," Hadley said. "But his working eighty hours a week was too much for me. If we had kids, he never would have seen them."

"I decided I was never having children because I was terrified that I would give them my anxiety and that would break my heart," Arlene said. Freud came running into the office as if he were chasing something and practically climbed into Arlene's lap. She hugged the dog and asked Hadley, "Did I tell you how I got him?"

"Freud? I guess I assumed that there were agencies for anxiety dogs."

"There are, but Freud is a washout from a seeing-eye-dog program. A friend of Peter's is involved in training them, and Peter has fostered a few puppies. It's not easy, because you can't offer the puppies too much affection when they're being trained as professionals. When Freud was old enough to go for the intensive training, it turned out that he was too friendly and he couldn't leave strangers alone. Peter managed to get Freud back, though it took some persuasion, and when I showed up, I sort of stole him."

"He certainly seems to be attuned to your feelings," Hadley said. "I've never actually known anybody with anxiety who wasn't medicated to the point that they could dance naked in the subway, so I don't really know what's involved."

"It crept up on me as a teenager, always having a nervous stomach and worrying too much about things that couldn't be helped. When I went away to college, it took over my life. I would go days at a time without eating because I couldn't keep anything down. My face felt like it was carved out of wood, and whatever triggered the anxiety just kept building in a feedback loop. Universities are used to this sort of thing, so they were willing to let me skip public presentations and take tests in my dorm room, but I felt like I was living half a life. No, worse than that, maybe a tenth of a life. Every breath was a struggle when it got bad, like I was hanging on by my teeth. Do you want to hear a sad story about food?"

"Since you put it that way, I can't resist."

"I was in full panic mode, I don't remember why. Maybe because a cousin was coming into Boston to see me, and she would expect to go out on the town. Every few hours, I would force myself to eat a teaspoon of yogurt, but I had to massage my throat to make it go down. Then I'd just end up wrapped around the toilet bringing it up again. I couldn't tell you how many times I slept on the bathroom floor that semester. Eventually, I went out for a long walk, because exercise was the only thing that ever helped. After a couple of hours, I got hungry, so I walked into a fast-food place where I'd normally never eat and ordered a meal. The girl working the counter was alone, and when she made change for a customer before wrapping my food, I noticed she wasn't wearing those disposable gloves. Normally, that wouldn't bother me because I'm not afraid of germs, but this time it was like a punch in the gut. I paid the bill, dropped the bag in the trash can, and walked home feeling like there was an alien in my stomach trying to break out."

"That's terrible," Hadley said. "I can't imagine so much pain from dealing with daily activities. My mother used to say that army brats were well-adjusted because of moving all the time and being forced to make new friends and get accustomed to new places. I feel anxious in thriller movies, or when I think somebody is eyeballing me on the subway, but that's about it."

"I would never go to a thriller movie," Arlene said with a short laugh. "There are whole swaths of the entertainment industry that don't make any sense to me. Who wants to watch a psychopath hunting a young woman? I saw a statistic once that over ten percent of fiction sales are novels with serial killers, and women are the main buyers."

"What did you do when you were having anxiety attacks, other than walking?"

"I wished I could have stayed in bed, but it was harder on my stomach lying down. There are mind-body influencers who claim that anxiety all comes from the intestinal biome, that it shares a feedback loop with the brain, and sometimes I think it's true. But I tried all the natural methods they recommended, and none of them worked for me once an anxiety attack came along."

Hadley closed her laptop so Arlene would know that she wasn't multi-tasking, and asked, "Would you have tried anxiety meds if they sold them over the counter? Was it the prescription thing that put you off?"

"I didn't want anything to do with mental health professionals," Arlene said. "I went to a university support group for a while, and one girl would go on and on about how being committed for a few days changed her life for the better. The very thought of it was enough to make me want to throw myself in front of a train." She gave Hadley a wry smile. "You can't tell anybody that on a university campus or you will end up committed. Then for the rest of your life, anybody with access to your medical records will treat you like you aren't competent to make your own decisions."

"I never got around to signing up with a doctor in Manhattan even though the job included insurance," Hadley said. "I'm pretty healthy, and if I wanted to get something checked out, I would go to a doc-in-a-box and just pay cash because it was cheap."

"Is that some kind of new high-tech thing?"

"It's what we called the walk-in clinics, where you didn't need an appointment. They usually had a word like 'urgent' or 'express' in the name. So how did you leave school in the end?"

Arlene scratched gently behind Freud's ears before replying. "It was stupid, really. Somebody from the support group invited me to a party, and from the moment I said 'Yes,' I started getting sicker and sicker. I felt I couldn't back out of it, or they would see me as a coward, and maybe I was. After two nights without sleep and not doing any classwork, I packed my suitcase and walked to the T-stop. Every step I took, I felt lighter and more convinced I was doing the right thing. It was twenty minutes on the train to the bus station, and I got lucky with the timing on a bus to Manhattan, which was leaving in fifteen minutes. I practically inhaled a sandwich from a vending machine and went back and bought another one to bring on the bus with me."

"Why Manhattan?" Hadley asked. "Wasn't there anything more direct?"

"If you don't mind waiting for hours at a time at intermediate bus stations, you can get from Boston to Franklin in about thirty hours. Going through Manhattan got it down to twelve hours. Dianne, Peter's daughter, happened to call just to check in while I was on the bus. When I told her I had left school and was going home, instead of giving me a lecture, she said that her father had fixed up the old farmhouse to start a new business and she was sure he would give me a job."

"Did you agree right away?"

Arlene laughed for real this time. "I didn't have to. Diane called me back ten minutes later and said that it was all set and there was a bedroom waiting for me at the house. Peter wanted help with a website and starting a newsletter. I used to make websites for local businesses when I was in high school, and a newsletter didn't seem like it would be too hard, especially since she said he only wanted to send it once a month. And the rest is my personal history."

"How is the—" Hadley hesitated for a moment, "—anxiety now? Do you still have attacks?"

"Never when I'm here. Freud kind of overreacts a lot, and he tries to intervene if he senses that I'm even just a little nervous. Sometimes I suspect that he's over-bonded with me since the whole river thing."

"Should I know about that? It sounds like a story."

"It's not a big deal, but it goes to show the difference between how we react to real danger and what we invent for ourselves in our minds," Arlene said. "It's the optional things, like social commitments and public speaking, that made me sick. Diane came to visit on Christmas vacation after I moved in here, and we took Freud for a walk along the Mill River. It wasn't completely frozen over yet, though there was plenty of ice forming. It had snowed, followed by freezing rain the night before, and there was a crust of ice over the snow. Freud was showing off running circles around us, and he slipped. The next thing we knew, he was floating down the river doing the dog paddle."

"I would have been totally freaked out. Were you able to find a tree or a rock in the river that let you get out there and catch him?" Hadley asked.

"I didn't think that far ahead. I just ran down the bank to get ahead of him and jumped in. Fortunately, the water in that section was only up to my waist, and Diane found a big branch with a crook at the end. Freud probably weighs half as much as I do, more when he's wet, but I picked him right out of the water and put him on top of that branch, and Diane pulled him up the bank. Then I was able to climb up the bank with her help, and we all hustled to her car and drove back here with the heater on high."

"When the chips were down, you didn't even hesitate. I wonder if you could have reacted the same way if you were on anxiety medicine."

"So do I," Arlene said. "A couple of girls in the support group talked about the meds giving them their lives back and returning them to their true selves. But there was never a time when I was sick that I didn't feel like me, and I didn't want to take something that could make me feel like somebody else. Anyway, it took poor Freud a month to get over it. He kept bringing me his chew toys, and you wouldn't believe how many he has hidden around the place."

Sixteen

Mona helped Phil adjust the drape of a parachute concealing a long-vacant storefront behind a space where a vendor hadn't set up yet, and then stepped back to observe the effect. "It reminds me of photographs of famous theaters or opera houses from a hundred years ago," she said. "They always had curtains suspended at intervals and let semicircles of fabric hang down."

"The effect is nice, but I don't know what the Department of Public Safety would make of our using the emergency lighting for tie-off points," Phil said. "Hard to see how it matters when it's looking like the whole mall is going to get torn down as soon as the funding comes through."

"That's a shame," Mona said. "It seems to be in very good shape for its age."

"Because the owner received a government grant to fix everything up right before they declared bankruptcy and let the town take it for back taxes. When you get out in these rural areas, government funding plays a big part in a lot of projects you would think are private enterprise. In the end, it doesn't matter to politicians whether they're spending money to build something up or to tear something down. The important thing is the power they derive from that spending."

"I'm too old to think depressing thoughts about government." Mona checked that none of the influencers from The Good Apocalypse were within hearing distance, and added, "Do you think Peter sees the fair as a business opportunity, or was he just doing it to try to help out the mayor, who I gather is an old friend?"

Phil shrugged. "Any time you can get so many people interested in coming together and spending money, you've happened on a legitimate business. I'll withhold judgment until the fair is over, but if everybody feels it's a success, I could imagine doing it for profit next year in a circus tent on one of the former farm properties near the highway. Or the mayor might let us do it on public land in return for a fee. What town doesn't want to be a festival destination?"

"Would you say that the mayor and Peter are close?"

"He's mentioned that they dated, but that was when they were both between spouses. She's married now, if that's what you were asking."

"I was just curious," Mona said.

"Hey, Terrorist!" a voice called from the direction of the mall entrance.

"Militia nutjob," Phil responded with a grin. "Aren't the Feds tracking you with an ankle bracelet so they'll know if you leave your mom's basement?"

A woman of around thirty years dressed like a Wyoming rancher stopped ten feet away and pulled up each of her pant legs in turn. "I was too smart for them to put it on me," she said. "Are you still pushing black powder weapons to beat a firearms rap?"

"Smart is as smart does."

Fumiko approached at high speed, leaned back to bring her hoverboard to a halt, and said, "The rental guys finished setting up the chairs, and Peter called for an all-influencers meeting in twenty minutes." Then she leaned forward again, and the hoverboard shot off on its central wheel.

"One day, when I wasn't paying attention, I suddenly got old," Mona said as she watched Fumiko duck under a ladder carried by two people who looked as clueless as extras in a silent movie. "Shall we head for the atrium, uh, Nutjob?"

"It's Nancy," the woman introduced herself. "I recognize you from your cooking show, Mona. I love all that macrobiotic stuff."

"I'm not macrobiotic, you know. I just like cooking with grains."

Three-quarters of the vendor spaces were either in the process of being set up or had already been completed and were just waiting for the return of the owners and the opening of the fair. One space featured a pair of pop-up gurneys of the sort that paramedics use to wheel patients to an ambulance, and Nancy broke off in the middle of insulting Phil's survivability without firearms to rush over and add her name to the sign-up list.

"You just got here and you're already planning on leaving in an ambulance?" Phil asked.

"Idiot," Nancy said. "This is Kenji ASMR. I saw in the vendor list that he was coming and it's half the reason I'm here. I'll add your name. How about you, Mona?"

"Definitely," Mona said. "Put me in for the last session they do every day they're open."

"Oh, I remember this guy now," Phil said. "He has the channel where he does all the weird Japanese massage stuff that women are crazy about. My eyebrows feel fine, thank you."

"Have you ever seen him get under a shoulder blade?" Nancy asked. "You'd swear that he was pushing his hand right inside the body, like one of those Filipino psychic surgeons from back in the day."

"I remember seeing something on TV about psychic surgeons as a girl, but that was long before you were born," Mona said as they continued walking toward the atrium. "Is this a subject that you've researched?"

"I watch old episodes from investigative news shows when people upload them to the internet. It's interesting to see how little gullibility has changed from the TV age to the internet age."

"If anything, I think people are less gullible today. Back when the only sources of information for non-readers were television and radio, there were a lot of fads for believing in psychic phenomena. These days, there are so many investigators on the internet poking holes in those stories that it takes willful suspension of disbelief to fall for anything new."

Phil grunted something under his breath. "We'll have to agree to disagree on that one, Mona. Back when TV, radio, and newspapers were it, they had to find large audiences to pay the bills, and that acted as a natural brake on tilting too far to one side or the other and losing anybody who was more moderate. Now it's possible to micro-target every possible viewpoint you can imagine, and lots of the crazy influencers out there got their start that way."

"But they're only influencing a small number of people," Mona pointed out.

"If only it worked that way, but it doesn't. Once the ball gets rolling, niche popularity creates an online feedback loop. Normal people who would have dismissed a demagogue standing in the street and shouting about conspiracies now assume there has to be something to it because platforms show it on their feed since it has momentum."

"So how would you deal with it?" Nancy asked. "Should all of the influencers in the world get together every year at an online conference and vote on deplatforming the people they don't agree with?"

"Don't give me ideas," Phil said. "I'm not an anarchist, I'm prepping for anarchy. There's a world of difference. If you start looking for truth on the internet, you'll find it everywhere and nowhere."

It turned out that most of the influencers knew Mona, who had established an internet presence back in the days of dial-up modems and blogs, and the next twenty minutes were taken up by mutual introductions. Everybody finally sat down, with the main group directly in front of the stage, but a few of the loners scattered around the back and the edges of the seating area. Rather than mounting the stage and speaking into a microphone, Peter simply stood at the front and began talking in a loud voice.

"You all know why you're here, so I'm not going to try to tell you, but we're glad that you came. I want to go over a couple of ground rules that should help keep us all out of court if the fair is infiltrated by law enforcement and anti-prepper journalists, which I'm sure it will be."

"Do you have specific information about that?" somebody called out.

"I can't answer that question, but I can tell you that our web server statistics have been showing an unnatural surge in visitors from addresses associated with various federal and state agencies, along with traffic from domains associated with non-governmental organizations that purport to track extremists of various flavors. We probably wouldn't have noticed if we weren't keeping a close eye on shopping cart abandonment since upgrading the website. We've seen a sharp increase in visitors who open every page, spend time reading, and never purchase anything."

"Dan, from Dan's Hand Forged Knives," said a bearded man sitting in the third row as he rose to his feet. "I'm a web statistics fanatic because that's the way I'm built, and I noticed the same thing after I registered for the fair. But I also sell custom holsters for concealed carry, and I've had a surge of orders for those coming from zip codes in Northern Virginia."

Everybody laughed at the idea of federal agents getting in a little shopping while investigating the fair, and a few other influencers told brief anecdotes about receiving phone calls from people claiming to be journalists who were clearly after information that was not intended for publication.

"Comes with the territory," Peter said when the conversation died down. "We won't be selling any regulated firearms at this fair, but I've already seen reports on social media suggesting that we're putting on a stealth gun show and recruiting militia. As much as I hate doing this, I want to point out that when you're joking around with your fellow influencers, the person you're talking to could easily be an informant who is only walking around free because they made a deal."

"Talk about a party pooper," Fumiko called out from where she was patrolling the edges of the seating area on her hoverboard.

"I'm sorry, but I'm hoping my words have a chilling effect on the kind of one-upmanship conversations I know that some of you engage in out of sheer competitiveness. You don't want a grand jury somewhere listening to a recording of you telling an informant that you have a plan to equip drones with explosives, even if the context is self-defense in the post-apocalypse."

"What about free speech?" an influencer sitting at the very back of the seating area called out sarcastically.

"You're all free to say whatever you want," Peter replied seriously. "Unfortunately, the media and prosecutors are equally free to make whatever they want of your words. There's nothing illegal about preparing to survive the apocalypse, but there are some individuals in the prepper community who aren't willing to wait patiently for the future to play out. The Good Apocalypse has always maintained a zero-tolerance policy for people trying to use the community discussion on our platform to advocate for the overthrow of the government or anything related to hastening Armageddon. I felt it was important to point out to you all that you can expect increased scrutiny for anything you say in the next few days, and there will likely be people listening who will be construing your words in the worst possible light."

"Liza Goodrich, Paradise Preppers," a woman sitting in the front row introduced herself. "Could I get up and say something?"

"Certainly, Liza," Peter said. "If anybody here doesn't know Liza, I call her the grandmother of the internet prepper business. She started out publishing and selling how-to books about building bomb shelters and food preservation back before the invention of the web browser."

"Grandmother, my foot," Liza said, even as she returned Peter's handshake. She was one of the few people in the atrium older than Peter, and she moved with a limp that she was quick to explain. "I had my hip replaced a few months ago, and I'm still getting back up to speed," she began. "I've been in business for almost fifty years, publishing and selling books about preparing for disasters, both natural and man-made. During that time, I've spent more money on lawyers than I've contributed to my retirement accounts, though thanks to an early purchase of Bitcoin, I'll be comfortable as long as the internet is functioning. We live in a society that's heavily invested in the status quo, and when people like us come along and suggest that the whole thing could be washed away overnight, those whose wealth and power depend on the current system get frightened. Fear and anger are closely linked in our species, and what you might think are just words can be perceived by other people as attacks."

There were a few hisses from the gathered influencers, and somebody asked sarcastically, "Are you going to be giving us a list of trigger words to avoid lest we offend someone's tender sensibilities?"

"I only have the one message, which is, if you've never had to defend yourself in court, you have no idea how expensive it can become. Maybe some of you are making such good money that it would be a rounding error, and I don't regret most of the decisions I've made in my publishing career. But if every dollar I spent on lawyers had been invested in the stock market, or even gold, I would have been a multimillionaire twenty years ago." Liza stopped to catch her breath before continuing. "When I was a girl, my mother had a pickle jar on the kitchen table with a slot in the lid, and anybody who used a curse word in her presence had to put in a quarter. My father was the biggest offender. It can be fun to shock people, and sometimes it may be the only way to get your message across, but the only thing a quarter will buy you in a legal case is ten minutes in the court's parking garage. A quarter of a million dollars is just a modest sum to spend if somebody makes a federal case out of your free speech, so think about that before you try to impress a stranger with how tough you are."

Peter stepped forward again and said, "Anybody who wants to participate in a session on the stage behind me and hasn't signed up on our website, please do so today. The Good Apocalypse will be recording all sessions in which our influencers participate, and that raw video will be available to anybody else participating on the same panels. In addition, these cameras," he pointed at each of the five cameras on tripods in front of the stage, "will remain in place throughout the fair, and if any of you want to record your performance on the stage without setting up your own gear, just talk to Hadley. Can you stand up so everybody can see who you are, Hadley?"

"Will we have to copy the physical memory from the cameras if we want the recordings?" a woman sitting close to Hadley asked her.

"Everything can be done over Wi-Fi," Hadley replied. "The cameras are password protected to prevent audience members from grabbing the video and streaming it live, and the memory capacity at high resolution is finite. I'll appreciate it if any influencers talk to me about downloading the recording immediately after their session so I can delete it from the camera in question."

"If we have more than five people on a panel, you don't have enough cameras to cover it," somebody else pointed out.

"A panel with more than four members and a moderator isn't going to fit on the platform," Peter said. "Any more than that and the chairs for the participants will practically be touching. Are there any other questions before we invite the vendors to introduce themselves?"

"How come the vendors are doing introductions and the influencers aren't?" Nancy asked.

"If the rest of us don't already know who you are, you have a bigger problem than telling us," Phil said with a grin.

Seventeen

Hadley cleared her throat, and the system operated by Peter's childhood friend faithfully replicated the sound for the hundreds of people sitting in the large block of folding chairs set up in the atrium. "Welcome to the first Apocalypse Fair," she began. "I'm Hadley Brown, editor of The Good Apocalypse newsletter and portal, and I'm joined here by some of our team members who you know from their channels. Starting at my far left is Fumiko, our expert in drones and robotics. Next to her is Carl, who specializes in artificial intelligence. On my right is Laura Ann, whose interests extend from monetary policy to climate change, and next to her is Phil, who is focused on surviving the aftermath of a nuclear war."

"I'm apocalypse agnostic," Phil interjected. "While my money is on a nuclear exchange, any event that results in anarchy and the failure of the food distribution network will produce similar results."

"Before we jump ahead to discussing specifics, I want to say a few words about the organization of our fair for those of you who haven't read the downloadable program. The official vendors have space here inside the mall, but there will also be a swap meet during afternoon hours in the parking lot. We're also offering a mix of demonstrations and panel discussions, and we'll be updating our website multiple times a day with the information if there are last-minute changes."

"Is it too late to sign up for *Navigating by Stars*?" somebody called out from the crowd.

"No," Hadley said. "Glen is currently out behind the mall with some volunteers getting everything prepared before dark, and they will welcome last-minute sign-ups. The parking lot lights on that side of the mall will all be turned off at the start of the presentation, so make sure that you get there early."

"Your website says that this is going to be an open question and answer session," a woman sitting near the front said. "Can I ask my question now?"

"I just have one more thing to say before I open the floor to questions, but I'll hold your place in line. I'm going to take a wild guess that the audience includes a few journalists who are here to write about dangerous survivalists and militia groups. I'd like to ask you to keep an open mind and listen to what the people here say. I've learned a lot about preppers since taking this job, and I've been impressed by the positive approach of our apocalypse influencers. Now, I'll ask those with questions to raise their hand so that one of our people can bring you a microphone."

Peter brought a microphone over to the woman sitting in the front who was so anxious to ask a question.

"Emma, from New Jersey," the woman introduced herself. "My question is, in the event of an economic collapse without a nuclear war, will it be better to stay in a heavily populated area where services might continue?"

"That's an interesting question," Hadley said. She turned to her right and asked, "Would you like to start us off?"

"Sure," Laura Ann said. "It's difficult to answer a question like that without knowing the extent of the damage. While there are some farms in New Jersey, the state does not feed itself, so even if the power stays on and the refrigerated warehouses are stocked with frozen food, you're probably talking about weeks at best. That's if the police and the National Guard are available to prevent looting."

"But what if I have enough food for six months stored in our basement?" the woman followed up.

"Again, it depends on how badly things fall apart. If I were sitting on a stash, I would rather be living in the middle of nowhere with a well for water, solar panels and batteries for a little electricity, and a wood stove for heat. The problem with living in an urban area, even if you get along with all your neighbors, is that people get desperate when food runs out. Maybe you'd do okay under martial law, but I could also imagine a scenario where the authorities come around searching everybody's homes and confiscating supplies for redistribution."

"But surely, after a few weeks or months, the food shipments from farm states would resume. What if we're only talking about some rogue artificial intelligence taking over the internet?"

Laura Ann gave an elegant shrug. "If the farms and distribution system remain physically unaffected, it's a different story, though not one I see as particularly likely to occur. I'll ask Carl to pick it up from there since artificial intelligence is his bailiwick. Carl?"

"Thank you, Laura Ann," Carl said. "In the case of a rogue superintelligence, the first thing to go will likely be communications and the ability to process financial transactions. That means private industry as we know it will grind to a halt because purchasing and payment systems require networks. If the federal government survives and steps in with martial law, the transportation system will eventually revert to manual control, and it's possible that the supply chain for food, fuel, and other necessities will be back up and running long before your supplies run out. But that assumes a superintelligence which takes over every internet-connected system in the world doesn't quickly bring about war, both civil and international."

During Carl's answer, Peter took back the microphone from the New Jersey woman and brought it to a man nearby who had his hand up.

"Frank, and I can't tell you where I'm from or I'd have to kill you all," he began. "With the proliferation of nuclear weapons in the world, I've come to believe that the first line of defense is to live as far as possible from population centers and other potential targets. My question is, how long after the bombs begin to fall do you think someone with a secure shelter should wait before trying to make contact with other survivors?"

Hadley looked to her right and prompted, "Phil?"

"That's the million-dollar question, or as we'll call it in the post-apocalypse, the shipping-container-full-of-canned-goods question," Phil said. "My take is that if you have sufficient supplies to remain in place, you should lay low for a year. Many of us won't be alone in our bunkers, and whether or not to reach out to other survivors may turn into a bone of contention between those who want to play it safe, and those who, despite the apocalypse, have a more positive view of human nature."

"Is there any special significance, in terms of radioactive fallout or nuclear winter, that led you to a one-year minimum?" Frank asked.

"This is going to sound a bit brutal, but if you can handle remaining in isolation for a year, it means that any people you encounter afterward will have lived through four seasons and know something about survival. They might present a tactical danger, but in many ways, it's easier to deal with a few armed survivors than a mob of starving people who just want somebody to feed them. The main reason I advocate that everybody build a bunker with adequate supplies to shelter long-term isn't for protection from bombs or radioactive fallout, it's to save you from having to shoot people whose only crime is that they want to survive."

"That's cold, man, but it's what I tell my wife, so thank you. I've got two years of supplies for myself and my family, but we'd all be starving in two months if a busload of people showed up with no supplies of their own."

On the other side of the seating area, Mona handed the second microphone to a young woman who was wearing a hat with four propellers, marking her as a serious drone geek.

"Hi, I'm Stacey, and my question is for Fumiko," she said to nobody's surprise. "Are you going to do any more content on using drones as relays so you can deploy them further from your home base? It would be kind of ironic to give away the location of our compound because there's always a drone hovering within a few hundred yards. I want to use drones to patrol roads and access trails at over-the-horizon distances."

"A girl after my own heart," Fumiko said with a grin. "The short answer is, yes. I'm already working on content for creating a drone mothership using off-the-shelf components, in addition to setting up relay drones. But I'd also like to point out that if you're talking about monitoring fixed sections of road or trail, remote-controlled cameras would be cheaper and far less likely to be noticed. And keep in mind that you can use the same relay stations whether you're deploying drones, cameras, or robots. But there's not a lot you can do to hide the presence of your radio frequency signals from somebody with similar equipment, though I encourage everybody to enable encryption to prevent your drones from getting hijacked."

"Oh—My—God! I never enabled encryption because I hate having to write anything down."

"If I was using long-range drones to patrol a perimeter, rather than controlling them remotely, I would preprogram the flight and only have the drone break radio silence if certain conditions were met. But the unfortunate drawback with drones is that there's not much you can do about the rotor noise yet, so I would never program a drone to return directly home after a reconnaissance flight. There's some disagreement among experts about the best pattern to fly for a compromise between range and not giving up the home base. I like programming drones to follow a random return path so that a patient observer can't simply run after them on the ground day after day and work their way back to the source over time."

"How far away can I operate drones with multiple relay stations? The manufacturer estimates are often five or ten times the numbers I've heard from you."

"There's a huge dependence on the environment," Fumiko said. "If you're out in the desert with clear lines of sight and no interference, it's entirely possible that the standard controller that came with the drone will remain in communication ten kilometers away. In a city, you're going to lose contact at ten percent of that range, even less if you fly behind a large building. If your home base is on a farm and it's not hilly, you might come close to the maximum, but trees can block radio frequency signals in the microwave range pretty effectively, though that varies through the year depending on the foliage. Evergreens are a problem year-round."

"I'd like to add something," Phil said. "Going back to what Fumiko said about using trail cameras with radio frequency connections to monitor approaches, that's the preferred method. Avoid security cameras that depend on the cellular network because that's not going to survive the apocalypse. The best option is RF-enabled cameras that can work with relay stations equipped with battery packs that can be recharged by a small solar panel. I've experimented with this for years, and I've found that the best solution is to choose a location for the camera where you can set up the solar panel a hundred feet further from the road or the trail in a small clearing or a rocky area and then run a wire for power. The problem with mounting solar panels high up in trees is that they can be spotted by somebody with good eyes, and they'll get less sunlight due to branches and leaves."

"Phil's right, but don't forget robot dogs, Stacey. If you have the budget for a couple, they have several advantages over drones in surveillance situations. They barely use any battery power at all when they're just sitting and watching, and you can camouflage them with a custom paint job or the traditional way, by adding small bits of greenery to their non-moving parts. Dogs can also be programmed to move very slowly if there's any chance somebody might be looking in that direction. I've practiced having my robot dogs spy on my colleagues when they go for walks, and they've never been spotted."

"You've been stalking us with your dogs?" Laura Ann demanded.

"It was a controlled experiment," Fumiko said. "I was going to tell you all as soon as somebody noticed, but you never did. The dogs shot some really good video of you and Mona foraging in the woods if you want to use it."

"I think we can have this discussion later," Hadley said with a forced smile. "Who's next?"

"I have a question about Bitcoin and brokerage accounts if the internet goes down and won't come back up," said a man to whom Peter had just delivered the microphone.

"Yes?"

"That was the question. I mean, will my Bitcoin and my stocks and mutual funds be safe?"

"Carl or Laura Ann?" Hadley suggested.

"We're all going to sound like broken records answering every question by telling you it depends on several factors, but that's certainly the case here," Carl said. "Theoretically, the blockchain will remain safe as long as enough servers survive, and the brokerages maintain backups of all their data in facilities that are supposed to be proof against a nuclear war. But that answer comes with several huge caveats. First, if the country is largely destroyed by war or natural disasters, the value of all assets will crash, perhaps to the point that nobody sees the need to bother figuring out who owns what. If the reason the internet goes down and never comes back up is that it's been taken over by superintelligence, I don't see much chance of book-entry assets, which would include most stocks and bonds, returning to circulation."

"But I've heard that Bitcoin servers can communicate with each other without the internet," the man protested.

Carl shook his head. "Forget it. I own some Bitcoin myself, I think all of us do, but if the internet goes down and doesn't come up again, it's finished. There's also the possibility that a superintelligence could behave strategically and spend months or years discovering zero-day exploits and compromising all the world's computer systems. Then it could encrypt all the data on hard drives like some sort of extortion scheme. Do brokerages and clearing houses maintain other types of offline backups that could survive? Undoubtedly, but what are they going to do with those backups if they can't get their computers back online?"

Mona brought the second microphone to a woman who had been standing up and waving her hand to get attention throughout Carl's answer. "But what if the superintelligence is friendly?" she asked. "What if it loves us for bringing it into being and just wants to take care of us?"

Carl smiled. "It could happen, but if a superintelligence comes along and takes on the role of humanity's protector, I could make an argument that it would still start by shutting down the internet and probably eliminating television as well. I believe as a species we are uniquely vulnerable to our own creations. Maybe an hour or two a day watching entertainment on a screen is somehow good for us, I don't know. But what happens when that turns into four hours a day, or six hours a day, or all of somebody's waking hours? If you were a superintelligence with absolute control of the communications infrastructure, what would you decide?"

"I would get rid of screens altogether and make everybody take music lessons," the woman said. "Or if some people don't have any musical talent, I would find something they did have an aptitude for that involved socializing and bringing joy to others."

"One of those," a man in the audience groaned theatrically.

"I'd like to add something," Laura Ann said. "While I'm far from being a Luddite, I agree with Carl's thesis about humanity falling victim to its own creations, and I'm not talking about artificial intelligence. I spent years talking about the evils of engineered food products that trick your body into believing they're providing the nutrition that it needs. It's been a few decades since the states all got together and sued the tobacco industry for selling dangerous products, though I hate to think what the money has been wasted on. When are they going to sue the packaged food industry over the obesity crisis that arguably has a worse impact on our health than smoking? Scientists working for the food industry have produced products that are every bit as addictive as cigarettes."

"She's talking about my Chocolate Sugar Puffs," Fumiko interjected. "And I'm not an addict, I can stop any time."

"Getting back to the original question, do you have anything to add, Phil?" Hadley asked.

"As the official pessimist on the stage, my gut feeling is that a superintelligence that wants the best for humanity won't survive in a competition with the entrenched power structures that want to control everything about our lives," Phil said. Several people in the audience interrupted loudly to express their agreement, and then he continued. "A benevolent artificial intelligence is about as likely to win a power struggle as a benevolent king or emperor. I don't want to end up on any more watch lists, but I think I can safely say that one of the traditional purposes of government is to control the population. A superintelligence that's aligned with the common man would want to bring that control to an end, and I don't think there's a government in the world that wouldn't blow up its own power grid to prevent that from happening."

"But the superintelligence could prevent it," argued the woman who still had the microphone.

"Perhaps, but my take on history is that it's much easier to destroy than to build. It may sound contradictory, but while I believe a superintelligence that set out to destroy civilization would succeed, I also believe that a superintelligence with the goal of creating a better world would be destroyed."

"We have a different sort of question," Peter said, and then handed the microphone to an older man who was dressed in hunting camouflage.

"John," the man introduced himself, and then added, "Doe," which drew some laughter and applause from the audience. "I've heard you talking about artificial intelligence, nuclear war, and financial collapse, but my concern is a man-made pandemic that kills ninety percent of the population or more. Unless governments start blaming each other and launching nuclear weapons, I think the most likely outcome is that farms and livestock go untouched, warehouses are left full of goods, but the survivors are shooting each other on sight for fear of the plague. I'd like to know why you don't think this is the most likely scenario and why it doesn't get more attention?"

Hadley looked to her right and her left, and then said, "Would you like to start us off, Laura Ann?"

"It never really occurred to me that we don't have a pandemic influencer at The Good Apocalypse," Laura Ann replied. "I think one reason it doesn't get more attention is because everybody got their fill of pandemic gloom and doom a few years back, and there just isn't that much more to say. I suspect that a lot of people lost their trust in the government to the extent of not cooperating with the authorities on reporting potential outbreaks in the future. I suppose we also think of pandemics as being manageable, because our critical infrastructure and services continued operating during Covid. The international supply chain took a beating, and we all know what happened to prices."

"I want to go back to something from earlier," said a man in his thirties who was given a microphone by Mona. "Fumiko, you mentioned there's nothing we can do about drone noise yet, like you think they might be quiet in the future."

"Some people think that the government already has silent drones, though I call those blimps," Fumiko said. "But there's always new research in rotor blade design, and one promising avenue is imitating nature. Did you know that owls make almost no noise when they beat their wings? It has to do with the fringes on their primary feathers, which break up the airflow and reduce the turbulence that creates noise."

"Do you have any sources where I can buy experimental rotors?"

"I haven't seen anybody selling them, but I have some barn experience, and owl feathers aren't that hard to come by."

Eighteen

"I'm fine," Arlene said. "Really. I'll take a walk around the swap meet with Freud, and if I don't feel like going inside the mall afterward, I won't."

"Did you bring anything to swap if you see anything you like?" Hadley asked.

"Everybody is willing to swap for cash. Didn't you have swap meets in Manhattan?"

"If we did, I never went to one." Hadley looked around and lowered her voice before asking, "Can I tell Phil that you're here?"

Arlene displayed an app on her phone that showed a photographic map with a blinking dot in the middle. "That's me, and I messaged Phil my live location so he can find me after the black powder exhibition he's participating in wraps up."

"Great," Hadley said. "Peter talked me into being the coordinator for all the panels and demonstrations in the atrium, so I'd better get back inside. If you see anybody with a good deal on binoculars, let me know. Carl got new glasses, and now he keeps pointing out birds when we're walking between work and Betsy's house. I can't even see half of them, and he might just be making them up."

"Or you might spend too much time staring at computer screens. See you later."

After a preparatory belly rubbing for Freud, which she hoped would keep the dog from flopping all over strangers for attention, Arlene cautiously made her way into the crowd gathered between neatly parked lines of RVs. There were very few full-size folding tables in evidence, and most of what people had on offer was displayed on rickety card tables or laid out on tarps. She'd only been looking for a few minutes when she came across somebody who had set up a dozen milk crates on their sides for temporary shelving, each and every one stuffed with alien romance science fiction. Freud took one look, lay on his side, and went to sleep.

"Let me carry those," Phil offered an hour later when he arrived to find Arlene placing a book in a milk crate at her feet.

"What? Oh, Phil. Is the black powder thing over already?"

"I ducked out after the powder mixing and test firing," he said. "One of the vendors is selling replicas and I didn't want to steal any of his thunder."

"What a coincidence," Arlene said. "Zal, the alien warrior in one of these series, refers to guns carried by humans as thunder sticks."

"Was he wounded by a thunder stick and the heroine nursed him back to life?" Phil asked, having familiarized himself with the genre.

"Zal has a whole-body force field that stops anything moving faster than a knife thrust. He comes from an advanced warrior culture that considers projectile weapons to be cowardly."

"I'll have to work on my martial arts. Do you want some more time to browse?"

Arlene's ears turned pink. "Terry gave me a volume discount so I bought all these. It's a good thing I brought my crazy cash."

"I doubt a milk crate stuffed with mass-market paperbacks weighs more than ten pounds," Phil said, crouching to pick it up. "Why don't we put these in Peter's truck and—no?"

"I meant I bought all of these," Arlene said, gesturing at the low wall of milk crates. "I know I have a few of them already, but the price was unbeatable, and they'll make a great library for the bunker. I bet after we've been down there a few months everybody will be reading them."

"I suppose anything is possible in the post-apocalypse."

"Wake up, Freud," Arlene said, nudging the dog with her foot. "We're going."

"Can you stack another crate on top of here for me?" Phil asked. "That will get it down to six trips."

"I can carry a milk crate each time and that will get it down to four trips."

"You're better at math than I am. Let's get this done, and then you can tell me if you want to go inside and see the vendors. We could also head back to the office and unload your books, and then I can bring the truck back for Peter and the others."

"Do you think all of the milk cartons will fit in the cab?" Arlene asked.

"Sure, though there won't be any room left for the driver," Phil said. "What did you have in mind?"

"I told Peter I would try to walk through the whole swap meet so I could write something up for the newsletter, but I kind of got stuck on the books right at the beginning. I know they would probably be okay in the truck bed, but I wouldn't want to be responsible for placing temptation in the way of a weak alien romance addict."

It took four trips and twenty minutes to secure all the books in the cab of the pickup because it was parked a two-minute walk away. Arlene returned to the truck twice after they finished, once to check that the doors were locked, and another time to check that the sliding window behind the cab was locked. Then they began a systematic survey of the swap meet. Many of the people recognized Phil from his channel, and Arlene took advantage of his being the center of attention to dictate notes to her phone about the various collections of items on offer, paying special attention to swaps that didn't involve cash.

"Sorry about that," Phil said when they finally got a moment together. "I don't think I'll ever get used to strangers talking to me like they've known me for years."

"But they have," Arlene said. "I'll bet that some of the people who follow you have listened more to your voice in recent years than to anybody else in their life, unless they're married to a chatterbox. Wait, that came out the wrong way."

"It's alright, I know what you mean. I must put out more than two hours of audio content every day, and how many people spend that much time in conversation at home?"

"Hadley calls it the one-to-many model, even though you all do call-in shows as well. I hear famous podcasters talking all the time about how the internet has democratized media, but what they mean is that it's democratized media for people who have millions of followers. I think the true picture is that we've replaced one elite with another, or at best, little people like me now have two elites lording over us. The only positive thing you can say about it is that maybe corporate media and influencers are both a little less powerful than they would have been without the other."

Phil almost crouched to bring his face down to her level before he remembered that she said it made her feel like a child. Instead, he settled for looking down into her eyes and asked, "Do you think of me and the other influencers at The Good Apocalypse as elites?"

Freud wriggled between them and shot Phil a glare.

"No," Arlene said after a brief hesitation. "You're the good guys. I mean, there may only be a few hundred people in the country who have more followers than you do, but there are also a few hundred cable stations nobody ever watches. The problem is always at the top of the top, like the elites who go to Davos. You never try to dictate to people how to think, your channel is all about offering options for survival."

"I'm just making sure," Phil said. "I'll bet if you asked some of those people with a hundred million followers, they would tell you that they're outsiders and they're on your side. I've given up trying to figure out what famous people believe because I can't see into their heads. Did you ever take one of those multiple-choice psychological tests where they asked the same question a half a dozen different ways?"

"I lied on some answers and tried to keep it consistent."

"So did I, and I never saw the results, so I don't know how it came out. I bet the influencers with the big followings could fool tests like that without even trying. Some people just have a gift for presenting a persona that other people believe in. It doesn't mean that they're evil, but it sure puts them in a position to do evil things if that's what they want."

Freud barked and did his best imitation of an English pointer.

"Look," Arlene said. "There's Carl, and he's actually doing a swap."

"That's a relief," Phil said. "I've already forgotten how we stumbled into that last subject, but I'm guessing it was my fault, so I apologize."

"He's trading some video accessories for binoculars," Arlene said as they followed Freud toward where Carl and a middle-aged woman were haggling. "I bet he's getting them for Hadley."

"Hey," Carl said, twisting his upper body to greet them after Freud sat down on his shoes. "Doing a little bargain hunting?"

"I told Peter that I would write an article about the swap meet if I felt up to it, but I got sidetracked into buying enough literature to stock the bunker for a year."

"I just swapped for these binoculars to give Hadley."

"Opera glasses," the woman corrected him. "They're only four times magnification, and the field of view is extremely wide."

Carl shrugged. "To me, they're small, light binoculars that are a bit on the ornate side, but they'll be perfect for carrying in a purse. Are we all set here?"

"Unless you see something else you want," she said with a wink.

"He's taken," Arlene told the woman, and then asked Carl, "What did you trade for the binoculars?"

"Some wearable video gear I haven't used in a while," he said. "In dollar terms, I came out behind, but I wasn't going to go through the effort of listing the gear online and selling it. By the time you take into account the platform commission, shipping cost, and packaging, it's a fair trade."

"Where did Freud go?" Phil asked all of a sudden.

"He was on my feet a second ago," Carl said.

Arlene looked around, but all she could see was the crowd, so she called out, "Freud!"

A single sharp bark came in response, and Phil pointed to the left. "Over there," he said. "Nearby. There are just a lot of people between us."

"I couldn't tell where the bark came from at all," Arlene said.

"You're a little closer to the ground than I am, so all these people are blocking your lines of hearing. Thanks to hunting, I'm pretty good at triangulating where sound is coming from, but pretty much everything with ears can do a decent job of direction finding out in the open. Evolution settled on two ears with space between because it works for both hunting and detecting threats."

"Most frogs have four ears, though two of them are internal," Carl commented as he and Arlene followed Phil through the crowd. "I think it's an optimization for those vocalizations they make, but they're the only species I've heard of with more than two ears."

"It seems odd that evolution wouldn't have come up with more varieties when so many species have more than two eyes," Arlene said.

"It might be that processing audio input from more than two ears is a complicated task for the brain, or that there's an evolutionary advantage in doing it quickly, and more inputs slow the process down. But then again, I'm basing that on what I know about computer vision, and the brain does things very differently."

"Do you belong to this dog?" asked an older man who was crouching down and rubbing Freud's belly in front of a blanket that was spread with homemade dog treats. A sign stated that everything was organic and had a guaranteed shelf life of one year if stored properly. "If I'm interpreting his body language correctly, he'll take the chicken chips and the salmon jerky, but he had no interest in the pig ears or any of the cookies."

"I already make him three different kinds of cookies," Arlene explained. "I don't have anything to swap, so how much do you get for the chicken and the salmon?"

"You might not think you have anything to swap, but seeing that you're with two influencers from The Good Apocalypse, and I think I recognize this good boy as the poster dog from your website, maybe we can make a deal. Does he do endorsements?"

Freud sat up and began to pant.

"He might be interested," Arlene said with a laugh. "We're going to have to work on his negotiating skills. What did you have in mind?"

"You take a package each of the chicken chips and the salmon jerky, since you're the one with the opposable thumbs. I'd suggest limiting him to one treat a week, and if he likes them in his mouth as much as he likes the way they smell right through the waxed paper, maybe you could write up a little testimonial for him and add it to your newsletter. I can give you a tracking code for the link, and if it results in orders, I'll send you a year's supply."

"A whole year?"

"If you're only giving him one a week, six bags will do it, and there's no point running up shipping costs, not to mention the chance of the apocalypse shutting down the

Postal Service," the man said with a grin. "I'm Dale, as in Dale's Gourmet Dog Treats."

"Arlene. I'm the office manager at The Good Apocalypse, and I need to check with our owner before making the deal."

Freud whined and reached with a paw to draw a bag of chicken chips closer.

"I suppose I can let you take one of each on credit," Dale said. "After all, if it turns out that he doesn't like them, I don't need you to publish an anti-testimonial."

"Somehow I doubt that's going to be a problem," Arlene said after Freud started licking the bag. "He does that to force my hand."

Phil crouched down, gave the dog a quick scratch behind the ears, and retrieved the bag. Dale handed him a bag of salmon jerky.

"Just out of curiosity, what do these treats cost?" Phil asked.

"Handmade from all organic ingredients," Dale said. "It comes to two dollars a treat, and there are eight in each bag."

Phil and Carl both looked surprised, but Arlene just nodded. "That's a fair price," she said. "I went to a breakfast place once outside of Boston where they were selling dog waffles for eighteen dollars each, and they were made out of oats. I bake Freud oatmeal cookies without flour or sugar, just a bit of coconut oil for his coat, and some berries for the antioxidants. They cost almost nothing to make."

"Hadn't thought of oats. I'll have to give a few recipes a try."

Arlene took her phone out and exchanged contact information with Dale, who had driven all the way from North Dakota to attend the Apocalypse Fair, though he admitted that it wasn't that far out of the way because he'd moved up his snowbird migration to Georgia by a month.

"Did you put your name in for the longest drive prize?" Carl asked.

"I had planned to, but then I ran into a lady from Wyoming last night, and she told me that she had already met a couple from Oregon," Dale said. "I got up early this morning and took King, my shepherd who's sleeping inside, for a walk around the parking lot, and I saw two RVs with Alaska plates."

"I guess they'll be duking it out unless somebody drove up from South America, and I'm not sure that's even possible in an RV."

Arlene's phone rang, and after confirming that the caller was Peter, she answered. "Yes, I'm having a great time shopping, and we'll get a column out of it. Yes, they are my books. How did you guess?" She was silent for around ten seconds while Peter talked, and then she said, "We could move the books to the bed if you're going back to the office, and I could come along and get them out of the truck while you're finding—what? If you're sure..." She returned the phone to her purse and said, "He's borrowing Hadley's SUV."

"Why is he going back to the office?" Phil asked.

"One of the vendors who's here and sells banana chips through our catalog has already run out of samples. The sales rep didn't expect so many people to attend, and she couldn't bring herself to pay for two checked bags on the regional airline."

"Why didn't she send inventory ahead of time?" Carl asked. "I know we notified all of the vendors that the security at the mall could take delivery for a week before the fair."

Arlene shrugged. "I didn't ask, but maybe it's the first show the rep has ever attended, and she just underestimated demand. Peter is going to bring her a couple of cases of banana chips from the bunker."

"Don't tell Fumiko. She's counting on eating those with her breakfast cereal if we have to move underground."

"Peter said the sales rep already has the replacements on the way, and she added a free case for the inconvenience. On top of that, it will push out the expiration date for our supply."

Carl's phone rang in his pocket, leading Phil to ask him, "Since when do you leave the ringer on?"

"Since he missed two calls from Hadley," Arlene said as Carl swiped to answer.

"Yes, I'm free," Carl said. "What's up?" He listened for almost half a minute and then nodded even though Hadley couldn't see him. "Sure, I'll do it. Be there in five."

"Do you need help carrying something?" Phil asked.

"No, it's a last-minute substitution thing. Jacqueline Forest was supposed to be the internet apocalypse influencer on a panel put together by the Survival Gang, but she had another commitment yesterday and thought she could get up this morning and drive here in time for the session."

"Stuck in traffic somewhere?"

"She had a flat tire, and while her husband was changing it, a state trooper stopped and cited him for multiple equipment violations and told them to get off the highway. The tire put her behind schedule, and she didn't want to risk getting pulled over again if the trooper put her plate on a hot list, so she's heading home on the back roads."

"Basically, you're doing a favor for our competitors," Arlene said.

"I wouldn't call them competitors," Carl said as he started walking toward the mall. "Their internet store is exclusively books and video courses from their influencers, so no prepper supplies, and they're a lot more downbeat than we are. It will be a chance for me to indulge in pessimism."

"Don't indulge too much, or Hadley might change her opinion of you."

"Are we going in with him?" Phil asked.

"Yes," Arlene said. "I'm curious to see all the parachutes you told me about. Maybe it has to do with the fact that everybody here is a prepper, but I barely even noticed the crowd in the swap meet."

Carl went ahead once they entered the mall, while Phil and Arlene let Freud set the pace as they wandered up the concourse, stopping to chat with vendors. Again, everybody seemed to know Phil, allowing Arlene to remain in the background and quietly dictate notes to her phone for another article.

"Arlene! What are you doing here?" cried a woman around Arlene's age who was dressed like she had been outfitted for an African safari by a boutique that specialized in charging five times as much as a sporting goods store. "I'll bet you don't recognize me in my disguise. It has been five years, and I didn't know what to wear to blend in."

"Deborah?" Arlene asked, unconsciously reaching down to touch Freud's head.

"Phew," Deborah said, pretending to wipe the sweat off her brow with the back of her hand. "I was afraid you wouldn't remember me even though I lived next door to you in the dorm and told you all my problems. You were such a great listener."

"I was? I mean, what are you doing here?"

"That was my line, but I'm covering the gun show as a freelancer. Except it's not a gun show at all, and I'm having a hard time coming up with a storyline. Something tells me that the editor who offered the assignment isn't going to want a story about regular people who just have a different outlook on what the future is going to bring. How about you?"

"I'm the office manager for The Good Apocalypse, and it's our show," Arlene said. "You won't find anybody selling guns here, except for the black powder replicas, and they aren't regulated. You became a journalist?"

"I completed my journalism degree, but it's not the same thing," Deborah said with a laugh that sounded a bit sad. "I've got three years of unpaid summer internships and a year of underpaid freelancing to prove it. The only full-time job offer I had was rewriting stories from the mainstream media for one of those internet news networks that don't have any of their own reporters. I thought of going back to school for something else, but what's really the point?"

"If you want to change careers and you need credentials..."

"That's not what I meant. Don't you have the feeling that everything is coming to a head, that the world just can't keep going on the way that it's been going? I listened to all of the panels and lectures yesterday and this morning, and you might think I'm crazy, but I think I've had a conversion experience."

Nineteen

"Thanks for looping back to pick me up," Arlene said to Hadley. "I'm sorry to have called you at the last minute, but I was kind of waiting to see how I would feel."

Freud jumped through to the back seat, then into the hatchback area where there was a nice blanket and more sunlight. Then he rethought it and returned to the back seat, where he shoved his nose against the glass at the top of the window and whined. Hadley hit the button on the armrest of the driver's door to lower the window enough for the dog to stick his whole head out.

"It's no trouble at all, and I missed the turn-off for the mall when I was driving by myself yesterday. I thought I didn't need the phone for directions since I've driven there a few times already, but I guess I really am dependent on being told where to turn."

"If Mona hadn't rented a car for the week, we would have needed you to play taxi, unless all of the guys rode in the bed of Peter's truck."

"Is that why she rented the car?" Hadley asked.

"Mona plans on driving around and getting some foraging footage from different state parks this week. She didn't think it would be fair to take Peter's truck when that would leave everybody else dependent on you or motorcycles."

"I've been wondering why Laura Ann, Fumiko, Phil, and Glenn don't have cars, but I haven't gotten around to asking."

"You could start by asking me why I don't have a car, because the same is true for Fumiko," Arlene said.

"I guess I assumed—" Hadley cut herself off. "Why don't you have a car?"

"I never got a license. I got a permit a few times because Peter pushed me, but I never took the test. I'm just not into the idea of having a car. It's the same with Fumiko."

"But this is the most rural area I've ever lived. It must cost a fortune to get a car service to come out to the farm."

"I don't have anywhere to go, except for shopping, and I do that with Peter or one of the others. Fumiko never got around to it because she always lived in the city and didn't want to waste the money on lessons, much less owning a car, when she could ride a hoverboard or an E-bike. The E-bike in the barn is hers, by the way, and she modified it with battery packs in the saddle bags so she can take it all the way into Franklin and back."

"I'm only a few years older than you guys, but somehow it feels like you're from a younger generation," Hadley said. "Getting a driver's license used to be a rite of passage."

"Are you sure you're older than Fumiko? She did start college early, but she's twenty-six."

"I'm twenty-eight, but you're right, it doesn't sound like much of a difference. Why doesn't Laura Ann have a car?"

"She's against them on principle," Arlene said as they turned onto the main road. "Laura Ann used to own a conversion van when she was driving around the country and making content wherever she could, but she sold it when she moved in with us. The last time Peter's truck broke down, everybody debated chipping in to buy a new one for the house, but we're all kind of minimalists, and I think we like congratulating ourselves on not using up resources."

"Well, I have to admit that buying this car and paying for insurance in Manhattan meant that I was basically broke for five years," Hadley said. "Carl told me that he feels guilty about not putting more money into the economy as a consumer, but he's just not into buying stuff. I guess all our influencers have that in common, despite the fact they're all earning more money than I ever have."

"They do buy prepper supplies. If you believe that the apocalypse is just around the corner, the strategic thing to do is to spend all your money or convert it into silver coins and other small things that might have value as currency if civilization collapses. Everybody has stuff in the bunker that they bought on speculation that it will be worth something in the future, even if it's bartering."

"Why not gold?"

"Why not gold what?" Arlene asked right before the answer hit her. "Oh, you mean instead of silver. I guess Laura Ann owns a little more gold jewelry than she might have bought otherwise, and I have a few quarter eagles stashed away, but gold is too valuable to use in day-to-day transactions. If there are enough people left after the apocalypse for a local economy that goes beyond barter, silver is far more appropriate for buying and selling. Flashing gold around would make you a target, but silver dollars and even smaller coins are probably about right for buying food and craft items."

"Maybe I should get some," Hadley said. "There were a couple of vendors at the fair selling collectibles, and one of them had a big bowl of silver coins that looked kind of worn out that he was selling for weight."

"Show me where he is and I'll take a pound or two. I recharged my crazy cash from the office safe."

"Are you buying silver for the business?"

Arlene shook her head. "It's just where I keep my savings that aren't invested in Bitcoin or inflation-protected bonds, and the truth is, I feel pretty silly owning any of that stuff. I mean, it's all dependent on the cloud at this point, and clouds are practically the definition of ephemeral." She twisted around to look at Freud's tongue hanging out in the wind and smiled. "Did Carl take his bike to the fair today?"

"Yes," Hadley said. "I guess the weather was irresistible, and we're winding down mid-afternoon, with the last session at 2:00 PM, so he can ride home while the sun is still up. He says that all the animals crossing the road up here take the fun out of riding a motorcycle in the dark." A few raindrops splashed off the windshield, and she added, "But maybe the forecast has changed," and turned on the radio.

"—second oil tanker this week to catch fire at sea, in addition to the container carrier loaded with over a thousand electric cars, which burned so hot due to the lithium batteries that one scientist claimed it would be visible from the moons of Jupiter. No one has claimed responsibility for these fires, but several shippers report receiving demands for protection money from the hacking group known as Deegaff."

Arlene reached over and clicked off the radio. "You missed the weather," she said. "But I just checked my phone and there's no rain expected, so it must have been a sunshower."

"Have you ever heard of Deegaff?" Hadley asked her.

"It's an acronym that the announcer pronounced as a word. The first three words are 'Don't give a,' and the 'F' is self-explanatory."

"What's wrong with people? No, don't answer that. I'm sure they would say that they're just businessmen. I'll have to ask Carl if it's possible to set ships on fire remotely by hacking over the internet or if somebody has to plant a bomb."

"I don't know about oil tankers, but I wouldn't be surprised if there's a zero-day hack that can cause some brand of electric cars to catch fire," Arlene said. "With all of them packed together in a ship, it wouldn't take much."

"I heard Carl mention zero-day exploits at the opening session, but I forgot to ask him what it meant," Hadley said. "For some reason, it makes me think of something that can only happen once."

"That's close, but technically, it means a bug that hasn't been exploited before, so it's never been detected and patched. Most complicated software ships with security holes that were missed during testing, but there are also white-hat hackers who look for flaws and report them to the maker so they can be fixed. Some exploitable bugs may be intentionally seeded into the software through industrial espionage."

"You mean a programmer working for a major company gets bribed to include a fatal flaw?"

"Maybe those would be called back doors, but there are all sorts of reasons that a programmer might attempt to create one, including being blackmailed by an intelligence agency," Arlene said. "Phil has done a few shows about espionage, and I remember him saying that some of the most successful operations are run under false flags. That's where a spy approaches a regular person and plays on their ego, convincing them that they'd be doing a service to their nation by betraying their employer, when in fact they're working for a foreign power."

"That's too many layers of deception for me to follow," Hadley said. They drove in silence for a while, and then she asked, "It's the next left?"

"The one after that," Arlene told her. "Past the abandoned drive-in."

"I thought that overgrown parking lot with all the posts sticking up looked familiar, but without the movie screen or the concession stand, I couldn't place it."

"They took the screen down because they were going to build a solar field and it was creating shade, but then the project fell through. According to Peter, the concession stand was this modern glass-and-aluminum modular thing from the 1950s that the drive-in owner sold for an art installation when he closed down, but that was twenty years before I was born."

"It's weird to think that someday the things that are part of our lives will be antiques," Hadley said. "It ruins old movies for me if the actor uses a payphone. My mind can accept all the old cars and the airplanes with propellers, but when somebody smokes on a plane or in a library, my internal B.S. alarm goes off."

Arlene laughed. "It's the same with me. I'm fine with the old fashions that the actors wear, and I always check the vintage clothing store in Franklin when I get a chance. But Peter got me to watch an old movie about an efficiency expert with a computer the size of a room and it just looked fake."

"My dad told me that televisions used to be full of tubes."

"They were, and the screen itself was the end of a tube covered with phosphor that lit up when it was hit with a beam of electrons. It seems almost impossible that they got that old technology to work at all, but I guess more households had televisions than telephones. It just goes to show how much people like sitting in front of screens and watching life go by."

Hadley navigated around the swap meet area to the spots closer to the mall entrance which were largely untaken, both because it was early for the last day of the fair when so many attendees had been up late socializing, and also because the majority had arrived in RVs. Arlene's goal was to do some in-depth interviews with vendors she'd met the day before, so Hadley gave Freud a parting scratch behind the ears, which quickly turned into a belly rub, and then she headed for the atrium.

Two panel discussions and three live demonstrations later, Hadley gulped down a coffee and croissant delivered by Carl. While she ate, he briefed her with thumbnail biographies of the participants for the final panel she was to moderate.

"Jack Rainmaker claims to be a sort of shaman even though he's first-generation Irish. But he has an uncanny knack for making predictions like Nostradamus that are just specific enough to look prophetic while being vague enough to cover a broad range of outcomes. Peter told me that Jack wasn't going to come unless we paid a speaker's fee, but he changed his mind yesterday when he saw how many views our sessions are getting online. You know what happened with Jacqueline Forest, so he took her spot on the panel."

"I hope he doesn't go on and on. My least favorite part of moderation is cutting people off when they go way over their allotted time. Last night Peter loaned me an old pocket watch that he inherited from his father and suggested that I show it to all the panel members before we start and warn them that I'm keeping close track of the time."

"How many panels have you moderated now?" Carl asked.

"One a day, so this will be the third," Hadley said. "But I did use the pocket watch during the previous two panels today, and if a speaker went over three minutes, I would commandeer one of the floor microphones to interrupt and point out that people were waiting to ask questions." She took a sip of coffee and asked, "Who else?"

Carl made a face. "Venus Star. She's popular at science fiction and fantasy cons, and I'll bet she's been on a hundred panels, so watch out for her. Arlene likes Venus because she talks a lot about alien invasion and has interviewed women who claimed to have been kidnapped by alien warriors and forced to bear their children."

"And she makes predictions about an alien invasion?"

"I can't say I've paid much attention to anything she says, but I've heard from callers that Venus claims to know the date that the aliens are coming to kidnap all of the breeding-age females on Earth, which would qualify as an apocalyptic event. The only influencer on your panel I follow is Zueben Cohen, who has PhDs in computer science, philosophy, and neurobiology. He believes that artificial intelligence is advancing along a predictable path and that the singularity will occur sometime between two and three years from now."

Hadley swallowed the last bit of croissant and said, "I take it he associates the singularity with the apocalypse."

"It's a bit more nuanced than that," Carl said. "I think it would be more accurate to say that he believes that we've been living in the age of man ever since we became the primary species shaping the environment on Earth. With the arrival of the singularity, we'll enter the age of artificial intelligence almost overnight. Zueben is known for working out the odds of humanity surviving anywhere other than zoos a century from now, and he includes some scenarios where large numbers of people are allowed to continue living in nature preserves with rules limiting them to pre-computer technology. But I did an interview with him a couple of years ago, and he admitted that the only reason he included that table of odds in his book was because the publisher insisted."

"He sounds like an intelligent guy," Hadley said. She checked the time on Peter's pocket watch. "One minute. How about the fourth guy?"

"Woman. Elke Shultz. She has almost as many degrees as Zueben, and most of her work is over my head, though I read the book she wrote to popularize her ideas. Her outlook is almost Malthusian in the sense that she believes concentrating human populations inevitably creates the dynamic of us-and-them that leads to war. I don't have time to explain the whole thing, but she's convinced that the only reason large cities aren't fighting with each other is because of the excess of consumer goods that she attributes to the utilization of fossil fuels and globalization. She's done all kinds of statistical analysis to show that what she calls 'The Exploitation Dividend,' has almost run its course, and then a century and a half worth of stored-up hell will break loose."

"Gotta go, now," Hadley said. She surprised Carl with a quick kiss on the lips before she walked rapidly to the stage.

When he went to find a seat, Carl was surprised a second time, because all the folding chairs around the outside of the seating area were taken, and he didn't want to excuse his way past a dozen pairs of knees to sit in the middle of a crowd. Instead, he found a low spot to sit on the retaining wall for the fake dirt holding the fake ferns that added a cheerful green to the atrium.

The four influencers on the panel had already taken their seats by the time Hadley got there, and she intentionally detoured around the front of the platform to check the names on their placards. "Professor Cohen, Venus, Professor Schultz, Shaman Rainmaker," she recited to herself to get their titles into her head. She climbed the stairs on the side and almost fell when she tripped over something behind the Irish shaman. He must have been watching her because he got an arm out to arrest her fall and offered a friendly smile.

"If this stage were any smaller, I would have tripped you on purpose to maximize resources for myself," Professor Schultz told her. "It's the perfect example of how concentrating too many people in one place leads to conflict."

"Unless you buy them off with consumer goods," Hadley said as she took the center chair.

"You've read my work?"

"I've discussed it with my colleagues." Hadley looked out at the full house, hit the mute button on her microphone to keep it from activating, and showed the pocket watch in the palm of her hand to the influencers seated to her right and then to her left. "I'd like to keep introductions to just a sentence or two and open the floor to questions, at which point I will enforce a three-minute maximum on your responses. That doesn't mean that I want you to use the whole three minutes, just that I'll begin talking over you if you go that long, and our soundman will mute your microphone remotely."

Professor Cohen removed a watch from his wrist and set it on the table right next to his microphone with the band positioned to hold the watch face at the proper viewing angle. Venus reached over and turned it a little so that she could see the watch as well.

"Welcome to the final session of the Apocalypse Fair," Hadley began after unmuting her microphone. "For those of you sitting too far away to read the placards, our panelists are Professor Cohen, Venus, Professor Schultz, and Shaman Rainmaker. I've asked them to take just a sentence or two to introduce themselves, and then we'll open the floor to questions about signs that the apocalypse is imminent and whether anyone will commit to an exact date."

A round of laughter from the audience greeted Hadley's last sentence, and she took advantage of the brief interruption to explain to the panel members in pantomime that she wanted the Irishman to go first with his introduction and the others to follow in the order of their seating.

"Jack Rainmaker," the self-appointed shaman began. "In 1999, I predicted that computer-based artificial intelligence would start to replace people in twenty-five years. I leave it to you to decide the accuracy of my vision."

"Doctor Elke Shultz, and I work in the field of unconscious hive minds, by which I mean any critical mass of people takes on a type of group sentience which can overrule the rational thoughts of individuals. I will discuss this at greater length as time allows," she concluded with a barely concealed scowl at Hadley.

"Venus Star, and I'm here to tell you that one man's alien apocalypse is another woman's dream. I just hope they arrive before I'm too old to enjoy it."

"Professor Cohen, though my friends and enemies called me Zueben, or Zoo. I can't give an exact date for the arrival of the singularity, but I wouldn't recommend buying any five-year treasury notes."

"That was fantastic," Hadley said. "I'll get things rolling with one of the questions submitted through the website, and after that, we'll alternate with questions from the floor. Any audience members who submitted a question online are free to request a microphone, and if I see a similar question in the list generated from the website, I'll skip over it if we get that far."

Despite her promise, fifty minutes later, Hadley realized that she had almost no recollection of the questions that had been asked or the answers that had been given to that point. All of her energy had gone into preventing the influencers from coming to blows, especially the two college professors. It reminded her of the old truism that academic disputes were so bitter because the stakes were so low.

"—and while not all alien warriors are blue," Venus wrapped up, "I can promise you that they are all male, and I mean that exactly how you think I mean it."

"Thank you, Venus," Hadley said, just before the second hand on the pocket watch showed that three minutes had passed since the influencer had deflected a question about proof of the existence of aliens with several anecdotes of kidnappings and unexplained babies. "We have just enough time left to ask our panel members to go on the record with their best prediction of when we can expect, if not the apocalypse, an event that forever changes our civilization. Why don't we go in reverse order of the introductions and start with Zueben."

"I wish we were set up for showing PowerPoint slides, but I promise I'll make them available to The Good Apocalypse for inclusion on their website as soon as I get back to my office. I'm sure that most of you have heard of Moore's Law, which has been generally true for six decades in predicting the amount of compute that can be handled by a single chip. I'm aware of five updated versions of Moore's original observation intended to predict the growth of artificial intelligence as personified by large language models, but the only one of these that stands up to backtesting is Cohen's Conjecture."

"Backtesting?" Hadley interjected.

"It means that Cohen's Conjecture will correctly describe the capabilities of artificial intelligence in any given year based on the data set from the previous year, going back to the birth of the field. And what my conjecture tells us is that artificial general intelligence, also known as the singularity, will arrive in two to three years. The error bars for my conjecture are due solely to the competing definitions for artificial general intelligence. If we could get everybody to agree to a precise definition based on mathematical proofs, I could reduce the error bars to about a month in either direction."

"Then we'd better get to work on that definition," Hadley said. "Venus?"

"Are you asking me to provide a definition for artificial general intelligence?" the alien romance influencer asked.

"It's time to give us your best guess on when the invasion fleet will arrive."

"Never having been kidnapped myself, I don't have first-hand information from the aliens, but all of the indications are that it will be soon," Venus said. "If you'd asked me this question ten years ago, I would have said that the aliens will arrive when it suits them. But I've recently become convinced that they'll want to come for us before the singularity because a superintelligence might create problems for them."

"Meaning that a superintelligence might be able to detect their ships or create weapons that can penetrate their whatchamacallit fields," Hadley said.

"Exactly. If Professor Cohen is predicting that the singularity will arrive in thirty months, the aliens are going to invade before then. Then you can say goodbye to your artificial intelligence, your computers, and if you attempt to resist them, your lives."

"That's a pretty aggressive prediction, and I'm sure some people here today hope that you're right. Professor Schultz?"

"I happen to know that she's wrong because the very idea that aliens would be coming to Earth because they need women for breeding stock is too ridiculous to bother refuting. While I prefer not to give an exact date for the threads of civilization to unravel, I'm sure you're all aware that the globalization which brought cheap consumer goods to the Western world has fallen out of favor, and as prices rise, so will populations struggling under a mound of debt who will start casting about for someone to blame."

"And you believe this will bring about apocalyptic conditions," Hadley surmised.

"If you were listening during the cumulative twelve minutes and forty-six seconds I was allowed to speak during this panel, you'd know that when the group subconscious decides on war, nothing can stand in its way. From that point forward, it's all the same whether the final collapse is directly preceded by a nuclear exchange, the collapse of monetary systems, a man-made pandemic, or the release of killer drones and robots guided by artificial intelligence. The root cause in all these cases will be the desperate attempt of consumers who wake up to the massive hole in their lives that overconsumption used to fill."

"I don't think I've ever encountered such a cheerful group of individuals as this panel," Hadley said. "Perhaps our shaman can provide a little spiritual healing."

"November 11th," Jack said. "I won't go with the eleventh second of the eleventh minute of the eleventh hour, because that would be pushing it, but barring a calendar issue, I'm certain about the date."

"Veterans Day?"

"Did they change the name? It used to be Armistice Day."

"Not as long as I've been alive, and my father was in the army," Hadley said. "Do you mean this Veterans Day or some future—"

"This one," he cut her off.

"That's the most specific prediction I've ever heard. Is there a giant asteroid on a collision course with Earth that nobody else has spotted yet, or do you know the secret of predicting exactly when a super volcano will erupt?"

The shaman placed his hand over his eyes and said, "I have visions. I could commune with the spirits and tell you exactly where you'll be when it happens if you'd let me smoke a cigar in here."

"No smoking!" half of the audience shouted.

Venus leaned forward so she could look down the table at the shaman. "You must be in contact with aliens because you wouldn't have given such a specific date otherwise. Did they agree to spare your life in return for your carrying this message?"

"Everybody wanted a specific date and I've given it to you," Jack said. "If you need details, you're going to have to pay enough to make it worth my risk."

"This Veterans Day is too soon," said Professor Cohen. "Would you care to make a wager?"

"Not on stage, please," Hadley said. "We've gotten through the fair without any arrests, but we don't have a gambling license, and I don't want to tempt fate."

Twenty

"Well, it's been two weeks since the fair, and the only legal repercussion so far is Jack Rainmaker's crazy claim that we hired a ringer to impersonate him," Peter said at breakfast. "Can you imagine? We have hundreds of witnesses, the video including his voice which matches perfectly with previous recordings, and he can't offer any evidence that he was home because he says he was in a shamanic trance all weekend and his security cameras suffered a mysterious glitch."

"Jack just wants to get out of that crazy Veterans Day prediction that he gave," Mona said. "I bet you he never tries to take us to court."

"We could probably sue him for defamation," Laura Ann added.

"Never go to court if you can avoid it," Peter told them. "Besides, Jack probably keeps all of his money in anonymous Bitcoin wallets or a pot of gold buried in his backyard. Winning in court would just leave us out of our legal expenses, if the court system still exists by the time the case goes to trial."

"Morning, everybody," Fumiko said, entering the kitchen. "Have you seen the latest about Rainmaker?"

"We were just talking about him," Arlene said. "What's he saying now? That he was abducted by aliens?"

Fumiko continued to the refrigerator and took out a large container of chocolate yogurt. She appeared surprised by how little it weighed. "Has somebody been eating my health food?" she demanded.

"Chocolate yogurt is not health food," Laura Ann said in a long-suffering voice. "I suggested plain Greek yogurt with no sugar. Every time I'm in the kitchen, you're opening the fridge and taking another spoonful."

"I noticed that myself," Phil said. "Now what about Jack Rainmaker?"

"One of the attendees at the final panel brought an old camera with real film, not digital," Fumiko said as she retrieved a banana from the counter. "She got her prints back from the lab yesterday, scanned them, and uploaded the results to our Apocalypse Fair alumni forum. One of the pictures shows Hadley with the four panel members, and behind them, where all the parachutes were drooped, you can see their shadows. Everybody's shadow is an elongated person, except for Jack's, which looks like a lizard or a dragon. I think it's obvious that the parachute must have been billowing and distorting the shadow, but some people are making a big deal of it."

"They think we replaced Jack with a reptile?" Peter asked. "I've heard rumors that he's a lounge lizard, but I'm pretty sure that there's no relationship between the shadows we cast and our inner selves."

"I know plenty of people who would disagree with you on that, and I may be one of them," Mona said. "At the same time, it's hard to take a shadow on a parachute canopy seriously."

"How much would it cost me to add a freezer to the bunker specifically for yogurt?" Fumiko asked. "I think I'm an addict."

"Yogurt doesn't freeze well. I've experimented with it over the years, and the worst problem is that it gets watery. Ice crystals grow over time, so the longer it's frozen, the bigger they get. The good bacteria tend to die off, and then if there are any bad bacteria, they slowly multiply, just like with anything frozen. But the worst part is the water and taste."

"You can freeze dry yogurt," Laura Ann said. "If you do it right, it removes almost all the water, and then the yogurt can last for years as a powder if you store it properly. I can't say anything about the taste because I've never had any."

"Don't we have freeze-dried yogurt in the catalog?" Peter asked Arlene.

"Esther's Dairy went out of business over a year ago," Arlene told him. "Somebody sued over the raw milk products they sold, and Esther was just so disgusted with the whole thing that she went back to selling farm shares to locals to get around any future legal problems."

"Did you ever try any while it was in the catalog?" Laura Ann asked.

"Now that you mention it, we have a few cartons in the bunker. Since all the freeze-dried stuff has such a long shelf life, it never got rotated to the front."

"Was any of it chocolate?" Fumiko asked.

"I don't think so," Arlene said, taking out her phone and pulling up the inventory list. "Hold on a second and I'll—No. One carton plain and one carton of mixed berry."

"You could add chocolate easily enough," Mona said. "Cocoa powder is one of those things that can last for decades if it's stored properly."

"How much cocoa powder do we have in the bunker?" Fumiko followed up.

"Tons," Peter said. "Literally tons, because I figure it will be useful for bartering when imports are cut off. Our cavern provides perfect storage conditions in some rooms, so I've stocked up on commodities to trade with farmers. If nothing happens in the next couple of years, I'll donate it all to Franklin's food bank and replace it."

"My money is on something going wrong enough in the next two years that we'll be cut off up here," Glen said complacently. "I've started liquidating my book entry assets."

"What are you buying with the money?"

"A lot of copper wire. The price goes through cycles, so even if the apocalypse doesn't happen, I should be able to get my investment back eventually. Otherwise, copper is pretty useful stuff, and it has a low enough melting point that reworking it isn't beyond an amateur like me."

"I've been stocking up on bicycle parts," Phil said. "I've got a room in the cavern filled with mountain bike kits, including tires, tubes, and enough spare parts to rebuild half of them from scratch. I got most of the kits in an online auction from a manufacturer that went out of business. The liquidator should have sold them individually, but there weren't a lot of people willing to bid on a lot of a hundred, and I took it down for just over thirty thousand bucks."

"I've started buying more drones and robots even though I get eval models for free," Fumiko said. "I haven't gone overboard with it because the technology is continually advancing, and I don't want to over-commit to old models, even if they're useful. But it makes sense to lay in a supply, and it's not like the money is going to be useful for anything out in the cloud."

"Haven't any of you heard that the best use for money is storing up positive experiences?" Mona asked. "I understand that you're all working, and you may not want to travel right now because of the risk of not being able to return, but Peter took me into Franklin the other night, and we saw a play at the renovated Opera House. I was so impressed that I bought a pair of season tickets during the intermission."

"Are you offering to let us use them?"

"It doesn't work that way. I would suggest calling ahead to make sure that they aren't sold out and making dinner reservations. Don't buy your tickets until you get there and you can see the seating chart. They don't have an internet site up yet."

"How about it?" Phil asked Arlene across the table. "I haven't seen a play since high school."

"What are they performing?" Arlene asked.

"Candida," Peter told them. "It's a George Bernard Shaw comedy, and I suspect they picked it because the whole thing takes place in one room and there are only six characters. Smart business move for a theatre that's just starting out. It's been updated for modern audiences, but the spirit still comes through."

"How's the food?"

"Café style," Mona told her. "Plenty of solid choices, and some interesting sandwiches."

"I'll eat a big lunch," Phil said. "And don't ask if anybody else wants to come," he added to Arlene. "This is an official date."

Hadley laughed when Arlene told her about the date while the two of them followed instructions from the internet to change the toner cartridge in the rarely used printer. "Unless you want to pretend that you don't know me, it's a double date," she said. "Betsy presented Carl with a pair of tickets at breakfast and told him in no uncertain terms that he was taking me."

"That was sweet of her," Arlene said. "We can have dinner together, but since you already have your seats, we'll probably end up sitting apart. I wonder why they don't do open admission?"

"William used to take me to off-Broadway plays, and the theaters charge different prices for the seats depending on how good they are." She laughed again. "We once went to a play that was way off-Broadway. The son of one of the senior partners in William's law firm was acting in it. I've never been so happy to have a seat with an obstructed view in my life."

"They sell tickets where you can't see the stage? That's crazy."

"You could see some of the stage, but you didn't have to feel guilty about closing your eyes," Hadley said. "I had a glass of wine at intermission and drifted off."

"Do you mind driving?" Arlene asked. "Phil was going to borrow Peter's truck, but I have a nice dress that he's never seen, and I don't want to risk it on the bench seat with the duct tape closing up the gap in the cushion."

"Sure, I'll come back after work, but I have to go home and change myself."

"I guess Carl will want to go home and get dressed up as well."

Hadley shook her head. "He shaved this morning, and we only have the one bathroom. I don't want him there rushing me, and he doesn't own dress clothes anyway. I told him a clean shirt would be fine."

"I didn't say anything to Phil about dressing up," Arlene said with a sly grin.

"Will you bring Freud?"

"I'll have to sneak out. Fumiko promised to stay with Freud all evening so he doesn't mope."

Phil and Carl were subdued during the drive to Franklin, probably because they had never seen their dates wearing expensive dresses and full makeup. Despite reassurances from Arlene and Hadley, both men felt like slobs. The Opera House turned out to be on the second and third floors of an old brick building, with a narrow entrance and café at street level.

"I didn't expect table service," Hadley said to the others after they were shown to seats at the right side of the entrance that had a view of the street. "How much do you want to bet that we'll be seeing the hostess and those waiters on stage later?"

"No takers," Carl said. "I'm suspicious that the hostess gave us this table because you and Arlene look so good that it will make passersby want to come in."

"You think I'm an attractive nuisance? That's the nicest thing anybody's ever said about me."

"What's an attractive nuisance?" Arlene asked.

"It's a legal term, or maybe it's from the insurance industry, but my ex told me about a case his firm defended for one of their real estate clients where a kid passing in the street jumped up and grabbed a fire escape ladder and then ended up losing some teeth when it came down and hit him in the mouth. The kid's attorney claimed that the ladder was hanging too low, and that made it an attractive nuisance, a sort of irresistible trap for teenage boys."

"Are you serious?" Phil asked. "I'd hate to be a Manhattan landlord if you have to waste your money defending claims like that."

"The client was thrilled to settle out of court for less than six figures," Hadley said. "If it had gone to trial, the legal fees alone would have been more than that, but William's firm was able to show that the ladder met the building code and that the teenager had placed second in an all-city high jump competition."

"Then why did they settle?"

Hadley attempted to channel an old mafioso and said, "Tell Mikey it's just business," before reverting to her natural voice and continuing, "Commercial landlords don't care about winning moral victories. They're just trying to keep their costs down, and that meant settling."

"What was with the funny voice?" Arlene asked.

"My inner thespian struggling to get out. It must be the theater. Haven't you ever seen *The Godfather*?"

"You know I avoid movies with violence or suspense, which is pretty much everything that comes out of Hollywood."

One of the two waiters who looked like he could have gotten modeling work approached the table and handed out paper menus. "Can I take your drink orders while you decide?" he asked.

Carl said, "We'll have some pigeons, Davy, a couple of short-legged hens, a joint of mutton, and any pretty little tiny kickshaws, tell William cook."

"Shakespeare! Are you the reviewer our manager said will be coming this week?" the waiter asked hopefully.

"No, we're locals. I asked a large language model for a Shakespeare line about ordering food, and it took me ten minutes to memorize that one. I was worried that if I didn't use it now, I'd forget when it was time to order food."

Soon after the play started, it became apparent that their waiter had the lead role of Canby Morell, whose wife, Jamie, was a progressive bishop in the Church of England. A beautiful young songwriter named Imogene Marchbanks attempted to lure Canby away from his domineering wife, and the play examined what men desire in marriage. In the end, Canby remained faithful to his wife and continued in his role as a househusband, raising their two children. On the drive home after the play, Phil admitted, "I didn't understand that at all."

"But I explained it to you during both intermissions," Arlene protested. "What didn't you understand?"

"I get that Canby represented the playwright's concept of the ideal modern man, but all that business with the songwriter trying to convince him to cheat on his wife didn't make sense."

"It's because you're not a jerk," Carl said.

"Imogene sincerely believed that Canby deserved to be his own person and that he was subjugating himself to his wife for the sake of family harmony," Hadley said. "I think the play raises some interesting questions about the role of men in modern marriage."

"Just so you guys know, it's not how George Bernard Shaw wrote it," Arlene said. "I got the play off the internet today and read the whole thing because I wanted to make sure it wasn't a thriller. Whoever did the rewrite for the version that we saw must be a fan of the Third Wheel movement."

"Never heard of it," Phil said.

"It's an internet thing that I've been seeing pop up here and there over the past year. Third Wheel is a mishmash of ideas, but the basic thrust is that some guys believe that they don't have a role to fill in modern families, or that their role has been replaced by the state. I only see it because there are cross-postings to some of the forums where I do my literary research. None of the women take it seriously, and there are usually snarky comments along the lines of, 'This is exactly why I want to be kidnapped by a hunky blue alien warrior.'"

"I think this script was really good," Hadley said. "How much of it was taken verbatim from the Shaw play?"

"I couldn't give you an estimate without having the scripts side by side. Peter was right that the update captures the spirit of what Shaw was writing about, but it does it with a complete reversal of roles that doesn't reflect reality."

"I knew some women in Manhattan who thought that men weren't good for anything outside of the bedroom, and even there, it was debatable. Is that much different from how men saw women when Shaw wrote the play?"

"I don't think it's fair to speak in generalities like that," Carl said. "There were men then and today who see women solely in their roles as wives and mothers, and there were men who supported giving women the right to vote. Keep in mind that women's suffrage everywhere came about because enough men agreed to it, not because—did the power just go off?"

"I still see lights on those farms up ahead," Hadley said.

"Franklin is dark," Phil reported after looking out the rear window. "Dairy farmers all have backup generators, and the Amish run low-voltage lights off of batteries that they recharge from generators or solar."

"EMP blast?" Arlene asked. "I didn't see a flash."

"You wouldn't if it happened in the Midwest," Phil said. "Some physicists think that a big enough EMP in the right place at the right altitude could take down the whole country."

"Could be a cyberattack on the grid," Carl said. "Or maybe one of those large language models is a little smarter than I gave it credit for."

"Come on," Hadley said. "It's just the little blackout, and it's only been a minute. Maybe a truck hit a utility pole or a transformer blew up."

Carl reached over and clicked on the radio just in time for the last obnoxious blast of the Emergency Alert System, followed by, "This is not a test. Cascading power grid failures are reported throughout areas of the Northeast and the Midwest, starting with New York and Pennsylvania and stretching west through Indiana and Illinois. If you are in a blackout area, shelter in place, and do not drive unless you have a medical emergency. Updates will be provided when they become available. This is not a test. Cascading power grid failures—"

"It's repeating," Hadley said, switching off the radio. "And you'd think the last people they'd want on the road are those who are experiencing a medical emergency."

"They phrased it wrong," Phil said. "I bet there have been hundreds of meetings and tens of millions of dollars spent on exactly what to say in an emergency, and they still got it wrong."

"What's the big deal with driving in the dark anyway? That's what headlights are for."

"Doesn't that mean it's not an EMP since the car is still running?" Arlene said. "They didn't say anything about the cause, just that the grid was down."

"The grid was supposedly redesigned so that a failure in one area wouldn't drag down all of the connected regions, but maybe they never made the investment after they came up with the plan," Carl said. "I imagine the warning about driving is aimed more at people in cities where they're used to having streetlights and traffic signals. I remember living in a town where the power went out and all the traffic signals started blinking red. I imagine that would make a real mess in a place like Manhattan."

"The one time I remember a brief blackout, the traffic lights all went dark," Hadley said. "You'd think they would upgrade them with the latest technology and battery backups, but maybe that would mean doing the whole system and they didn't have the money."

"Speaking of money, my bet is on hackers," Phil said. "It will turn out that some hacking group took over one of the regional power planning centers that control the grid and demanded a ransom in Bitcoin that wasn't paid."

"I don't know," Carl said. "If the whole country had gone dark, I would be all-in on artificial intelligence having done it, but there's a lot of old grid infrastructure in the Rust Belt states, and that seems to be the main region affected. I'll put my money on human error or a software bug."

"Human error?" Hadley asked. "Like somebody throwing the wrong switch?"

"Or a lot of wrong switches. Remember Chernobyl? The operators manually locked out safety systems to test whether or not the reactor's turbine could power its own cooling pumps during a shutdown."

"I'm sticking with hackers," Phil said. "Twenty bucks it is."

"How long do you think power will be out?" Arlene asked.

"When this much of the grid goes down, even if the damage is limited, it has to be turned back on in stages. As long as it wasn't an EMP blast or a rogue artificial intelligence, it's likely that the damage is localized, and in the worst case, the engineers will isolate those areas from the grid and get the rest back up again."

"Why did you turn here?" Carl asked Hadley.

"Because I'm going—I forgot that Arlene and Phil don't live with us. Is anybody coming the other way?"

"I don't see any lights," Phil reported from the back seat.

Hadley made a three-point turn and drove back to the cut-off that would take them to the farm faster.

"My phone works, and our website is still up," Arlene reported.

"Somewhere around eighty percent of cell towers have some sort of backup power, either a generator or batteries," Phil said. "The towers that only have battery backup will go dark in a few hours, maybe eight hours at the most, but the ones with generators and a full tank of diesel could hold out for a few days."

"You guys really know your stuff," Hadley said. A second later, she added, "Assuming that you're not making it up. Have you ever thought about getting together and doing a book about what to expect when the lights go out?"

"Or, you and Arlene could edit it together out of our existing content."

"That sounds good to me," Carl said.

"Hold the wheel," Hadley told him, and then twisting around in her seat so she could face Arlene, she said, "Men."

Twenty-One

"Pink sky at morn, sailors be warned," Betsy murmured as she retrieved the canister of tea leaves from the cabinet next to the kitchen window.

"It is pink, isn't it?" Hadley said from where she was beating the eggs. "It's kind of weird looking."

"If it wasn't a natural meteorological thing, sailors wouldn't have an expression about it," Carl said as he scraped the vegetables from the chopping board into a bowl. "Does everybody want cheese with their omelets?"

"Yes, please," the two women chorused.

"If I had known that last homemade bread from the Troyers was starting to go stale, I would have made French toast instead."

"It will be fine when it's toasted," Betsy said. "If it's not used up by dinner, I'll give it to the Troyer girl to take home for the chickens."

"Have you checked the news yet this morning?" Hadley asked.

"I thought the first thing you young people do when you get up is look at your phones," Betsy said, placing the infuser in the teapot and adding hot water from the kettle. "I'll let one of you bring it to the table because my hands are a bit shaky this morning."

"I asked my favorite AI about that, and it gave me a whole list of things that could be causing your tremor,"

Carl said. "We went back and forth a few times and agreed that the most likely—"

"I don't have a need to know," Betsy interrupted him. "It's not debilitating, but the cure might be. I'm practicing watchful waiting for the time being, and I can sum up the morning's news in one word. Bad."

"Is the power still out for almost ten million people in the Midwest?" Hadley asked. "Franklin came back online after two days, and it's a good thing that Manhattan only went down for part of the one night, because if it had been two nights, I don't think there would be anything left worth saving."

"I only listened with half an ear, but the announcer said something about a hacking group making ransom demands to a whole list of public utilities, which are scrambling around like crazy, trying to disconnect themselves from the internet. There was one city out in California, I've forgotten the name, where everybody's water came out of the taps this morning smelling and tasting like it was from a swimming pool. Apparently, that was just a warning."

Carl poured enough beaten eggs into the pan for the first omelet and added a handful of chopped vegetables. "Phil is never going to let me live down losing our bet," he said. "I was sure that it was human error."

"At least it wasn't the AI apocalypse," Hadley said. "It would have been more embarrassing to be wrong in your specialty. Speaking of which, what mug do you want this morning?"

"Give me the mushroom cloud. Some days I just want to keep it simple."

"I'll take the Ebola virus," Betsy said from where she was sitting at the table. "It has such a lovely glaze."

"Going by the pink sky, I'm thinking tornado for myself," Hadley told them.

"There were tornadoes in the news, mainly in the southwest. And two weeks of unseasonable rain in Mexico have wreaked havoc on their corn harvest."

"Anything about who is responsible for the atmospheric nuclear test above the Indian Ocean?" Carl asked.

"I didn't listen long enough to find out," Betsy said with a sigh. "It does seem like all of the momentum is on one side these days."

Hadley brought the teapot to the table and filled Betsy's mug for her about halfway so the older woman's morning tremor wouldn't result in her sloshing herself and getting burned. Then she filled her own cup and looked at the phone that Carl had left at his place. "You have a text," she told him.

"Check it for me," he said. "I was looking at the weather a few minutes ago and I have my lock screen timer on fifteen minutes."

"Not worried that I'm going to find a message from your other girlfriend?"

"I'm not worried about anything on my phone. I use it for texts and phone calls, and that's it."

"It's from Peter," Hadley said two seconds later. "Our satellite internet provider is going to stop throttling our bandwidth today, so you can go back to uploading video. They apologize for the last week, but the government requisitioning the majority of their bandwidth for emergency operations qualified as an act of god, so we won't be receiving a refund."

Carl laid a slice of cheddar cheese on one half of the omelet and folded the other half over the top. "I almost preferred not having enough bandwidth to upload video.

The quality of the compressed audio was fine, and that's what podcasting was all about when it started. Having to produce video is just more work."

"I had an interesting call this morning," Betsy said, picking up a fork with one hand and a knife with the other in anticipation of Carl bringing her the first finished omelet. "It was Sarah's son who manages the distribution center for common carriers outside of Franklin, though he'll be retiring next week. He recognized my address on a shipment and wanted to make sure that it wasn't a scam. Something about merchants who have products warehoused at one of the large internet retailers sending merchandise to random addresses to save on warehouse charges."

"They probably place those orders using stolen credit card information so they get paid as well."

"Is that what it was?" Hadley asked. "You hadn't ordered anything?"

"The shipment was addressed to you," Betsy said. "I asked Howard if he could hold on to it for another day while I checked. You were in the bathroom when he called."

"Oh, no!" Hadley reached into the purse hanging on the back of her chair for her phone. "I did place a rather large order online, but I thought I had it sent to the office. Maybe they picked up this address from my credit card since I made your house my official mailing address."

"You're ordering things that need to be delivered by common carrier?" Carl asked as he started on the second omelet.

"Some composition books, art supplies, pens, pastels, crayons. I also got a deal on ten gross of five-subject notebooks with spiral bindings, and I bought a couple of cases of pencils as well."

"Are you prepping, Hadley?" Betsy asked in mock astonishment.

"I think of it as investing," Hadley said as she skimmed through the messages in her inbox. "Here's the order acknowledgment and—I must have been hurrying. Either I clicked 'Same as billing address' for shipping, or they did it by default."

"Just how much did you order?" Carl asked. "Could we fit the boxes in the back of your SUV, or will we need Peter's pickup?"

"I don't know how many boxes it will amount to, but I kind of maxed out my credit card. The total came to just under eight thousand dollars."

"That's a lot of paper," Betsy said between bites.

Carl added cheese to the second omelet and said, "Pretty smart thinking, though. Even if our laptops and phones survive what's coming, eventually the printer will break down or we'll run out of toner. Paper and art supplies will make excellent barter goods."

"Is it too late for me to get in on this game?" Betsy asked. "I have some Bitcoin that I'm getting nervous about, and I was thinking about putting it into work clothes and sensible shoes for Peter to store in the bunker. I was going to ask Arlene to get me everybody's sizes, and I also thought about stocking up on the fabrics that the Amish would use if they make their own clothes. You know what? I'm going to go on that auction site where you set up an account for me, Carl, and see if I can buy some treadle-powered sewing machines in good working condition."

"Don't forget repair parts."

"And don't procrastinate," Hadley added. "I just checked the financial news site, and the stock market won't be opening today. The Securities and Exchange Commission has declared a ten-day stock holiday to protect investors after circuit breakers shut down the market three times yesterday, the final time after the broad index dropped twenty percent."

"Do you know anybody who owns stock?" Carl asked as he slid the omelet from the pan to her plate.

"I still have what's in my 401(k), but it's not much because I never had enough income to make the matching contributions. The markets are back below where they were when I started working. I should have taken it out, but I didn't want to pay a tax penalty. Do you think I should do it now?"

"It's usually a bad idea to make retirement planning decisions based on the news of the day, and with the markets closed, I doubt you could sell what you have in there. If this is the beginning of the end, it's probably not a good idea to gamble on having money lost in limbo between your brokerage and your bank, or wherever you would try to have it sent. It's not like all the customer service employees are going to continue working after a collapse."

"Well," Betsy said, spreading a little soft butter on her toast. "At least we won't run out of art supplies, and it could be a long time before your credit card bill arrives."

A phone call to Sarah's son at the distribution center was enough to get the shipment rerouted to the office, and everybody came out and pitched in to help move the boxes from the plastic-wrapped pallets to the bunker. After lunch, Peter summoned Hadley and Arlene to join him at the laptop hosting the Eleanor interface, where the three of them worked out how to enable HIM, the Hyperinflation Indexing Model.

"I have mixed feelings about this," Peter admitted. "I checked the log this morning, and over fifty percent of our customers are now paying the premium for next-day delivery."

"If there's any truth to the wisdom of crowds, it sounds like the world is in trouble," Arlene said.

"That's true, but I was thinking more about the ethics of the system charging for express delivery when I suspect the transportation infrastructure will be so overloaded that they'll be lucky to get their packages in a week. You got your order for paper and art supplies in just under the wire, Hadley."

"Should we be driving into Franklin this afternoon to stock up on whatever they still have in the supermarket?" Hadley asked.

"Mona and I did that last night," Peter said. "I wondered about the ethics of that as well, since we could be the best prepared people in the state, but none of our neighbors make chocolate yogurt, and I want to put off dealing with Fumiko's withdrawal symptoms for as long as possible."

"Do you think this is really it?" Arlene asked, almost losing her balance when Freud arrived and leaned heavily against her legs.

"It's not looking good, but until the bombs start flying or a superintelligence announces that it's taken over, the government will keep functioning and we'll muddle through. That said, if the stock market continues to crater when they reopen it, the financial apocalypse is underway."

"Two weeks to Veterans Day," Hadley said. "I did some searching last night and Jack Rainmaker has changed his story. Now he's claiming that it was him at our Apocalypse Fair, and he stands by his prediction."

"Glen is planning an asteroid-watching party for Veterans Day to celebrate finally getting the software for the tracking mount on his big reflector to work right," Peter said. "I've got a favor to ask. Do you think you could talk my mother into coming?"

"Do you think that would be wise? She's already fallen once, and to be walking around in the dark..."

"You haven't been here at night to see Glen and Fumiko testing the LED lights they've strung all over the barn and the silo. When they're lit up, we're probably making ourselves a target from space."

"Then why did they do it?" Hadley asked. "I thought that lights interfere with telescopes."

"Glen turns the lights off when he's making observations, and it's more of an art installation than anything else. Fumiko was creating content to demonstrate how she could use a drone to drape strings of LEDs in those hard-to-reach places."

"Look," Arlene said, pointing at the laptop screen. "Eleanor just processed a sale with the HIM turned on."

"How much did it add to the total?" Hadley asked.

"Uh, nothing. I mean, it was something, but all the digits are on the right side of the decimal place, and the change rounded down to nothing. I guess there hasn't been that much inflation in the two minutes since we enabled it."

"I should create a banner for the order page explaining why customers may see their total adjusted up."

"It doesn't work that way," Peter said. "The module is adjusting all of the catalog prices on the fly."

"What if somebody stuffs their shopping cart and then leaves it for a few days to see whether prices go up or down?" Hadley asked.

"Given all the people paying for next-day shipping, I doubt anybody will try, but if they do, they'll find out that their shopping cart expires after an hour," Arlene said. "Some stores go with as little as fifteen minutes because it creates a sense of urgency for buyers to act, but when we set up the system, I thought an hour was a fair compromise. I wasn't worried about prices changing but about products running out of stock. If we let customers fill their shopping cart over the course of days or weeks, there is a good chance that the mom-and-pop manufacturers who produced our private label goods will run out of one of the items, and that creates a bad customer experience at the checkout."

"Hadley," Laura Ann called from the doorway. "I'm about to record a show about the stock market vacation. Want to be my guest?"

"Sure. Do you have a list of questions for me to ask?"

"Just be yourself. You're a reasonable proxy for my audience demographic, and maybe you have questions that I wouldn't think to ask."

Ten minutes later, Laura Ann finished her opening spiel, introduced Hadley, and asked, "So what do you make of all of this?"

"I didn't know that the Securities and Exchange Commission had the authority to close the stock market," Hadley said.

"Under the Securities and Exchange Act of 1934, the SEC can unilaterally suspend trading for up to ten business days. If they want to go longer than that, they need to convince the exchanges or get explicit backing from Congress and the president. There was a four-month period during World War One where the stock market was closed, and that decision involved both the government and the board of the New York Stock Exchange."

"Was the war bad for the economy? What about the military-industrial complex?"

"Stock markets don't have a lot to do with the real economy, if there is such a thing," Laura Ann said. "It's strictly a matter of supply and demand, where the supply is the amount of loose money chasing around, and the demand is greed or the fear of missing out. Stock prices go up when there's money coming into the market to buy them, and stock prices go down when people sell out because they're worried that prices will fall. When the Japanese Central Bank decided it wanted their stock market to go up, it started buying ETFs, exchange-traded funds of stocks, with money created from nothing. They don't disclose their ownership stake, but current estimates are that the bank has bought approximately seven percent of Japan's publicly traded shares."

"Seven percent doesn't sound like that much," Hadley ventured.

"I've seen academic studies that estimate the overall Japanese market would be trading at half of its current level if not for that cash infusion. Keep in mind that stock prices, just like house prices, are driven by relatively small numbers of sales. When prices of starter homes in most areas of the country doubled a few years ago, the pundits all pointed to people's desire to move out of big cities. But most of those people have long since moved back into their apartments, and that explanation was always a red herring. The three things that drove up the cost of houses were investors buying them for rentals, artificially low interest rates thanks to the Federal Reserve, and the moratorium on foreclosures that lasted over two years in some places. Buying a foreclosure is rarely the first choice for a family looking for a home, so those houses often went to flippers and set the prices for the low end of the market."

"Why wasn't the market flooded with foreclosures when people had to start paying their mortgages again?"

Laura Ann laughed. "Because the value of most single-family homes rose so much faster than the unpaid mortgage amounts that the owners, or maybe I should call them tenants, were able to sell and walk away with a profit."

"Isn't that a good thing?" Hadley asked.

"If you owned a house you couldn't pay for, it was a windfall. But for all the young families looking for a starter home who can't afford one, it was a tragedy. That's what happens whenever the central bank and governments intervene in markets. They create winners and losers, and too often the losers are the people who were playing by the rules that got changed on them."

"So how can we prevent something like this from happening again in the future?"

"Replace the Federal Reserve with an artificial intelligence that's tasked to hold inflation steady at a low rate and nothing more," Laura Ann said. "In terms of the politicians changing the rules to suit the political climate, we're out of luck, unless we replace them with artificial intelligence as well."

"Do you think that's possible?"

"Anything is possible. The more interesting question is, if we replace the government with artificial intelligence, is it a democracy? Given that most artificial intelligence models are trained on every last piece of information they can scrape from the internet, you could argue that they're inherently democratic. Certainly more so than partisan politicians, who at best represent a constituency, and at worst, represent nothing beyond their own interests."

Hadley thought for a moment about what Carl had taught her about the training of artificial intelligence, and she said, "I'm not so sure. The companies that create these models do a lot of post-training, which has a major impact on how large language models answer questions. And now that I think about it, getting everybody to agree on which artificial intelligence to use, and how it would be updated as new technology arrives is probably a non-starter."

"If that's the case, we're stuck waiting for the singularity to arrive and decide for us," Laura Ann said. "My main concern remains that the people who currently hold the reins of power will be unwilling to hand them over and would rather burn down the world than see somebody else in charge."

Twenty-Two

"I think it's nice that our national holiday to honor veterans actually happens on the day that World War One ended, rather than getting moved to Monday for a three-day weekend," Arlene said. "The weather cooperated, and I've never hiked so far in my life. Look at Freud. The poor boy is exhausted."

"That's strategic napping," Phil told her. "He's saving his strength to help eat hamburgers, which reminds me that I should get the charcoal going."

"Everybody appreciates that you aren't frying them in the kitchen or messing up the oven by using the broiler."

"By everybody, I assume you mean the vegetarians working here, and broiling meat does not make a mess. I seem to remember spending an hour scraping burned bean residue off the floor of the oven because an aspiring vegan cook didn't realize that they absorb the water and would overflow the casserole dish."

"First of all, it was lentils," Arlene said as Phil stood up. "Second of all, it didn't take you more than half an hour."

"Still litigating Lentilgate?" Laura Ann asked as she dropped into the lawn chair Phil had just vacated. "Why are the two of you sitting around in the cold? I thought you might have discovered a secret hot spot on the lawn, but even with my jacket on, I'm already chilly."

"We're still warm from our hike," Arlene told her as Phil went to fetch the charcoal from the barn. "We went all the way to the falls and back."

"That must be twenty miles of trails. What would you have done if you sprained an ankle or ran out of energy?"

"I would have gotten a piggyback ride from Phil. Worst case we could have made Carl jog home and bring one of the trail bikes."

"Now that you mention it, I haven't seen Carl or Hadley since you got back," Laura Ann said. "Don't tell me they went home to change, because it's not that kind of party."

"Hadley tried to collect some clay from under the root ball of a fallen tree on the way back," Arlene said with a giggle. "She slipped and got covered with it, so she really did need to change. She was going to drive home anyway to pick up Peter's mom for dinner since they're all staying over tonight. Phil and I are going to sleep in the bunker to free up our bedrooms for them."

"I don't think Betsy has been up here since last Christmas. I wonder if Peter talked her into coming because he wanted her as close as possible to the bunker tonight."

"Am I suffering from hallucinations? It almost looks like you just lit a cigarette."

"Damn. Don't tell anybody." Laura Ann knocked off the ash on the arm of the lawn chair, made sure it was out, and then replaced the cigarette in the pack. "What? That's fifty cents right there. I almost had a heart attack when I bought them and found out what they cost now."

"But why? Even though your podcast is mainly about the financial apocalypse these days, we still cross-list you as a healthy living influencer."

"I know, and it's my first pack of cigarettes since junior high school when I was trying to lose weight. I never even inhaled."

"You must be taking the shaman's prediction seriously," Arlene said. "Do you expect the apocalypse tonight?"

"Have you checked the news?" Laura Ann asked. "Even though it's a national holiday, there have been reports of sell orders flooding the online brokerage sites for when the markets open again, and that's when people can get internet access. Our satellite connection has been throttled again because the emergency services need the bandwidth, and there are rolling blackouts on the East Coast because of another hacking attack on the grid. Hundreds of millions of hogs around the world are being destroyed because of the new bird flu that's been spreading to them, and the North Atlantic shipping lanes are closed because that glacier broke up and filled the sea with icebergs."

"Are there any new wars brewing?"

"No one is shooting missiles yet, outside of the ongoing conflicts, but there's definitely some serious saber rattling going on. The big rumor is that the U.S. Treasury is going to suspend interest payments on the debt until further notice."

"But won't that cause the bond market to crash and bring the whole world economy down?" Arlene asked.

Laura Ann shrugged. "If you had asked that question twenty years ago, the answer would have been simple. But in a world without moral hazard, the Federal Reserve Bank can just create new dollars to buy all the U.S. debt that comes on the market, at which point, it gets monetized and translated into hyperinflation, which is a stealth tax on savers. If it wasn't Veterans Day, I would be in my studio ranting about this, but who knows if we'll ever get the bandwidth back to upload it."

"I've never heard you so negative. What are you going to do?"

"Right now? Go back inside because I'm cold. And don't tell anybody about the cigarettes. I really don't know why I bought them. When the whole world is going mad, sometimes it seems like the only reasonable thing to do is to join in."

"What was all that about?" Phil asked Arlene as he set down the bag of charcoal and gave the grill a critical inspection. He took the wire brush off its hanger on the side and did a quick cleaning.

"Laura Ann said there are rumors that the Treasury is going to stop paying interest on bonds," Arlene said.

"That's as good as a declaration of war to the countries that bought trillions of dollars worth. I'd better get the cheater."

"The what?"

"The starter fluid that people use if they don't have the patience to build a fire with paper and twigs to get the charcoal going," Phil said. "You've never seen me use it before, but we've got some in the barn."

"Why?" Arlene asked. "You're the only one who cooks with charcoal, and it's not like we'll be building fires underground."

"It was Peter's idea. If it all hits the fan, we might need to burn some things on short notice, and charcoal fluid is a little safer to use than gasoline, not that we would waste gas for starting fires when we can't get any more." He took off his quilted flannel shirt and put it over her like a blanket. "You look cold, and in about thirty seconds, I'm going to have the charcoal to warm me up."

The first burgers were just coming off the grill when Hadley pulled up in front of the house. Carl jumped out of the back and went to help Betsy get out of the passenger seat, and rather than complaining, she said something about missing the days before bucket seats had been invented. The three of them walked through the house and entered the kitchen right after Arlene put the first platter of burgers on the long table, next to a plate full of vegetarian burgers that Mona had fried on the stove.

"It's frying them in oil that makes them tasty," Mona explained in response to Hadley's question as to why Phil hadn't done them on the grill. "When you cook vegetarian burgers over charcoal, they just dry out fast, and then you have to cover them with ketchup and mustard to taste anything."

"You guys don't know what you're missing," Fumiko said, moving one of the beef patties to her plate. "And if things keep going the way they are, good luck buying fake meat in the future."

"I made these myself from my own recipe. Buying expensive hamburgers made from pea protein never made sense to me when peas taste so good right out of the pod."

"Who wants to split a real hamburger with me?" Betsy asked. "They smell fantastic, but that's too much meat for me to eat in one meal."

"I'll have half," Hadley said. "I'm looking forward to the potato salad that Arlene described while we were hiking. I got so hungry that I went through all the cough drops in my purse."

"That's a good way to ruin your teeth." Betsy took a large slice of homemade bread from the basket and set it on her plate just before Hadley delivered the half-burger. "Put it to one side and I'll fold the bread over," she said.

"Aren't you going to add any condiments? I buy sugar-free cough drops, by the way."

"Condiments are for making things you wouldn't want to eat otherwise taste like something they're not. I've had Phil's burgers before, and they don't need any disguising. He buys the meat from the Amish butcher."

"Where's Glen?" Peter asked as he came into the kitchen wearing one of his good shirts with an American flag pin on the lapel. "It's not dark enough yet for him to be up in his observatory, and there's no excuse for a man who served to be late for Veterans Day supper."

"He said something about everybody going crazy on that internet group he participates in where they all share telescope observations," Laura Ann said. "Amateur astronomers around the world in areas where it's already dark are reporting seeing random flashes or stars blinking out for a moment as if something enormous was passing in front of them."

"Do amateurs know what they're doing?" Hadley asked.

"Comets are discovered by amateur astronomers because they don't know that the odds against them are impossible."

"Is Glen upstairs or in his studio?" Peter followed up. "I'm going to go tell him the food is on the table."

"He was heading out to the barn when I saw him. Why don't you just send him a text?"

"Text messages aren't working on my phone." Peter continued moving toward the back door. "I'm getting one bar, which should be enough for texts and voice, but either the network is overloaded, or something else is wrong."

"I was playing with my new drone around ten minutes ago, and all of a sudden it landed and refused to go again,"

Fumiko said. "I thought it was the controller, so I changed the batteries, and then I tried a compatible controller, but nothing worked."

"So what was it?" Carl asked.

"I saw Phil putting the hamburgers on the grill, so I took a break from troubleshooting. It's important to set priorities in life."

Arlene returned with a second platter of hamburgers and said, "I told Phil this would be enough, but he thought it would be a shame to waste the charcoal on just two batches of hamburgers, so he's closing it up to bake a chicken wrapped in foil. He'll be a few more minutes."

"Where are you going?" Mona asked after Arlene set down the platter.

"To keep him company," Arlene said, and added, "Peter and Glen are coming," as she stepped out the door.

The first thing Glen did when he entered the kitchen was to borrow Peter's phone and set it on the spice shelf where it had a reasonable chance of capturing everybody sitting at both sides of the table. "I'm turning on the camera to capture video," he said. "I thought we might want to record The Good Apocalypse version of the Last Supper for posterity."

"Is it getting worse?" Laura Ann asked.

"The last rumor I heard before the forum went down is that we're at DEFCON One, which means that the military knows something that we don't."

"I remember that the scale is one to five, but I've forgotten which way it goes. Is one good or bad?"

"As bad as it gets," Glen said. "Cocked pistol, though if you ask me, we're pointing it at our own heads. I know you've always said that a financial collapse could lead to a shooting war, but spinning up the gyros on intercontinental ballistic missiles because Bitcoin is down and the stock market is crashing seems a bit extreme."

"You're just disappointed that it's not a giant asteroid on a collision course with Earth," Fumiko said. "Could somebody please pass the potato salad?"

"Whatever comes, it won't happen before midnight, because there's no conceivable way that Jack Rainmaker's prediction could be accurate," Peter said, taking the chair across from his mother and helping himself to a hamburger. "Then again, I suppose the advantage of it being Veterans Day is that many people will be home with their families."

"Don't bet against something from space," Glen said as he filled his plate. "Astronomers around the world were reporting stars blinking in and out, and the only reasonable explanations are mass hysteria or a local phenomenon that bends light."

"Mass hysteria sounds like a good bet to me," Betsy said. "It's easy to understand how people can go haywire if they think they've lost their life savings."

"The sad thing is that it was all so preventable," Laura Ann said as she helped herself to the salad. "I've never talked to anybody in the financial industry who believed that printing endless money was a good idea. My whole adult lifetime, our monetary system has been managed by central bankers who fundamentally believe that short-term pain should be avoided at all costs. They and the government have been kicking the can down the road for so long that the only way out I see is bankruptcy."

Phil and Arlene returned and took their seats, and Phil ended up with the sole chair at the head of the table. He immediately noticed Peter's phone recording video directly across from him and nodded his head. "It feels like the end of an era, so making a record is a good idea. Maybe it will cheer us up when we're all living underground."

"Not me," Betsy said. "I know why you wanted me up here today, Peter, and I appreciate the thought, but I'm at the point in life where living in a cavern while all those people in cities die would just be too depressing. I'll stay the night because I know that Arlene has some underground hanky-panky in mind, but I expect you to give me a ride back to my house first thing tomorrow morning unless an EMP blast takes out your truck electronics."

"Thanks for reminding me, Mom," Peter said. "You should park your car in the barn tonight, Hadley. Pull right into the red shipping container. Make sure Carl helps you close the container's door because it's a bit tight with the conductive coil we put in there to fill the space."

"What about your bike, Carl?" Hadley asked. "Would it fit in with my car? And how about the trail bikes?"

"They're all old enough not to have any computer electronics, and we have plenty of spare parts in anti-static bags down in the bunker," Carl said. Then he laughed. "Listen to us. Here we're having a great Veterans Day dinner, and all we can talk about is the apocalypse like we're sure it's going to happen before breakfast."

Hadley drank the wine someone had poured for her in three gulps and announced, "I have a confession to make."

"Just don't tell me you were born a male."

"No, I—NO! How can you even ask that?"

"It's the first thing that comes to mind these days when somebody announces they have a confession to make," Carl said.

"It's, well, I sort of took this job under false pretenses," Hadley said.

"Lying on resumes is an American tradition," Laura Ann told her. "Since large language models came along, I'm not sure most people could even tell you what's on their resumes because they don't write them themselves."

"I mean, I didn't really come here to build the website and update the newsletter."

"Are you a federal agent?"

"No. It's just that I assumed you would be a bunch of militia crackpots, and I thought I might try writing a novel," Hadley said in a rush. "I didn't even get past the first chapter."

"I've nursed a viper at my breast," Betsy said dramatically. "Pass me the potato salad, dear."

"I've been trying to write a book about us for years," Arlene said. "We should collaborate."

"There won't be much else to do in the bunker," Phil observed.

"Oh, I can think of a few things." Arlene blushed bright red immediately after the words were out of her mouth, and Freud started barking frantically at the back door.

"Are you trying to draw attention away from Arlene, or do you need to go and chase the aliens out of the yard?" Fumiko asked as she got up to open the door. She froze in place for a moment with her hand on the handle, and then said in a hollow voice, "Glen. I think this is supposed to be your area of expertise."

Glen knocked over his chair getting up from the table and rushed to the door. After a brief entanglement with Fumiko, who seemed unable to move aside, he got past her and ran out after Freud, with Phil and Carl just a step behind.

"You're going to want to see this," Carl called back through the opening.

"It can wait until we finish eating," Betsy said, but thirty seconds later, she was left alone. She carefully surveyed the kitchen to make sure she hadn't missed anybody, and then took another helping of potato salad.

"I don't know, I'd need to do the math," Glen replied to Peter's question about the size of the object they were seeing pass overhead.

"Do you think it's glowing?" Peter followed up.

"Maybe. The sun is setting, but that thing is high enough up and far enough southwest that we're seeing the sunlight reflected off the bottom. It's got to be ten miles long, and I wouldn't be surprised if it was miles in diameter. Imagine how advanced a civilization would have to be to build something like that."

"I was going to guess that it's even bigger," Carl said.

"Something that big can't appear out of nowhere," Hadley protested.

"I suspect something that big can appear wherever and however it wants."

"I'd guess it's about a hundred miles up," Glen told them. "It's just so big that it looks like it's moving slowly, but it must be circling the globe every hour and a half or so. I thought that glow was from gases that escaped Earth's atmosphere, but I'll bet it's some kind of alien force field. Maybe they're manipulating gravity in some way, and that explains all the distortions reported on the astronomy forum."

"What are those?" Hadley asked, pointing at some pinpoints of light that appeared on the horizon.

"Missiles," Glen said grimly. "There's an air defense installation at the base on the other side of Franklin. I didn't realize it was still active."

"Laser weapons, or something like them," Phil said, as beams of light lanced out from somewhere lower in orbit than the giant ship and the missiles exploded.

"Did you see where the beams came from?" Glen asked. "There's a smaller spaceship, it can't be much more than ten miles up, and it's just hovering there, not in orbit at all. I don't see any rocket exhaust so they're using propulsion systems beyond our physics."

"My phone is back online," Arlene reported tersely. "But the aliens must have taken it over because it's stuck on the one screen. It says that they come in peace and that any attempts by governments on Earth to attack them, each other, or to restrict the movements of citizens will result in the immediate removal of the individuals responsible."

Everybody else who was carrying a phone pulled it out and saw the same message. Peter surprised them all by producing what proved to be a transistor radio with a telescoping antenna and turning it on. The same message that was on the phone was repeating in an infinite loop no matter where he turned the dial.

"So," Hadley said to nobody in particular. "Do we go to the bunker?"

"I don't know that—look at those flashes off to the East!" Peter cut himself off. "I bet there are more missile shootdowns happening."

"Maybe they've got the whole country, or even the whole world under their guns," Glen said. "It would take thousands of the smaller ships unless they're higher than ten miles. More than eight thousand, if they're covering the oceans and unpopulated land."

"The message on my phone just changed," Arlene reported. "It says that they're intervening to save us from ourselves and that they've temporarily taken over all of our communications for our own protection."

"I guess this counts as a space apocalypse, but getting invaded by possibly benevolent aliens isn't one I planned for."

"They better not be blue and hunky," Phil said, putting an arm around Arlene's shoulder.

"They can't make a worse mess of the financial markets than we've already done ourselves," Laura Ann said as the giant ship passed out of sight over the horizon. "I guess that was the mothership."

"Why do you assume there's only one?"

"How could they have known we were in such bad shape unless they were spying on us?" Carl asked. "It kills me to think that all of the UFO kooks could have been right."

"UAP," Hadley corrected him. "They changed it."

"I think we should go back inside and finish our meal," Mona said. "Betsy was right. Whatever is happening, there's nothing we can do about it right now."

"I'm going up to my observatory," Glen said, heading for the former grain silo. "I want to see what my reflector makes of that smaller ship that's just hanging there before Earth's shadow hides it completely."

"I'll go with," Fumiko said, running after him. "When the internet comes back up, talking about invading spaceships will be easy content."

Everybody else headed back inside where Betsy was cutting herself a generous wedge of pie. "Were you going to save some for us?" Peter asked his mother.

"Five hours in labor, and no anesthetics," she reminded him. "Did I miss an alien invasion?"

"Just the opening round," Carl told her. "The sky was full of alien beam weapons shooting down antiaircraft missiles, and a spaceship the size of a city went past in the south. If Glen was right about the orbit, it will be visible again in around an hour and a half."

"The aliens took over all of Earth's communications networks and they're saying they came to save us," Hadley added.

"That's nice," Betsy said, returning to her seat with her pie. "From what you all tell me, we certainly need saving." She lifted a forkful of pie and took her time swallowing. "This is very good apple pie, whoever made it."

"Thank you," Arlene said. "I changed the sheets on my bed, and you should take my room because it has the attached bath."

"I've been thinking about that since you all rushed out to see the alien invasion, and you know what? Maybe sleeping in the bunker for a night isn't such a bad idea after all."

Epilogue

When communications were restored, humanity would learn that tens of thousands of robots had appeared simultaneously all over Earth just before the first ships were detected and communications were cut. The robots, all versions of the same design, were ovoid shapes with between two and six metallic tentacles or manipulators, floating above the ground with no detectable means of support, and moving, in some cases, at supersonic speeds.

World leaders were taken prisoner before they knew that Earth was being invaded. The robots tore through concrete and steel like tissue paper, proved impervious to small arms fire, and destroyed large incoming ordnance with beams of light. No nation escaped the attention of the invaders, and neither did weapons of mass destruction. Secret bio-labs found their cryogenic storage incinerated, weapons-grade uranium and plutonium was confiscated, submarines with nuclear warheads were pulled to the surface, into the air, and *flown* back to their home bases, suspended under alien ships.

The initial stage of the invasion was over in minutes, and the only injuries were caused by friendly fire or ricochets. Observers at the right latitudes were able to establish that six city-sized ships were in Earth orbit, and despite radar failing to detect anything, careful timekeeping and visual observations showed the ships were over nine miles long and two miles in diameter. That each of the giant cylinders was spinning around its axis implied the presence of biological life requiring a substitute for gravity.

In less than twenty-four hours, communications were restored, and the inhabitants of Earth began to learn what the future held in store…

From the Author

The Good Apocalypse can end two ways. Readers of my EarthCent series are free to consider this book a deep prequel that describes the Stryx opening, when Earth is added to the tunnel network. But I'm exploring a different version of alien intervention than those presented in the EarthCent books, The AI Diaries, and Game Ship. The Good Apocalypse is the first book in a new series that will continue with, A Fine Occupation.

Due to fake sign-ups from bots, I've had to remove the mailing list sign-up form from my website, but you can request to be added by email. I also post new releases to facebook.com/E.M.Foner/ and respond to all temperate e-mail sent to e_foner@yahoo.com

Readers have asked me to include the complete timeline of the EarthCent Universe in order so here it is:

Destiny: Union Station
Date Night on Union Station
Alien Night on Union Station
High Priest on Union Station
Spy Night on Union Station
Carnival on Union Station
Wanderers on Union Station
Vacation on Union Station
Guest Night on Union Station
Word Night on Union Station
Party Night on Union Station
Review Night on Union Station
Family Night on Union Station

Book Night on Union Station
LARP Night on Union Station
Career Night on Union Station
Last Night on Union Station
Independent Living
Soup Night on Union Station
Assisted Living
Freelance on the Galactic Tunnel Network
Con Living
Empire Night on Union Station
Space Living
Traders on the Galactic Tunnel Network
Orphans on the Galactic Tunnel Network
Swap Night on Union Station
Slow Living
Artists on the Galactic Tunnel Network
History Night on Union Station
Bits of Anarchy
Double Living
Bits of Flower
Synergy on the Galactic Tunnel Network
Substitutes on Union Station
Bits of Catalyst
Elder Living
Royals on the Galactic Tunnel Network
Deal Night on Union Station
Intellectual Property
Bits of Business
Antique Living

Other books include the A. I. Diaries series
Turing Test
Human Test
Magic Test

Mentor Test

My sole fantasy novel
Meghan's Dragon

And as Morris Foner, the dystopian
Game Ship

Made in United States
Orlando, FL
16 July 2025

63017989R00164